PE A

'It's only an anniversary, Kim. It doesn't *mean* anything.'

'Doesn't it?' Kim looked unconvinced. As far as she was concerned, Jack and Beth's first wedding anniversary should be a major cause for celebration. She looked disapprovingly at Beth, and then, detecting a hint of sadness behind her smile, she grinned. 'I'm sure he hasn't forgotten.'

Beth's expression suggested otherwise.

'I bet,' continued Kim, 'he's got some romantic surprise planned. Just you wait and see.'

This time it was Beth who looked unconvinced. Jack had already given her a surprise this morning – he had disappeared.

K PR ACTICE

Also by Tom McGregor

Between the Lines, the Chill Factor
Between the Lines, Close Protection
Peak Practice
Kavanagh QC

TOM McGREGOR

PEAK
PRACTICE

PAN BOOKS

First published 1995 by Pan Books

an imprint of Macmillan General Books
Cavaye Place London SW10 9PG
and Basingstoke

Associated companies throughout the world

ISBN 0 330 34130 8

Copyright © Tom McGregor 1995

The right of Tom McGregor to be identified as the
author of this work has been asserted by him in accordance
with the Copyright, Designs and Patents Act 1988.

All rights reserved. No reproduction, copy or transmission
of this publication may be made without written permission.
No paragraph of this publication may be reproduced, copied or
transmitted save with written permission or in accordance with
the provisions of the Copyright Act 1956 (as amended). Any
person who does any unauthorized act in relation to
this publication may be liable to criminal prosecution
and civil claims for damages.

135798642

A CIP catalogue record for this book is available from
the British Library

Typeset by CentraCet Limited, Cambridge
Printed and bound by Firmin-Didot (France),
Group Herissey. No d'impression : 31081.

This book is sold subject to the condition that it shall not,
by way of trade or otherwise, be lent, re-sold, hired out,
or otherwise circulated without the publisher's prior consent
in any form of binding or cover other than that in which
it is published and without a similar condition including this
condition being imposed on the subsequent purchaser

CH**A**PTER 1

Jack Kerruish both looked and felt uneasy. He had always considered himself a hearty, outdoors type but there was something about this particular outdoors activity that troubled him. As a doctor he knew perfectly well what it was – yet also, being a doctor, he, typically, refused to admit it. Shrugging into his heavy cotton overalls he cast another covert look at the entrance to the abandoned lead mine. It would be all right, he tried to tell himself. Concentrate on the people you're trying to rescue. Don't think about claustrophobia.

'You all right?' Alan 'Tommo' Tomlins, the larger-than-life leader of the cave-rescue team, gave him a strange look.

'Fine.' Jack had already sensed a combative, competitive personality in Tommo and he was damned if he was going to show any weakness in front of him. Anxious to change the subject, he stepped back towards the Land-rover, heaved out the metal 'ammo' box containing his medical supplies and then turned back to Tommo. 'It's a school party, is it?'

Tommo nodded. 'Yep. Reported overdue two and a half hours. Teacher and a party of three.' Then he nodded in the direction of the mine entrance. 'Probably got themselves lost inside . . .'

Jack, against his inclination, followed Tommo's gaze. Holdale Mine was situated in a particularly windswept and forbidding part of the Derbyshire Dales. High up on a ridge, it was also surrounded by a few pieces of abandoned, rusting machinery that had somehow evaded the clean-up operation after the death of the mine. They simply added to the utter desolation of the scene, thought Jack. The school minibus and the other Land-rover sporting the cave-rescue logo, parked nearer the entrance, confirmed that the desolation was combined with possible disaster.

Then, accompanied by Andy Corrigan and Chris Palmer, the other two occupants of their Land-rover, he and Tommo walked up the slope towards the mine entrance. Before they got to it, a man emerged from the second Land-rover. Like Jack and his companions, he was wearing a hard hat, heavy boots and overalls. As he approached, he looked up at the threatening rain-clouds and smiled grimly. 'Lovely day for it,' was his succinct greeting.

Chris Palmer nodded in assent and then turned towards Jack. 'This is the medic.'

The man smiled – less grimly – and held out his hand. 'John Cleary, Rescue Co-ordinator.'

'Jack. Jack Kerruish.'

'Glad to have you with us. I hope we won't need your services. No offence, but it's best to be prepared. And the situation,' he added with emphasis, 'is not looking good.' After checking that all four men were ready, he headed uphill again – but away from the mine entrance.

'I thought we were going in to find them.' Tommo, puzzled, gestured back to the unwelcoming darkness of the mine.

'Not unless you can walk through walls. Pickstone Shaft's come down. A rock-fall. The tunnel's blocked.' Cleary's bleak words highlighted just how bad the situation had become. With those words, he went back to his own vehicle and extracted a map of the mine workings. Jack looked over his shoulder as he indicated the location of the rock-fall on the map. 'We think,' Cleary explained, 'that the kids are there. They're either buried under the fall or trapped behind it. The digging party from my vehicle is

2

already in there. As soon as they've finished it's yours. Two girls, one boy, female teacher aged twenty-eight.'

'What were they doing there?' Nothing on earth, Jack thought, would induce him to enter a redundant mine of his own volition.

'A-level geography trip. School sends a party down every year to look at the old lead workings.' Cleary shrugged. 'It's supposed to be as safe as houses.'

At that moment, Tommo joined them. Neither had noticed that, while they were talking, he had returned to his own Land-rover. Without ceremony, he thrust something into Jack's arms. 'That fit you?' he asked.

Jack looked in astonishment at the bundle: it was a wet-suit. He looked, uncomprehendingly, at Tommo's set features.

Cleary, too, was confused. 'What the hell's all this about?'

Tommo, now unzipping his overalls and preparing to don his own wet-suit, looked up in grim determination. 'We're going to get 'em, aren't we? The mine is connected to the Ravensgill Caves,' he continued. 'There's a way in from there.'

Cleary looked horrified. 'I know that, Tommo, but . . .' He paused and looked at Jack. He also knew just how dangerous the Ravensgill Caves were. The entrance to them wasn't called Devil's Throat for nothing.

But Jack knew nothing about the caves or their inherent dangers. 'What's the problem?' he asked.

Tommo, impatient to get going, almost snapped at him. 'They're trapped in the mine, right? There's a system of natural caves lets into it about a mile from here. If we use it we should come in roughly fifty metres the other side of the rock-fall.' He gestured towards the mine entrance. 'We can't wait for the diggers. They might not even be able to clear the fall, for Christ's sake.'

'Yeah but, come on, Tommo,' pleaded Cleary, with sidelong glance at Jack. 'He's not a caver.'

3

'No. He's a *medic*. He needs to get to them *now*.'

Cleary, aware of the urgency but fearful for Jack, looked at him. 'You done one of these before?'

Jack, slightly annoyed that his capabilities were evidently in doubt, began to unzip his overalls in preparation for putting on the wet-suit. 'I'm on the GPs' volunteer list but . . . well, I've never actually done a rescue.'

It was Tommo who asked the burning question. 'What are you like with confined spaces?'

All eyes, suddenly, were on Jack. He avoided looking at Tommo as, after a slight hesitation, he answered, 'Same as the next man.'

Still not entirely convinced, Tommo nevertheless turned back to Cleary. 'You've seen the weather forecast and you know how much rain there's already been. If we leave it too late, there's a risk of flooding and they could drown. If they're buried under two tons of rock then we've *got* to get a move on. It's pointless going in without a medic.' With another gesture at Jack, he added, 'If he says he's all right, I say get on with it.'

'We're all volunteers, Jack,' said Chris Palmer quietly. 'There's no pressed men.'

Not, thought Jack, until now. He was aware that the rescue attempt hinged on his agreement to enter what he now suspected were narrow, dangerous and waterlogged caves. 'I'll be fine,' he said. Then, trying to disguise his trepidation under a veneer of humour, he added, 'I'll just have to phone the wife first.'

The remark did not have the desired effect. All four men looked at him as if he were a wimp. And Tommo gave him a look that redefined the term 'withering'.

Embarrassed, Jack looked serious again. 'It's . . . er, our first wedding anniversary.'

*

4

'It's only an anniversary, Kim. It doesn't *mean* anything.'

'Doesn't it?' Kim looked unconvinced. As far as she was concerned, Jack and Beth's first wedding anniversary should be a major cause for celebration. She looked disapprovingly at Beth and then, detecting a hint of sadness behind her smile, she grinned. 'I'm sure he hasn't forgotten.'

Beth's expression suggested otherwise.

'I bet,' continued Kim, 'he's got some romantic surprise planned. Just you wait and see.'

This time it was Beth who looked unconvinced. Jack had already given her a surprise this morning – he had disappeared.

They hadn't had much in the way of conversation that morning, admittedly, but Beth was sure, when she had left to conduct the usual Saturday morning emergency surgery, that Jack hadn't mentioned he was going out. Indeed, she had left him wallowing in bed and wearing a contented, sleepy expression that carried no suggestion of imminent activity. Yet now, with surgery nearly over, he was not at home to answer his wife's repeated phone calls. Perhaps Kim was right. Perhaps he really was planning a romantic surprise. Lost in thought and with no more patients left to see, Beth sat at her desk and absently twirled her wedding ring round her finger.

Marriage, she mused, was both a marvel and a minefield. She had assumed – arrogantly, she now conceded – that because she had married at the age of thirty-seven, she was mature enough to know everything about human relationships. She was a doctor and she had married a doctor. Hadn't both of them experienced, through their patients, every facet of married life?

The answer, of course, was no. No matter how much you thought you knew about it, no matter how many successes and failures you had witnessed, your own marriage was always different, always presenting unexpected challenges. Much like your own babies, Beth supposed. But that was another matter, one that Beth found herself strangely unwilling to broach with her husband. She loved Jack, and she knew that he loved her. Yet sometimes she felt that she had married a child. Jack the Lad was a nickname that could have been invented for her husband. Beth had no doubt whatsoever that he was and would remain faithful to her; it was his extramural rather than any extramarital activities that worried her. Jack was always rushing in where angels feared to tread; always ready for new challenges, always hopeful of finding a solution to every problem.

Beth grinned to herself as she recalled the day when, nearly three years ago, she and Will Preston had invited Jack Kerruish to join them as a fellow GP at The Beeches Surgery. At first Beth had been reluctant to take him on: she had been doubtful that this restless, energetic man who had spent years practising in underdeveloped regions of Africa would be able to settle down in a small Derbyshire town. Will, who had sensed that her reservations were partly born of an inherent resistance to change, had persuaded her that Jack Kerruish was just the man they needed to enlarge the practice and – it went unsaid – bring it into the twentieth century. They were, Will had implied, stuck in a rut. Beth, born and bred in Cardale, had taken over The Beeches from her father. Will, although an 'incomer', had blended into the community and, with his laid-back charm and film-star looks, become a trusted and valued member of their small society. Yet Will had insisted they needed change and they needed to expand and that Jack was the man to help them.

Life, Beth thought as she turned to the window at the sound of the rain that was now lashing down, had certainly changed.

The Beeches had become a fundholding practice, a business with its own budget to manage. They had more staff, including a fund manager who had once been, oddly enough, their bank manager. Will's rocky marriage had finally collapsed and Beth, of course, had married Jack. Three years ago she wouldn't have dreamed that any of this could have happened. Then she frowned: three years ago she wouldn't have been tying herself up in knots wondering why her husband had gone walkabout on their first wedding anniversary.

A minute later Beth was shaken out of her reverie by the shrill sound of the telephone. She suspected it would be Kim announcing another patient but she hoped it would be Jack.

The moment she picked up the receiver she knew from the fuzzy reception that it was Jack calling from his mobile.

'Beth . . .'

'Jack! Where are you?' Beth didn't even try to disguise the relief in her voice. 'I've been trying to call you for ages.'

The crackle on the line told her that Jack was outdoors, the tone of his voice that it was an emergency. 'I'm at the lead mine at Holdale. Cave-rescue called me . . . The mobile's being playing up.'

Beth, not sure if she had caught all of what he had said, had nevertheless heard enough to alarm her. 'A cave rescue? You going to be all right?' She was one of the few people on earth who knew of Jack's fear of confined spaces.

'Yeah . . .' The crackle on the line rendered Jack's next words unintelligible. '. . . Kids got themselves stuck after a rock-fall,' she managed to decipher. 'Probably need a doctor.' Then, after a short pause, Jack's tone became softer. 'Look, Beth . . . about today . . .' But it was no use. As Beth cradled the phone to her ear, the line went dead.

She looked in annoyance at the dead receiver and, with a weary sigh, replaced it. For a moment she stood motionless as a tingle of fear shot down her spine. Since their marriage, she had thought constantly about her husband.

Inevitably, not all of those thoughts had been charitable; the closeness of their relationship combined with the fact that they were also colleagues and volatile personalities had sometimes led to moments – even days – of friction. But the one thought that had never occurred to Beth was that she might lose Jack. Now, with visions of him clambering around in dangerous caves, trying to fight his claustrophobia, she was forced to entertain that possibility. It made her feel physically sick.

Almost instinctively, she reached again for the phone and dialled the familiar number of Isabel de Gines, her friend, mentor and surrogate mother. Isabel had always been there for her. Never one to dispense advice without being asked, she was always there to help in moments of crisis, to comfort and to talk things through. Beth had a sudden, urgent need to hear her voice.

Yet she was to be disappointed. After several rings and no answer, she hung up, this time in anger. Then she grinned ruefully: Isabel, after all, had a perfect right to go out. And if Beth, when she reached fifty-nine, could have anything like Isabel's energy then she would be truly blessed. Isabel had so many interests, and so much to give. Yet now, in her edgy state, Beth couldn't help wondering why. Was it because her husband, the person she loved most in the world had been taken away from her?

'Really, girl,' she said to herself as she sat down and reached for the stack of files at the corner of her desk, 'get a grip. The is not the attitude of a sane, sensible doctor.'

Five minutes later, the sane, sensible doctor was interrupted once more. 'Beth?' It was Kim at reception. 'There's a Marie McKenner here who . . . er, insists on seeing you?'

'I don't think I know her.'

'She's Jack's patient, but . . .'

'. . . but he isn't here, I know.' Beth paused. Uncharacteristically, she didn't feel like chatting with the bonhomie that was always required when seeing a new patient. 'Can't Will see her?'

'Gone home.' Kim's voice radiated disapproval. If she, the practice manager, was prepared to man reception on a Saturday morning, she didn't see why Will couldn't fulfil his proper role and remain at the practice throughout morning surgery.

'All right, then. Do you know what it's about?'

'Something to do with anti-depressants.'

'On a Saturday?' Beth was surprised because a request for anti-depressants could hardly count as an emergency. They took several weeks to have any effect and Jack would undoubedly have made her aware of that.

'Yes.' Kim, who also knew it, was not, however, going to enter into a discussion about it. 'On a Saturday.'

Beth grinned at Kim's frosty tone. 'Okay, then. Send her in.' She pushed aside the file she had been reading and, thirty seconds later, forced a smile as Marie McKenner, followed by Kim, entered her room. Kim, unseen by Marie, rolled her eyes, deposited the woman's file on Beth's desk, and walked out again.

Beth opened the file and cast a sidelong, though kindly glance at her new patient. Her immediate impression was of a woman, probably in her mid-thirties, who was leading a stressful life that was getting worse by the minute. She looked worn down and depressed. She also looked angry. 'Sit down, please,' said Beth, in her friendliest manner. Taking a card from the file, she leaned across the desk and smiled. 'You said that Dr Kerruish wouldn't give you anti-depressants?'

Marie, tight-lipped, stared across at Beth. 'Yes. That's right . . . but I've had 'em before, off my last doctor.' She glared at Beth and then shrugged. 'I don't see what all the fuss is about.'

'Did Dr Kerruish explain that anti-depressants aren't a

cure for stress, Marie? They'll only mask your symptoms—'

Marie waved a dismissive hand and interrupted her. 'He went through all of that. I could have hypnosis, stress management . . .' Her tone made it abundantly clear what she thought of those alternatives. 'I said I'd try to win the pools. He thought that would be a good idea.' Again, Marie glared at Beth, letting her know that her opinion of Jack wasn't too favourable.

'I could refer you for counselling,' Beth suggested.

Marie took a deep breath. 'I've got four kids, a husband who's in Cardiff – at least that's where he says he is – me brother's sleeping on the sofa . . . I haven't got time for counselling.'

Beth remained silent.

'Our house is bedlam at weekends,' continued the distraught woman. 'Saturdays are the worst and – and I don't think I can stand much more.' She looked at Beth in genuine appeal. 'Are you going to give me something?'

This time it was Beth who drew a deep breath. No, she thought, I can't give you something. I want to know what Jack said to you, and I don't believe anti-depressants are the answer. 'I can help,' she said evenly, 'but not with drugs.'

Marie just looked at her. Then, abruptly, she stood up and went to the door. 'Thanks.'

'Marie! Wait!'

''S all right, love. I'll just book an appointment before I'm ill next time.' With that, the door slammed and Marie McKenner walked back into the life from which she so desperately needed respite. Beth sighed and put her head between her hands. That woman, she thought, doesn't need anti-depressants; she needs a six-month break. I know the feeling.

*

As Marie McKenner walked out of The Beeches, Jack Kerruish was preparing to walk into a situation that was already beginning to fill him with something approaching terror. The entire cave-rescue team, now high on the ridge that marked the entrance to the Ravensgill Caves, was squatting in the mud beside a narrow gap in the rock. As the rain poured down on them, Jack's only solace was the wet-suit he was now wearing. He was miserable enough as it was and getting soaked would have been the last straw. The gap in the rocks, which Tommo was inspecting with a practised eye, looked hardly big enough for a small animal to crawl through – let alone an adult male with a case of medical equipment.

'Your mission,' said Tommo, 'should you wish to accept it.' Then, seeing Jack's expression, he stared intently at him. 'Think you'll get through there?'

Jack shrugged. 'Do me best.'

'Looks worse than it is,' mused Tommo. Like hell, thought Jack. 'It's a squeeze getting in, but once you're past the entrance, you could drive a bus through the cave.' Without further ado, Tommo slid further down into the quagmire surrounding the gap and started to crawl through it. Jack, as he had been instructed, pushed the medical kit in front of him and began to follow. Andy and Chris would bring up the rear: Jack didn't dare look at them. He didn't want them to see the expression on his face.

Two minutes later it was impossible to see the expression on anybody's face. The wet darkness enveloped the men as they crawled into the cave, through a narrow rift and deeper into the caverns. Only their headlamps, flickering with each movement, cut through the darkness. Only the sound of their heavy boots, scraping against the grit and wet rock, penetrated the eerie silence. For Jack, it was even worse than he had expected. Yet for Tommo, scrambling ahead with swift efficiency, it was all in a day's

11

work. The only thing that kept Jack going was the knowledge that Tommo was trying to rile him.

'I'll tell you what, mate,' panted the latter as he turned to pull the medical kit down a narrow ledge, 'you should've seen the last one we had.'

'The last who?'

'Doctor.' Suddenly Tommo's face loomed in front of him. The light from Jack's hard hat illuminated Tommo's eyes: they were hard and amused – and mocking. 'Got himself in a right state, he did.'

Chris, now level with the others, asked who they were talking about.

'The last doctor we had,' said Tommo. 'Nearly left him down there, didn't we, Chris?'

Chris, remembering, laughed without humour. 'Oh, yeah. *Him!*'

'I never bother with 'em,' continued Tommo as they forged ahead.

'With what?' asked Jack.

'Doctors.'

'Me neither.' At least that's true, thought Jack. Can't remember when I last consulted one. Being married to one probably didn't count.

They continued in grim silence as they descended deeper into the narrow network of caves. Just as Jack was wondering if they'd ever be able to find their way out, Tommo spoke again. 'Think they're God, don't they? Some of 'em, anyway.'

Jack bit back the reply he wanted to make. Tommo, he told himself, was being deliberately provocative. Don't rise to the bait. Don't antagonize the man. Your life, after all, is in his hands.

Twenty minutes later Jack made the appalling discovery that his life was indeed in danger – and that Tommo didn't seem to care. 'I'm stuck,' he called to the others, now slightly ahead of him in an even narrower part of the caverns. He knew it was a feeble cry: the smallness of the space in which he was confined seemed to restrict his voice as well as his movements, and had he shouted, the echo of his cry would have rebounded straight onto him. He was lying flat on his back with his nose touching the hard rock above. The others, he knew, had managed to wriggle through this horrifying, claustrophobic channel but he was stuck.

There was no reply from the men ahead. Jack felt panic welling within him and his next words betrayed desperation. 'Tommo? I'm stuck.' The words reverberated back and outright fear gripped him as he lay there, unable to move, beset by visions of being stuck for ever.

Tommo, however, had heard the second cry. He inched back to Jack and, with his customary brusqueness, addressed the back of his head. 'You're the same shape as when you got in there, aren't you? That means you can get back.'

Somewhere within Jack, the voice of reason agreed with Tommo. With considerable effort, he began to move back.

'Push with your legs . . . I said your legs! That's it! Now use your back . . . yes, that's it! Go on, you're nearly there.'

Grunting with the effort, Jack found himself suddenly able to move more easily. 'Now back towards me,' said Tommo. 'Yes, easier this time. And don't panic!'

Finally, Jack was out and, panting with exertion, found himself facing Tommo, his face illuminated in the harsh light of the man's headlamp.

'So what was the problem?' Tommo appeared to relish Jack's fear and humiliation. Jack just stared at him.

'You all right, Jack?' Chris called from further down the tunnel. His voice, in stark contrast to Tommo's, was all concern.

'Yeah! I'm fine.'

It was Jack's forced grin, his clear desire not to betray

just how scared he had been, that suddenly made Tommo soften. He peered closely at Jack, a worried frown creasing his brow. 'You sure you're all right?'

'Yeah.' Jack nodded. 'I'm fine.'

For the first time since Jack had met him, Tommo managed something approaching a grin. 'Wouldn't want to lose yer.'

'Thought you left the last medic down here?' Jack, too, managed a smile. The ice, he thought, was beginning to melt.

Tommo raised an eyebrow. 'Yeah, well, you don't want to listen to half the things I say.'

'That's all right' replied Jack. 'I don't.'

Tommo, who had begun to turn back towards Chris and Andy, suddenly looked at Jack again. 'Nice one, Jack.' Then, with a curious mixture of embarrassment and respect, he added, 'Tell you what, you're the first one who's answered me back.'

Jack nodded. This is going to be OK, he thought. I think I've found a friend.

Forging ahead into the tunnels, the men carried on without further conversation until Jack bumped into Tommo. With a restraining hand, Tommo indicated for him to stay where he was. Then he spoke. His words carried with them a curious echo. Jack looked upwards, thinking that, at last, there was space all around them. Yet the space, the source of the current of air suddenly chilling his face, came from below. 'We're at Devil's Throat, Jack,' said Tommo, almost in awe. 'Now we go down.'

Against his better judgement, Jack looked down. The beam from his headlamp illuminated . . . nothing. For the first few feet he could follow the sheer walls of rock and then the light faded. Jack felt a stab of fear. Just when he thought this nightmare rescue operation was getting better, it seemed to get worse. And now, faced with the descent into some unseen hellhole, it had got infinitely worse.

While Tommo and Andy began drilling pitons into the area of rock above the drop, Chris picked up the mole phone he had been carrying with him. A direct radio contact with John Cleary, it was their only link with the outside world.

The news from above ground was not good. After a fuzzy, crackling conversation with Cleary, Chris turned to Tommo. 'It's raining. Buckets.'

Jack looked at Chris in surprise. 'So why's that a problem? We're down here—' Noticing the worried looks of the others, he lapsed into silence.

'The problem,' said Chris, 'is that the water backs up. The whole mine and cave system can flood.' He looked down at the sheer walls of Devil's Throat. 'It may already be flooding down there.'

Wordlessly, Jack followed his gaze. He strained to hear any sounds that would suggest water down below, but there was nothing to hear and nothing to see.

The descent wasn't as bad as Jack had expected. They connected the steel ladder to the pitons and lowered themselves, one by one, into Devil's Throat. As instructed by Tommo, Jack looked neither up nor down; he just climbed down with his face pressed almost against the rock until his feet touched the ground. His profound relief at reaching the bottom was short-lived: he was standing in six inches of water.

Chris, again on the mole phone to John Cleary, was relaying that information to the team leader. Unknown to Jack, Cleary's major worry was Jack's own well-being. The diggers, he told Chris, were beginning to make some headway at the entrance to Holdale mine: they would soon be through to the trapped party. If the underground team were in danger they were to get out – and if Jack Kerruish couldn't handle it, then they must bring him up. Cleary didn't doubt Jack's commitment or bravery. He was highly impressed by him. But he was a realist. No matter how brave or willing Jack was, he had no experience as a caver, and there was no point in courting disaster. With the news of the flooding in Devil's Throat, Cleary was only too aware that disaster could be just round the corner.

'What's the problem?' asked Jack as Chris replaced the mole phone in his belt attachment. 'The cave's filling with water, yeah?'

Tommo nodded. The cave wasn't the problem: it was the narrow passage they would have to negotiate to get to the cave connecting Ravensgill with Holdale Mine and thus with the stranded party. Tommo stared at Jack. 'What are you like at holding your breath?'

'Er, how long would I be under?'

'Six . . .' Tommo looked at Andy for corroboration, 'seven seconds?'

'Could we get the injured through? On the way back?'

Tommo shook his head. 'No. We'll stay with 'em till the digging party breaks through. You can treat 'em. I'll help the diggers from this side.'

'What is the alternative?' Jack asked with a hint of desperation.

'We all go back.'

'In that case, it better just be seven seconds.'

It was longer than that and it was nearly the last straw for Jack. Tommo's earlier snorts of derision had now given way to outright encouragement and support: this was the worst and the most dangerous rescue operation he had ever been faced with, and it was bad enough for him, Andy and Chris. He couldn't imagine what it must be like for Jack.

It was hell. Like Tommo before him, Jack had to wade into the dark, swirling pool of muddy water and, as the water rose above his head, he had to keep walking. It was the most unnatural feeling in the world: Jack felt as if he were being compelled to commit suicide. He also had to place his entire trust – and his life – in Tommo's hands. Tommo said it would take only a matter of seconds before he reached the air-pocket at the other end. He had even demonstrated, by doing the journey first to secure a shot line for the others to follow, that it *was* only a matter of seconds. But neither that proof nor the now-secured line could erase the doubt from Jack's mind as he waded into the dark expanse of water.

'All right?'

The words were the most comforting Jack had ever heard. He was through. Tommo was crouching on the narrow ledge at the other side of the flooded passageway. Coughing and gasping for breath, Jack stumbled towards him. 'I banged my head,' he wheezed as he gestured to his flickering lamp.

'You're all right.' With quiet efficiency, Tommo inspected Jack's hat and the lamp. 'It's not damaged.' As he helped Jack on to the rock ledge, he added, 'Save your energy while you're in here. Try and relax. I'll be straight back. Just going to get your gear.'

Jack couldn't trust himself to speak. He was surveying, with mounting horror, the tiny space in which he now found himself. Tommo, sensing his unease, pointed towards a tiny gap in the rock just above the waterline. 'We'll be going through there in a minute. After that it'll be plain sailing.' He clapped Jack on the shoulder. 'Soon be out of here, mate. Don't worry.' Then, with a forced smile, he plunged back into the water. Jack followed Tommo's hand as it gripped the shot line until, like the rest of him, it disappeared underwater.

Silence closed around him. It was the sort of silence, he thought, that you could *hear*. Profound, eerie and solid. He was beginning to panic again. He tried to collect his thoughts and focus his mind on something – anything –

other than his present circumstances. But all he could think of was the silence, the foetal position into which the tiny ledge forced him, the rising water behind and in front of him and the tons of rock above.

His headlamp flickered and went out. The darkness was now as impenetrable as the silence and Jack realized that he could take no more. The reappearance of Tommo and the arrival of Andy and Chris did nothing to alleviate his mounting panic. The sudden rush of water, the flickering lamps on the men's helmets only emphasized the horror of the situation: four men huddled underground, above swirling torrents of water on a ridge no bigger than a cupboard. Jack didn't even register the words of comfort from the others. His only concern was that he had to get out – now. Suddenly he jumped back into the water.

'Jack!' Chris shouted. 'Where are you going!'

Tommo and Andy joined him in the water and tried to restrain him. Tommo's grip was fierce yet his words were gentle as he helped Jack back onto the ledge. 'Take it easy, will yer? You're all right! Just breathe . . . keep breathing . . . that's it.'

Breathing deeply as instructed, Jack began to get himself under control. Panic slowly gave way to intense embarrassment: he, Jack Kerruish, the fearless doctor, had been reduced to a quivering wreck in front of these men. He had exposed himself as the weak link in this otherwise strong human chain.

The others, however, were only concerned for his welfare, not for any displays of bravado. At a look from Tommo, Chris and Andy forged ahead through the narrow gap that would take them to the collapsed mineshaft while Tommo remained with Jack.

'I've, er, I've never done that before.' Jack tried a tentative smile.

Tommo grinned broadly. 'Probably won't do it again, eh? How're you feeling?'

'Better.' Jack breathed out again and nodded in confirmation of his own words.

'You've done great, Jack.'

'I feel a bit of a prat.'

Again Tommo grinned. 'You should see me on ladders.' Suddenly, he was brisk efficiency again. 'We're nearly there,' he said, as he made to follow Andy and Chris. 'Straight through Dead Man's Finger, down Abraham's Drop and then—' He stopped, noticing Jack's horrified expression. Looking slightly abashed, he added, 'Well, it's not me that names these blasted caves, is it?'

Whoever did name them had some sense of humour, thought Jack. But Tommo had not been lying. After a few minutes' crawling through the aptly named Dead Man's Finger and a hair-raising abseil down the sheer walls of Abraham's Drop, they found themselves in the mine, in man-made passageways carved in search of lead. Jack breathed more easily in the clear, wide walkways and he even detected light somewhere above them as they walked along briskly. Light at the end of the tunnel, he thought. I'd never have believed it a few minutes ago.

Ten minutes after they entered the mine they found the trapped party. Faint sounds that they soon identified as weak calls of 'Hello' and 'Anyone there?' led them to the four people who had been stranded for five hours. Their one flashlight had long since run out: they had exhausted their meagre store of supplies and they were all weary, desperate and frightened. The teacher leading the party was huddled, still trying bravely to remain on top and in charge, against the well of the mine. One leg was stretched out before her and her face was racked with pain. She, like the three teenagers with her, had difficulty in fighting off tears of relief at the arrival of the rescue party.

Jack, heartily relieved both to have located them and to be able to switch back into doctor mode, began to examine

19

them for injuries. He was relieved to discover that only Caroline Royal, the teacher, was injured. Looking at her leg, he suspected a fracture. Then he reached for his medical bag while the other men dispensed chocolate and extra clothing to the three teenagers. Chris, once more, was in contact with John Cleary above ground. 'We've found 'em!' he shouted into the phone. 'Teacher's got leg injuries, one kid's in a bit of shock . . . No, no hypothermia, but you're going to have to get an ambulance organized.'

Tommo and Andy lost no time in establishing the extent of the mine collapse. The passage leading to the entrance was completely blocked by a mound of fallen rock and timber, indicating that the entire mineshaft had collapsed. Worse, more rock and rubble were suspended precariously above them. If the incessant rainfall above caused further movement of the soil, they wouldn't be just trapped – they would be buried.

Tommo and Andy set to work on establishing the safest way to proceed. A chink of light indicated that one portion of the landslide, at least, was not impenetrable. With great care, they began to remove a few of the looser stones around the gap and soon it was wide enough for Tommo to crawl through.

'Careful, Tommo!' urged Andy. 'It's loose this—'

But Tommo was already wriggling through.

'Does it go right through?'

'Hold on.' Tommo's voice, faint now, carried an element of doubt. Chris, standing nearby and still on the phone to John Cleary, smiled at his view of Tommo's flailing legs. Then he frowned as he listened to Cleary's urgent questions. 'Yeah . . . that's right. But we'll need—'

That unfinished request was the last communication John Cleary was to hear from the trapped party. Chris, below him in the mine, looked round in horror as Tommo's feet disappeared from view and were replaced by tons of rock hurtling down towards him.

By three o'clock Beth was seriously worried. All afternoon she had tried to avoid listening to the alarm bells sounding in her mind. Kim, equally worried, had begun to irritate her with her well-meaning yet incessant visits to her room to offer coffee, tea, biscuits and sympathy.

By half past three Beth had had enough. Surgery was long over, Kim was about to depart – and still there was no sign of Jack. Picking up her coat, she left The Beeches and drove – rather faster than was advisable in the pouring rain – to Holdale mine.

The sight that greeted her did nothing to boost her flagging spirits. Numerous vehicles were parked around the entrance to the mine – evidence of the swelling ranks of villagers. The Cardale grapevine had obviously been working overtime, and the mine rescue was obviously still in progress. She noticed a man in a hard hat standing at the entrance to the mineshaft, speaking into a mobile phone while directing the team of diggers gathered near him. As she approached him, she noted, to her surprise, that Marie McKenner was standing beside him. Marie, looking even more worried than she had at the surgery several hours ago, tried to brush past him.

'Sorry, love.' John Cleary held out a restraining arm. 'Can't go in there.' Then, clipping his phone to his belt, he took her by the shoulders and gently steered her away. Seeing her anguished expression, he smiled sympathetically and added, 'You're really not supposed to be here.'

Abruptly, Marie turned to face him. 'Alison,' she said. 'Alison McKenner. She's in there. I'm her mother. Have you found her yet?'

He cleared his throat and tried again to steer her away. 'Let's get out of the way.'

'I only want to know if they've found her!' Marie's voice rose to a high wail.

After a moment, Cleary said 'there are men inside looking for them. I'm sure we'll find them. It's just that—'

'Marie?' Both Marie and Cleary looked up in surprise. The latter didn't recognize the new arrival. Marie, however, did. Glaring at Beth, she sniffed loudly and ran a hand distractedly through her hair.

'Marie?' said Beth again. 'Why don't you come with me? We're only in the way here.' As the woman was incapable of making any sort of decision, she smiled at Cleary and drew her away from him. Cleary nodded his thanks. The last thing he needed was to be surrounded by hysterical women, however justified their distress. Leaving Marie in Beth's capable hands, he walked back towards the diggers, unclipping his phone to speak once more to Chris Palmer beneath the surface.

Because his head was bent over the mouthpiece, he failed to notice that every bird in the vicinity, as if obeying some pre-recorded signal, suddenly took flight. Barely a second after they collectively swooped away from the mine, a low rumbling came from the bowels of the earth. A moment after that Cleary lost contact with Chris as, horrified, he turned towards the entrance to the mine. The rumbling increased in volume, the ground beneath his feet began to shake and, like Beth, Marie, the diggers and everyone else at the site, he looked in disbelief at the mine. The rumbling stopped, and in its wake a huge cloud of dust billowed out of the entrance. And then an ominous silence settled.

The episode was over in a few seconds, yet for Beth, Marie and the other parents, friends and villagers gathered at the site, it seemed both to take an eternity and to happen in slow motion. Beth was unaware that she was holding one hand to her mouth in silent horror as she watched the diggers nearest the mine entrance cough and splutter as they fought for breath. Marie McKenner, too, was struck dumb. Standing beside Beth, she turned and saw her expression. Their earlier encounter was forgotten as they were united in their distress.

Marie peered closely at Beth. Something told her why her reaction had been so great. 'You got someone in there?' she asked.

'Yes.' Beth looked as if she were trying to dissociate herself from her own words. 'My husband.'

Marie looked blank. She wasn't even aware that Doctor Glover was married.

With a sad half-smile, Beth enlightened her. 'Doctor Kerruish.'

Marie was taken aback. 'Oh . . . I didn't know . . . I, er . . .' Then, lapsing into silence, she looked again towards the mine. 'My Alison,' she said. 'I told her she wasn't to go on this.' She shrugged. 'Tell her not to do it and what's the first thing she goes and does? Should've told her to get stuck. None of this would have happened.' Then, with a shy look at Beth, she added, 'Your husband – he'll look after her, will he?'

That, thought Beth, was the only certainty of this ghastly affair. 'Oh, yes,' she said. 'He will. You can be sure of that.'

'I'm . . . er, sorry about this morning. I speak before I think.' Marie was embarrassed. 'You live in our house, you have to.'

Beth's smile told her there was nothing to be sorry about.

'Funny,' Marie continued, 'I'm all here now, y'know. Suddenly I feel calm and capable. Maybe I don't need pills. You never really know what you've got till it's gone, do you?'

Oh how I wish that you hadn't said that, thought Beth.

*

As soon as the dust had settled, John Cleary and the team of diggers went back into the mine to inspect the damage. It quickly became obvious that the new rock-fall had sounded worse than it was – from their perspective, at least.

For those below ground it was a different story. While the school party, Jack and Chris had been far enough down the passageway to avoid being hit by any of the falling rocks and timbers, Tommo and Andy had not been so lucky. Andy, by flattening himself against the rock wall, had somehow managed to escape serious injury. Tommo, however, had borne the full brunt of the fall. Still conscious as Jack scrambled towards him, he was clearly in great pain and was having difficulty in breathing. With the help of Andy and Chris, Jack managed to pull him clear of the fallen rocks and set about examining his wounds.

He was horrified by what he saw. Gently unzipping Tommo's wet-suit, he discovered that his injuries were horrific and extensive. The garment had been designed to keep out water but had proved an ineffectual barrier against anything more substantial. Jack sucked in his breath as he realized what had happened to Tommo. Something – a sharp timber or jagged rock – had hit him directly on the chest and penetrated through the suit, through his skin, deep into his body. Tommo's laboured, agonized breaths were easily explained: the object had also punctured his lung.

Jack looked in desperation at Chris. 'The phone?'

Chris shook his head. 'Dead.' He couldn't trust himself to say any more. He was staring at Tommo in undisguised horror. The man had always seemed indestructible. Now his mortality was revealed in the cruellest way.

'We have to get him to a hospital,' whispered Jack. '*Now*.' Then he looked towards the rock-fall that separated them from their rescuers. 'Any sign of help?'

'I'll . . . I'll go and see.'

Jack looked back towards the schoolchildren and Caroline Royal who, despite her pain and the discomfort of the splint that Jack had made for her leg, was still trying to keep up their spirits. Jack smiled at her in grateful acknowledgement. He couldn't, he knew, leave Tommo. Then, reaching for the box containing his medical supplies, he frowned. There was only one thing he could do for Tommo at the moment – and he baulked at doing it. Tommo's pain would be made even more intense.

Tommo was trying to speak. Jack silenced him with a hand on his mouth. 'You've punctured a lung, Tommo. There's air getting into your chest.'

'Aye,' rasped the injured man. 'Wondered why I was feeling so cold.'

Jack grinned. It was typical, he thought, that Tommo should try to make light of the situation. 'I can put a tube in your side,' he continued. 'It'll relieve the pressure, make your breathing easier.'

Tommo nodded, wincing in pain as he did so.

'I want you,' said Jack, as he got out a scalpel and a Venthlon needle, 'to concentrate on thinking about something else.'

Again Tommo nodded.

'This brain walks into a pub one night, right?'

'A brain?'

'Yes. It walks into the pub and it says to the landlord, "Can I have a pint of bitter, please?", and . . .' Here Tommo winced again as Jack began to cut away his wetsuit. '. . . and the landlord says, "I'm not serving you, you're out of your skull!"' Tommo, with difficulty, started laughing at the joke, and Jack used the opportunity to cleanse the intended injection site. Then, biting his lip and concentrating hard in the dim light of the tunnel, he urged Tommo to keep very still as he took the Venthlon needle and inserted it into his side.

Tommo's roar of agony was almost as loud as the sound

of the tumbling rocks that had led to his accident. Out of the corner of his eye, Jack noticed the school party looking on in horror. As Tommo's screams subsided, he held his shoulders. 'It's OK now, Tommo. It's in.' With a swift, practised movement, he opened the valve of the needle. 'There! Is that better?'

Tommo's eyes were moist as he looked up and, with the beginnings of a smile, nodded.

Behind them, and with infinite care. Chris and Andy were pulling the rocks away from the scene of the latest fall. They worked in silence for several minutes until, as Chris bent forward to pull at a large, loose rock, he heard a sound. Holding up a hand for Andy to be quiet, he leaned forward and listened. A few seconds later he heard the sound again. This time it was closer – and unmistakable. It was the sound of digging.

Six hours after Jack had ventured below ground at Ravensgill Caves, he emerged from Holdale Mine. Exhausted and disorientated, he blinked fiercely at the light. Sunset, he realized with some surprise, must have happened hours ago: the brightness that nearly blinded him was from the huge arc-lights that had been erected at the mine entrance.

As soon as he came out of the mine, the paramedics rushed in with stretchers for Tommo and Caroline. Once he was able to see clearly, Jack began to feel even more disorientated. Tommo had made him promise to accompany him to hospital, and the last thing Jack would ever do was abandon a patient. Yet now, suddenly, he was standing in front of the person who meant more to him than any patient.

'Beth?'

'Jack.' Suddenly shy, Beth smiled and turned to Isabel who, since her arrival an hour ago, hadn't moved from her side. 'We . . . er, we thought . . .' But Beth had no time to finish: hordes of people swarmed towards Jack.

Tearful parents, Marie McKenner among them, congratulated him for rescuing their children, while many of the other locals cheered him as the hero of the day. Jack was both bemused and annoyed: as far as he was concerned, he hadn't done anything. ⎪

Will, wrapped up against the chill of the evening in a Barbour and long scarf, came up and clapped him on the back. 'Well done. Must've been a nightmare for you.'

'But I didn't do anything!' Jack wailed.

Beth forced her way back towards her husband. 'Are you all right?' she asked. Jack, she thought, was looking decidedly manic.

'Yeah . . .' Jack's hands fell to his side as he looked around. This was hardly the moment for an intimate reunion. 'Look, can we talk about it later? It was a bit of a rush this morning and the first thing I knew—'

Beth grinned. 'There's always next year.'

Then, staring deep into his eyes, she added, in a softer tone, 'Happy anniversary!'

'Yeah. Happy anniversary.' Again they were interrupted, this time by the paramedics rushing towards the ambulance carrying Tommo's stretcher. 'I – I said I'd go with him.'

If Beth was disappointed, she did a good job of not showing it. 'Sure. Is he badly hurt?'

'Very.' As Jack made to follow the stretcher, he was suddenly reminded of the joke Tommo had been trying to tell him when their rescuers had broken through the rock barrier. He hadn't got the answer, maybe Beth would. 'What's the difference between God and a doctor?' he asked her.

Without hesitation, Beth replied, 'God doesn't believe he's a doctor.'

Somehow, the joke broke the ice between them, and Jack, his face streaked with mud and wet from his recent exertions, leaned over and kissed her. Then, somewhat guiltily, he looked over towards Tommo's ambulance.

Beth's voice was gentle as, with a light touch on his shoulder, she pushed him away. 'Well, go on, if you're going with him.'

Relieved and happy that the most appalling day of his life was nearly over, Jack jogged up towards the ambulance. In one long-legged stride he lifted himself into the vehicle and addressed his new friend. 'Told you, Tommo,' he boomed, 'wild horses wouldn't keep me away!'

But he was too late. Tommo's face, so vibrant and full of life even when he had suffered ungodly pain, was now still. For a moment Jack was frozen in shock. Then, behind him, a light went out. He looked back towards the entrance of the mine in time to see the last arc-light being extinguished and the mine disappear into the blackness. For Tommo, he reflected bitterly, there had been no light at the end of that tunnel.

CH**A**PTER 2

Isabel de Gines was more relieved than she would ever admit that Jack had survived the mine rescue unscathed. As they had watched, in mounting trepidation, the progress of the diggers, Beth had confided to her not only that Jack was an inexperienced caver but that he suffered from claustrophobia. Isabel, true to form, had not even tried to console Beth with platitudes: she had simply offered comfort as a physical presence and, if Beth had so wished, as a shoulder to cry on. If she had been somewhat more subdued than usual, Beth hadn't noticed. For that Isabel was relieved. She had something to tell Beth – and she hadn't been sure the time was right.

Two weeks later, she still wasn't sure the time was right. Yet she was aware that her out-of-character indecisiveness was beginning to have an effect. The other evening, when she had gone round to visit Jack and Beth having run out of excuses for refusing invitations, the latter had accused her of trying to avoid them. Beth's manner had been light-hearted, yet Isabel had seen that she was hurt. They had never had any secrets from each other and if Beth suspected that Isabel was being evasive then she had every right to be annoyed. But still Isabel had hesitated. She had assured both Jack and Beth that she had just been busy – which had been largely true. For Isabel not to be busy would have been worrying indeed. Today, as on the first Saturday of every month, she was busy doing the flowers in church. An avid gardener and expert on floral arrangements, she found that activity cathartic, pleasing and peaceful, and today she derived a special satisfaction from her work. As she finished, she stood back to admire the effect. The sun was streaming through the stained-glass windows and as its rays refracted off the flowers they seemed to herald a new brightness: a great hope and a suggestion of promises fulfilled.

So lost in thought was she as she collected her baskets, gardening gloves and various other tools, to leave the church, that she was unaware of having left anything behind. Only the appearance of Father Kelly, waving frantically as she prepared to drive off, nudged Isabel out of her reverie. As he approached, she wound down her window, smiled and then grimaced as she realized what he was holding.

'My eyes are keen enough to spot them,' he panted as he drew level with the car, 'but I fear a few of our lay members could have done themselves a mischief with these.' Then, laughing, he handed Isabel the secateurs she had left on the front pew.

Isabel smiled. 'I'm sorry. I must've been miles away.' She reached for the lethal-looking instrument and deposited it on the passenger seat. 'Thank you, Father.'

'It should be me thanking you.' Father Kelly was beaming from ear to ear. 'The church looks a picture.'

Isabel was pleased: she had made a special effort with today's arrangements. Then, as she reached for the ignition, Father Kelly bent closer to her. 'I've heard,' he said with mock severity, 'a vicious rumour.'

'Oh?'

'Yes. I'm sure there's no truth in it – but the grapevine tells me that you're withdrawing from the rota.' At that he waved a finger in good-humoured admonishment. 'We rely on you, Mrs de Gines. I've already pencilled you in for next Easter.'

For a moment Isabel looked as if she were a million miles away. Then, pulling herself together, she smiled at the priest. 'I assure you, I'm not withdrawing from anything, Father.' With that, she gave him a cheery wave and drove off. Father Kelly didn't see the frown that replaced her serene smile. She couldn't, she realized, keep quiet for ever. Soon she would have to tell Beth. Then, suddenly, she brightened again. She had just thought of another excuse not to tell her: there was a flu epidemic in Cardale and all three doctors at The Beeches were run off their feet. The last thing Beth needed was to be pestered by her. Stoically ignoring the little voice in her head that told her she was procrastinating, Isabel smiled at her ingenuity and headed home.

The flu epidemic had not been a figment of Isabel's fertile imagination. Cardale, high on the Derbyshire Dales, suffered from extreme weather in winter and its residents, in turn, suffered severe bouts of cold and flu. It was typical, thought Will Preston as he marched down the High Street, that one of the oldest and most vulnerable residents should suffer in silence. Alice North, so Kim had informed him, had appeared at The Beeches and then, realizing that she hadn't made an appointment, had departed again because she 'didn't want to make a fuss'. Kim had tried to make her stay, to fit her in, but Alice would have none of it. At nearly eighty and all alone in the world (her daughter, she had been known to admit with a derisive snort, might as well be dead as she lived in Canada), Alice had lived through enough to know that a little bit of flu never hurt anyone. She had also, in common with many old people, lived long enough to believe that she was immortal.

Will, however, believed otherwise. On hearing what Kim had to say, he decided to nip down to Alice's after surgery and berate her for being a troublesome old bag. That, he thought with a smile, was the sort of language to which Alice responded best. She hated being mollycoddled and loved a good fight – she and Will were old sparring partners. The constant bickering between them was merely a manifestation of the warm relationship they enjoyed. Alice had a soft spot for good-looking young men, and Will admired people – elderly ones in particular – who were prepared to accept everything life threw at them. Some people, he thought as he approached Alice's unprepossessing front door, just didn't know when they were lucky. His estranged wife, for one.

He frowned as he thought of Sarah and the conversation they had had the other day. It was she who had walked out on him, and now she wanted back. He was, she had said, no longer the weak man he had become in the latter years of their marriage. She seemed to have missed the irony that a strong Will simply wouldn't put up with a renewed bout of her tantrums. Will had pretended not to understand what she was after and they had parted friends. Friends armed with divorce papers.

Alice, predictably, put on a show of disgust at seeing Will. 'It's only a bit of flu.' Then she glared at him. 'Can't seem to shift it myself but then I don't s'pose you can do much about it either.'

Will refused to rise to the bait. 'It still doesn't excuse your behaviour, Alice. Marching out of the surgery was hardly good medicine, was it?'

'If I'd stuck there much longer,' she snorted, 'I'd have come out with more than I went in with. To look at some of 'em waiting you'd think they were at death's door. And all over a bit of a chill. 'S not worth the fuss.'

Will grinned and produced a thermometer. 'Maybe I could be the judge of that?'

Alice grudgingly put it in her mouth. 'Oh, I don't need stirring over,' she mumbled. 'Get enough of that from her next door.'

Will, although interested in whoever 'her next door' was, refused to enter into further conversation until he was done with the thermometer. They sat in silence, Will smiling amiably, Alice looking mutinous.

'So who,' he asked as he reached for the thermometer a minute later, 'has moved in next door?'

'Right nosy-parker. Can't sneeze but she's on to it.'

Will grinned. It was par for the course for Alice to find fault with her neighbours and, anyway, calling someone a nosy-parker was, coming from Alice, almost a compliment. 'Well,' he said, 'you *have* got a temperature. It's nothing extreme, though.'

Alice was delighted. She would have been mortified if he'd come to her house for no reason. 'Could have told you that myself,' she growled, 'and saved you all this faffing around.'

Will ignored her. 'Hopefully this means you're on the mend. The most important thing in the meantime is lots of fluids.' Then, getting to his feet, he shivered and looked around the austere room. 'And a bit of warmth in here wouldn't go amiss. It's as cold as the grave.'

'It's the draught.' Alice, for once, wasn't on the defensive. 'I keep turning the fire up, but the heat goes straight out the window.'

'Mmm. Well, if you're still feeling poorly in a couple of days we'll sort something out.'

But Alice had no intention of feeling poorly for that long. 'I'll be as right as rain by then. Like I say,' she added with a glint in her eye, 'it weren't worth bothering you with.'

Will was still smiling as he walked back up the road towards his car. He wondered how Alice would react if he told her he regarded her as a breath of fresh air. His smile vanished as he realized that she would probably hit him. Looking at his watch as he reached his Range Rover he frowned and then retraced his steps as far as the dry-cleaners on the corner.

Ten minutes later he was back at The Beeches. Laura, the new nurse, was standing in reception with Jack and Kim. They all fell silent as he entered with a cellophane-wrapped dinner-jacket slung over his shoulder.

'What's this?' asked Jack. 'Fancy dress party?'

'Ha, ha.' Will looked down his nose. It was an expression that, unfortunately, came easily to him. Those who didn't know him assumed, from his upper-class drawl and 'that' expression, that he was aloof, snobbish and supercilious. Jack, who was as down-to-earth as they came, had disliked him on sight at their first meeting. And now, years later, even though they were firm friends, they could still rub each other up the wrong way.

'Don't tell me you're moonlighting?' continued Jack. 'Calling the numbers at bingo?'

Will, adopting an ever more supercilious look, sailed past him without responding. He knew Jack was only teasing, but he sometimes found his brand of humour just a little tired.

'I wish,' said Kim, as Will disappeared into his room, 'you wouldn't rile him. It's his business where he goes of an evening.' Her cryptic smile suggested that she knew exactly where he was going.

'Meaning,' said Jack, 'you know something I don't.' With an evil glint in his eye, he went up to Kim and raised his hands in mock-attack. 'You'd best tell me, else I'll tickle yer till you do.'

Kim, unimpressed, stood her ground. 'You're just a big kid, aren't you?'

The big kid, however, was a great deal bigger than her. 'Oh, all right, then. All I'm saying is Trevor's been round him like a bee round a honey pot and that he's been getting a lot of phone calls from someone called . . . Hargrave?'

Jack suddenly stopped fooling about. 'Hargrave? Patrick Hargrave?'

'Yes. Why? Who is he?'

But Jack had already gone straight to Will's room.

Entering without knocking, he saw Will getting changed, aided by Trevor. The latter was already fully kitted out in evening dress. Both men looked up in surprise as Jack rushed in and, without preamble, asked what on earth they were doing messing about with Patrick Hargrave.

'I'm surprised you even know who he is, Jack,' said Will drily.

'Course I know he is. Everyone's heard of Hargrave. Conservative Party king-maker.' Jack's last words were not spoken in awe.

'And I thought you only read the sports pages. That,' added Will, as he narrowed his eyes like a cat and concentrated on tying his bow-tie, 'and the kids' supplements on a Saturday.'

But Jack refused to rise to the bait. 'What exactly does he want?'

'Well – and not that it's really any of your business – it's what he can offer that interests me.'

'And that is?'

It was Trevor, irritated and impatient, who answered the question. 'Will,' he announced with a proud smile, 'has been asked to consider allowing his name to go forward.'

Jack, who had always suspected that Trevor hero-worshipped Will, looked both annoyed at the interruption – and uncomprehending of the statement.

'It's for a vacant ward,' Will explained. 'A seat on the council.'

'It'd be very prestigious for the practice,' Trevor added, as he handed Will his jacket.

'I haven't even been selected yet. Haven't even made up my mind.' Will, too, suspected Trevor of hero-worship and at times it made him feel uncomfortable. This was one of those times: Jack was looking distinctly unimpressed.

'What brought all this on?' he asked. 'Will Preston, champion of the people?'

Will, irritated by his tone, rounded on him. 'It's all a big joke, isn't it? That's your problem, Jack. You like shouting about causes, about injustice. But I never see you getting involved.'

The dig was unfair – and both men knew it. Jack, open-mouthed, stared at him. 'OK,' the latter said in apology, 'that was unfair. But,' he added in a more conciliatory tone, 'how often are we asked to operate with one hand tied behind our backs? Arguing about funding, about facilities. Only our voice never gets heard. Because we're shouting from the sidelines.'

Jack was unconvinced. 'At least that way I know what I'm shouting for.'

'Yes, but the Left hasn't got a monopoly on caring, Jack. That's too easy—'

'So,' Jack interrupted, 'your lot are going to change their spots, are they? After fifteen years of slavish dedication to the great God "private"? All because of you?'

Will's eyes flashed with anger. 'It's best not to get involved, is that it? Stay pure instead. Better to throw up my hands in horror and blame someone else? No, Jack, I'm sorry. We're not separate from the human race. Medicine isn't some Trappist order.'

Jack, surprised by Will's vehemence, held up his hands in mock surrender. 'OK, OK, I was only asking.' Turning to leave the room, he couldn't resist adding, 'I'm sure, at the very least, you'll get a nice dinner out of it. That lot certainly know how to enjoy themselves.'

Will glared at his retreating back and turned to Trevor. 'Sour grapes,' he said with a pitying smile.

That, again, was both unfair and untrue – and Trevor knew it. Yet he didn't bother to respond: he knew Jack and Will too well to think that it would be any use intervening in their personal and political differences. Neither did he have any desire to do so. When Trevor had joined the three doctors at The Beeches as their fund manager, he had quickly realized that their different personalities and views contributed, paradoxically, to a healthy working relationship. When Jack and Will disagreed, Beth would step in as the voice of reason. And if, as was sometimes the case, they were behaving like overgrown schoolboys, Beth wouldn't baulk at treating them as such. And if Beth herself was at loggerheads with either Will or her husband, the other would similarly intervene. Trevor, mild-mannered and generally unassuming, had initially found this clash of strong personalities more than a little alarming.

His wife, however, had soon put him right. Cast in a completely different mould from her husband, the volatile and voluptuous Leanda lost no time in telling him that the best thing he could do was stay on the sidelines. After all, as she had archly declared, Trevor now held the strongest hand: the purse strings. As fund manager, he controlled The Beeches' annual budget and, while that didn't mean he could do exactly what he wanted with the money, it did, he had to concede, make him an integral and important part of the team. So Trevor, secure in the knowledge that he knew more about balancing budgets than the others, had learned not to intervene in any clash of temperaments. And if he did appear to favour Will over the other two doctors it was only, he would insist, because he shared a passion with him: golf. That they had political views in common was a new, and not unwelcome discovery. Trevor, while interested in politics, knew he lacked the clout and force of personality to be elected as a Conservative councillor. Will, though, was perfect material. A dedicated professional, he was also charismatic, forceful when he wanted to be, and a respected member of the community. It had been Trevor who had dropped a word in Patrick Hargrave's ear about Dr Will Preston, and it had been he who had persuaded Will to attend the Conservative Club annual dinner-dance.

Will, flattered and intrigued, found himself becoming increasingly interested in pursuing an interest in politics. The driving force behind The Beeches becoming a fund-holding practice, he now found that, having successfully established it as such, he had more free time on his hands. A born-again bachelor during the week, he relished the weekends when his two sons stayed with him, yet he often found himself at a loose end in the evenings. Politics would provide him with another outlet for his energies. And, as he began to realize while chatting to Patrick Hargrave an hour later, it would give him more clout in the closed, often snobbish community of Cardale.

'The real choice of candidate will be made at the selection meeting on Sunday,' Hargrave was saying. Then, gesturing expansively towards the body of the room, he added, 'Functions like this just give the members the chance to check you're "one of us".' With that, he chuckled. The implication was not lost on Will: Hargrave had already decided that he was 'one of us.' Will, not sure whether to be flattered or annoyed, looked round the room. The grand reception room of a country-house hotel, it was a fitting venue for a Conservative bash. Elegant without being prohibitively expensive, it was accessible to the less wealthy supporters as well as the 'movers and shakers' of the local political world. And Patrick Hargrave was most definitely of the latter category: he was one of Derbyshire's biggest landowners. Will, deciding that annoyance at being so easily pigeon-holed was churlish, turned back to him and smiled. 'Well . . . I can't guarantee they'll go away reassured. If they ask too many questions they may find they don't get the answers they want.'

'Good,' Hargrave said approvingly. 'No harm in stirring 'em up a bit.'

Will was pleased by his companion's response, and surveyed the room again. His gaze alighted on Trevor who was, embarrassingly, watching him to see how he was performing.

Hargrave, too, was looking at Trevor. 'He's with your practice now, isn't he?'

'Mmm. Managing the fund – among other things. I think,' he added with a grin, 'he sees himself as my campaign manager.'

But Hargrave saw no cause for amusement. 'The backbone of the Conservative Association, folk like Trevor. The foot-sloggers of this world. Always ready to shove leaflets through doors at election time.' Then, after a contemplative sip of his drink, he looked back at Will. 'Strictly speaking, as chairman, I have to remain scrupulously neutral at this stage.'

'Of course.'

'But, off the record, William, you've got my vote.'

Will was knocked off-centre by this sudden, direct admission. 'Isn't that a bit premature?' he said, after a moment. 'I've yet to put my case.'

'Ah, but you're not a yes-man. That's what I like. That's why I approached you. We've already got too many of them. What we're short on are those who know what they're talking about.'

Will could feel himself reddening. He hadn't expected such an immediate show of support from such an important source, and he wasn't quite sure how to react. 'Er . . . thank you, Mr Hargrave,' he mumbled.

'Patrick, please.'

A moment later the maître d' announced that dinner

was about to be served and the smartly dressed, high-spirited gathering filed through to the dining room for a five-course dinner that turned out to be every bit as sumptuous as Jack had intimated.

As Will – seated next to Patrick Hargrave's large and somewhat overbearing wife – tucked into a a delicate roulade of smoked salmon with dill sauce, Alice North, back in Cardale, was struggling to get by on altogether less appetizing fare, and in a distinctly less favourable environment. The already inclement weather had worsened and high winds, sweeping down from the craggy dales surrounding the village, began to howl through the streets. All of them, it seemed to Alice, were converging on her house.

In the process of making herself a warm drink, she was diverted from her task by a sudden gust of wind from an air vent near the cooker. With considerable difficulty, she picked up a kitchen rag in an attempt to thwart the draught. Weakened by flu, she barely had enough strength for the task – and none left to boil the kettle. With a weary sigh, she left the kitchen and padded, breath rasping, through to the sitting-room. Slumping into the chair in front of the television, she leaned back against the cushions and closed her eyes.

She was still in the same position twelve hours later, when her 'nosy' neighbour found her.

CHAPTER 3

'Morning. How was the dinner?'

'Oh, God, not you as well.' Hassled, slightly hung-over and more than a little late for his morning's appointments, Will was in no mood to be needled by Beth as well as Jack. Then he noticed her expression of complete bewilderment.

'All I asked,' she said frostily, 'was how the dinner went. I wasn't aware that was an invitation to bite my head off.'

Will had the grace to look sheepish. 'Sorry.' He put a hand to his head. 'I'm feeling a bit . . . well, and I thought you were going to do a Jack on me.'

'I'm not Jack. And what *is* "doing a Jack" anyway?'

'Oh, well, he gave me a lecture on politics yesterday just as I was going off to the dinner. I thought he might have told you.'

'No, he didn't actually. We're not joined at the hip, you know. We don't tell each other absolutely every tiny detail of our lives.' Beth was aware she was sounding more annoyed than she felt. She wasn't annoyed with Will anyway, just with his, and most other people's, assumption that she had lost her status as a separate being when she had married Jack. Half the residents of Cardale, she was sure, had expected her to stop being a doctor and devote her life to washing Jack's socks the minute she had married him.

Will's attention, however, had been caught by the sight of three hulking six-foot specimens of manhood perched precariously on the waiting-room chairs. 'No,' he said. 'I should jolly well hope you don't tell him everything. I suppose you know,' he added, with a wink and a nod in their direction, 'what they're saying about those firemen of yours?'

Beth, grinning, leaned forward and whispered, 'I know. And . . . it's all *true*.'

With that, they both burst out laughing and Will, glad that the difficult moment had passed, left Beth to 'her firemen'. They weren't, of course, hers at all; they were just the latest in the ever-increasing line of patients being treated at The Beeches since they had become fundholders. Beth, initially the most resistant about the prospect of being a business and managing their own budgets, had long since conceded that it had been a good move. Apart from giving The Beeches a reputation for being professional and highly organized, it also meant they were more able to seek the best consultants, advice and treatment for their patients. In consequence, more patients came their way.

The Cardale and District Fire Service had been a case in point. The station officer, David Gilzean, an ambitious man in his mid-thirties, had been keen to switch his department's health care contract away from the county medical officer in order to prove that he knew how to handle his own budget and, equally important, that he was aware of supporting local businesses – of which The Beeches was one. Beth had been delighted and had emphasized how good it would be for his men to know that their health was going to be looked after by a local doctor in whom they could learn to confide. Gilzean, oddly, had not been interested in that concept. Confiding in someone, he implied, suggested that one's mental health was in doubt. And none of his staff, he had told Beth, would have any problems on that front.

Beth, knowing how closely mental and physical health were related, had bitten her tongue. Time, she knew, would tell about that. Yet she had to admit the three firemen currently waiting in reception looked physically and mentally in tip-top form. The fourth, she mused as Will headed for his own room down the corridor, was the one she was worried about. George Milton, in his late forties, was the eldest of the firemen in the Cardale and District service. He was the only one with whom Beth was personally acquainted: she had known him for over a year and she had been a doctor long enough to know that George's health was not the same as it had been twelve months ago. There was something, she suspected, that he was not telling anyone.

Ten minutes later, however, she was beginning to think she might have been mistaken. Laura Elliott, the new practice nurse who had replaced Ellie Ndebela a month before, had just put him through a rigorous physical test, and Beth was now testing his blood pressure. 'Well, George,' she smiled, 'your BP's fine. Your recovery rate would put a lot of people half your age to shame.'

George, heartily relieved, grinned from ear to ear. 'Sounds about right. Fittest grandad for years, that's me. Got a few more years at the sharp end in me yet.'

Beth moved behind the screen to the sink. George, who hadn't been at all chuffed when his teenage daughter Vicky married and almost immediately became pregnant, was now the proudest – as well as the fittest – grandad in Cardale. His three-month-old granddaughter was the apple of his eye, and Vicky had long since been forgiven. Beth, who had looked after her throughout her pregnancy, had enjoyed watching the process by which the Milton family had become reunited. And so delighted were the whole family by her solicitude during those months that they had invited her and Jack to tomorrow's christening. Beth hadn't wanted to accept: she wasn't, she protested, a family friend. Jack, predictably, had told her not to be daft. Yet now that she was employed in a professional capacity by the district fire service, she was even more reluctant to attend. As she was obliged to report to George's boss on the state of his health, the last thing she wanted was to be involved at a personal level with his family. Still, she thought as she washed her hands, at least George is in perfect health.

'Well,' she said, as she emerged from behind the screen, 'that's fine. You're looking at a clean bill of health.' Then, seeing George's expression, she frowned. 'George?' Suddenly George snapped to attention, and the vacant stare of a few seconds ago was gone. Yet that expression had been enough to ring alarm bells in Beth's mind. 'Did you hear a word I said just then?'

George, thinking fast, grinned apologetically. 'Sorry, Beth. Miles away. Got me mind on the christening and that. What were you saying?'

Beth, unconvinced, tried the oldest trick in the book. Positive there was something wrong with his hearing, she moved behind him and then spoke again. George, however, was on to her: he shifted position so that he was facing her as she spoke. 'I was saying that you've got the all clear. Apart from . . . George, why didn't you tell me you had trouble with your hearing?'

George bridled. 'Who says I have?'

Beth shot him a don't-try-to-fool-me look.

'All right, all right. It's not enough to call trouble.'

'So?' Beth folded her arms. 'Tell me.'

'Just a bit of ringing. Like a whistle. But not all the time,' he added.

'Enough to obstruct your aural facility, though? You should have said.'

George, floundering, tried to brush it off. "S not as if it means anything, is it? It's more nuisance than owt else. It's probably a bit of wax got built up. I'll clean 'em out.'

Beth sighed and moved back to her desk. 'I'm sorry, George. If it was just that I would have spotted it. I'm going to fix you an appointment. I want you to have an audiogram.'

'Oh, come on, Beth's not worth all that bother. I mean,' he added with a pleading look, 'how's it going to look on yer report? How's this going to look if . . .?'

But Beth, although sympathetic, was no longer listening. Neither, as she bent to write on his medical notes, could she see the expression in his eyes. George Milton was panic-stricken.

Two hours later, Will's emotions were more complex. Anger and guilt competed with grief as he made his way to Alice North's house. Why, he asked himself for the hundredth time, hadn't he noticed? Why had he so readily assumed that Alice had flu? He allowed himself little relief that her symptoms had been consistent with flu: Will was her doctor and he should have got it right. Furthermore, it was a bitter irony that Mrs Roberts, the neighbour of whom Alice had complained, was the one who had found her – the one who had called the ambulance and then contacted Will to tell him the news.

That news was not good. The consultant gave her a fifty-fifty chance of survival. Rushing to the hospital the minute he was free after morning surgery, Will had drawn little solace from knowing that Alice was a fighter: she would have to battle hard to recover from the carbon-monoxide poisoning that had induced her coma and the hypothermia which had gripped her during the night. And it was all his fault.

Silently berating himself, head bowed and hands thrust angrily into his pockets, Will trudged towards Alice's house. He supposed vaguely that, as well as thanking the neighbour for noticing that Alice had failed to take her milk in that morning, for registering that the curtains hadn't been opened and for calling the ambulance, he was going to try to find out how Alice had managed to poison herself. So lost in thought was he that at first he failed to register that Alice's front door was wide open. When he did notice, he started to run towards the house. The last thing Alice needed was a burglary.

Yet it was a policeman, not a burglar, who greeted Will in the hall. Relief flooded through him as he addressed the stocky constable. 'Oh, I saw the door open. I thought it might be a burglar or something.'

PC Martin smiled. 'No, no. Just securing the house. Er . . . you the neighbour?'

'No. Mrs North's doctor.'

'Ah. Well, we've just had the fire investigation mob down this afternoon. Trying to locate the source of the problem.'

'Did they find anything?'

'Oh, yeah.' PC Martin grinned. 'They don't miss a trick. Here, I'll show yer . . .'

Leading Will into the house, he made straight for the kitchen, opened the large cupboard in the corner and pointed to the ancient, decrepit water-heater. 'There,' he said. 'Leaking like a sieve, that thing.' Then, moving over to the sink, he pointed to the air-vent that Alice had blocked the previous night. 'Normally the fumes would escape – or at least some of them – but she's blocked up all of these. 'S like that all over the house. Poor old bird's been breathing in carbon monoxide from this antiques roadshow.'

Will was horrified. This was the first time he had been to this house without Alice's eagle eye watching over him and, with the leisure to inspect it, he only now appreciated just how dilapidated were many of the fixtures and fittings. PC Martin, however, anxious to lock up and be on the move, ushered him out before he had a chance to look further.

'Tell you what,' continued the policeman as they exited

into the street, 'I don't know who the landlord is but he needs taking out and shooting.'

'What will he be charged with?'

'Charged?' Martin looked surprised. 'Oh, no, it's not one for us, Doctor. It's a civil case – if that. We won't even investigate it. After all,' he added, with heavy irony, 'it's not criminal, is it?'

Will, fuming with the injustice of it all, found himself walking away from the house in as bad a mood as he had arrived in. Yet this time there was a difference: this time he could do something about the sort of social injustice that led to old ladies being poisoned – albeit not deliberately – by rapacious and uncaring landlords. If, that is, he was elected to the council. Even if Alice North died as a result of what had happened, her death, Will resolved, would not be entirely in vain.

Alice didn't die. By the next day she was out of her coma and, though still pale and weak, had regained much of her customary belligerence. While hugely relieved, Will made a point of treating her in his normal, abrupt manner.

'I can't see how you expect anyone to operate as your GP,' he said, scathingly, 'when you consistently fail to confide in them.'

Alice, defiant, avoided his eye. Still stranded in her hospital bed, she felt herself at a distinct disadvantage with Will towering over her.

'Flu symptoms?' he persisted, '"A bit of a chill"?'

'If I didn't know you better, Doctor Preston, it'd sound like you were feeling guilty about summat.' Alice's look was fierce – and knowing.

Ouch, thought Will. 'So,' he said after a moment, 'how are you feeling now?'

'Stupid. All this bother.' Alice gestured around her. 'What's the cost of all this?'

'It's for your own good, Alice. And just for once in your life you're going to let someone else be the judge of that.'

'Going on and on about the cost of beds . . .' Suddenly Alice lost interest in her new theme as a thought occurred to her. 'Is my house locked up? I don't want burglars.'

'Yes. The police have seen to that.'

'Humph.' Alice clearly felt much the same about police as she did about doctors.

'Alice . . . who d'you rent your house off?'

'Why? Don't tell me they want to evict me for being a nuisance?'

'If anything,' said Will with a derisive snort, 'it should be the other way round.'

'It's not the council. I pay me own way.'

Will wasn't surprised: Alice's resistance to being 'looked after' spread to every area of her life. 'So who is it, Alice?'

'Hargrave Holdings. Why?'

That was the last thing Will had expected to hear. '*Hargrave?*'

'Aye. He owns half the houses down there.'

'*Patrick* Hargrave?'

Alice shot him a withering look. 'Aye. There's only one Hargrave round these parts. You ought to know that. Mind you,' she added, 'I've no time for landlords. All rogues, the lot of 'em. Compared to what some have to put up with, though, Hargrave's not been so bad.'

Will, shocked by Alice's revelation, was also unconvinced by her protestations of loyalty. He stood rubbing his chin in silent contemplation, already revising the speech he was going to make to the selection committee this afternoon. Hargrave, he mused, was in for a shock.

If Will was feeling uncomfortable at Alice's bedside, Beth was feeling even more so as she stood in the living room of George Milton's house, making polite conversation –

and wishing heartily that she was elsewhere. The unhappy result of her medical examination of George had been embarrassing enough, but to be standing here at his granddaughter's christening party was making things infinitely worse. That, and Beth's dislike of christenings anyway, was making her feel miserable. Vicky, George's daughter, had just been extolling the virtues of motherhood, which, nowadays, made Beth feel like screaming. Beth Glover, the capable and independent doctor, was the last person anyone would suspect of feeling broody – but that was exactly how she felt.

Managing to excuse herself from Vicky, she went straight from the frying-pan into the fire: she found herself face to face with David Gilzean.

'Doctor Glover?' Gilzean looked half-puzzled, half-amused. 'I didn't know you'd be keeping an eye on my lads off-duty as well.'

Beth's smile was rather more frosty than she intended. 'This is purely social, Mr Gilzean.'

Gilzean didn't appear to notice her ill-humour. 'I'll put aside a morning next week to go through your reports.' With a cryptic smile, he added, 'They should make interesting reading.'

Beth, unsure of how to reply, just nodded. There was no love lost, she knew, between George Milton and David Gilzean. The latter had long been looking for a way to get rid of George from his team and now, thanks to Beth, it looked like he might be able to do so. Feeling even more wretched, Beth edged through the throng to Jack. She noted, with wry amusement, that he was holding court to a bunch of Vicky's girlfriends.

'Jack,' she teased, as she grabbed his arm, 'you're old enough to be their father.'

Jack was incensed. 'I'm not that old!'

Beth grinned. 'Look, I'm going to say goodbye to Pam and George, then I'm off. I did promise Isabel.'

'Did you?'

'Yes, I *told* you, Jack. A girls-only dog-walking session.'

'Oh, yes, I forgot.' Jack looked towards the table, laden with food and drink. 'I might hang on then. George has laid on a good spread. Be a shame to see it go to waste.'

'Hmm.' Beth, also looking around, was scanning the room for her host. 'Any idea where he is?'

'Upstairs.' Jack chuckled. 'Getting in fresh supplies.'

George was indeed upstairs, but he was singularly failing to fetch the fresh supplies of drink. Climbing the stairs, he had felt himself breaking out into a cold sweat; his vision had become blurred and his breathing more and more difficult. He had managed to stumble into the spare bedroom – and the next thing he was aware of was Beth standing over him. 'George! Are you all right?'

Blinking hard, still disorientated, George managed, 'I'm – I'm fine, Beth. Nothing I can't deal with.'

At that, Beth closed the door behind her and sat on the bed as George, seemingly indeed fine, rose to his feet. 'Has this happened before?'

George, reluctant to reply, was cornered nonetheless. 'Once.' Beth looked at him. 'Well . . . twice at the outside.'

'George, blackouts aren't something you can just shrug off.'

George sighed in defeat. 'I know that. But not here, eh, Beth? Not now. Today's special.'

His plea had the desired effect. Beth, both touched and concerned, looked speculatively at him. 'When's your next shift?'

'Tomorrow. Late.'

Beth stood up. 'You're to ring in sick. I want to see you first thing. Is that understood?'

George, knowing she would brook no argument,

nodded in assent. 'I'd best get cleaned up.' Then he smiled and tapped the crate of beer he had come to fetch. 'There's people downstairs going without.'

Beth, silent and thoughtful, followed him down the stairs. It was at times like this that she hated being a doctor, being responsible both for lives and livelihoods. It was at times like this that she needed Isabel.

If Beth was looking forward to their afternoon of dog-walking on the moors, Isabel was dreading it. Yet she had decided that enough was enough; Beth had to be told and there was no point in delaying it any further.

An hour later, the two women, warmly wrapped against the bitter cold and biting wind, strode across the moors as they had done hundreds of times before. The dogs, Isabel's Molly and Beth's Connal, bounded on ahead. Isabel, who had been steeling herself to confide in Beth, found instead that Beth, silent and self-absorbed, appeared to have even more on her mind. 'Problems?' she asked, after a particularly long silence. 'D'you want to talk?'

Beth gave her the benefit of a rueful smile. 'Can't.'

'Oh. Patient confidentiality?'

'Mmm. Mostly it's trying to get people to see that what you're doing is in their best interests – and sometimes doubting that it is.'

This, thought Isabel, was most unlike Beth. 'Beth Glover? Self-doubts?'

But Beth was not in the mood for levity. Suddenly she waved her arms in a gesture of helplessness. 'Why are people so stubborn?' she almost shouted. 'Sometimes I just don't want to play God. To have . . . the power of life and death.'

Isabel looked sidelong at her friend. Then, drawing in her breath, she answered, as if to herself, 'You don't, Beth.'

For a few moments more, both women strode on in silence. Isabel, leading the way, reached her favourite part of the moor: a high, craggy outcrop, it was the perfect vantage-point from which to view the dales in all their rugged beauty. She thrust her hands deep into her pockets and surveyed the landscape in silence. Then she turned to Beth. Her voice was slightly strained as she spoke. 'You know, Beth, there'll come a time when I'm not here for your problems.'

Beth, however, failed to pick up on Isabel's serious tone. Bending for a small stone, she tossed it in front of her and watched it gather momentum as it rolled down the hillside, rattling around as it made its way into the valley below. 'I can't go back to writing to agony aunts,' she said flippantly. 'Haven't done that since I was sixteen.'

Isabel would normally have replied with an equally throw-away remark. But this time she stared straight ahead, tensed, and seemed to withdraw into herself. For the first time, a seed of doubt, a flicker of fear, crept into Beth's mind. 'Isabel?'

'I'm sorry, Beth.' Isabel's voice was terse, distant. She still refused to meet Beth's eye. 'This isn't easy. I have cancer of the pancreas. It's at an advanced stage.'

That moment would stay with Beth for the rest of her life. Even years later, she could cast her mind back and visualize Isabel standing proud and dignified, immaculate as ever, and delivering the most devastating words Beth had ever heard. Yet the one thing Beth would never be able to remember was her own reaction to the news: her system, she later realized, had simply shut down. Her body treated the news as it would a physical trauma; it enveloped itself in numbness.

Isabel, unable to bear the silence, turned to her friend and saw that she was trying, yet failing, to say something. 'Please,' she urged, 'don't ask me anything medical. It's a bit late to tell you this, but the inner workings of the body have always bored me senseless.'

Almost in desperation, Beth latched on to the easiest way to respond: as a doctor. 'There are new ways of treating cancer.' She could hear her own voice: flat and wooden, it was devoid of emotion. 'It needn't be fatal. You can't just give up.' How many times had she said those words – and to how many people? How many times had she urged people to believe them? Beth had always tried to believe that where there was life there was hope. But now, looking at Isabel, she knew with a sudden, dreadful finality that this time there was no hope.

'I've not given up, Beth.' Isabel was still staring, unseeing now, into the distance. 'The choice was out of my hands. In different circumstances I would have fought. Tooth and nail. But the carcinoma is inoperable. They found it too late.' Then she shrugged and looked at Beth with a weary smile. 'I've been through all of this.'

Beth, suddenly, was hurt, and angry with her closest friend for keeping this secret, for excluding her for the first time from the details of her life. She knew it was a childish, petulant reaction, but she couldn't help herself. 'When?' she barked. 'Who with?'

Isabel, amused despite herself, smiled again. 'A friend. A very good surgeon. He's been very kind. The pain,' she added, 'is bearable.' Now the two woman locked eyes and Isabel registered Beth's bewilderment, her pain and her impotent anger. 'I never meant to exclude you, Beth. It was something I had to come to terms with first. To make my own decisions. Now I *have* made them. You see . . .' Isabel looked away again, yet Beth knew that she was looking into herself. '. . . I now know that I don't need to cling to every last breath, to try to cheat myself an extra day, an extra month, while the cancer just spreads. I love life, but I'm not afraid of death. Not spiritually.' Then she looked once more into Beth's eyes. 'I have made my peace, Beth.'

Beth, blinking furiously, returned her gaze. 'Who . . . who have you told?'

'You. I couldn't go on without telling you. I'd feel that I'd let you down.'

Beth had to bite her lip before the words came out. 'You've never let me down.' Then, unable to control her emotions, powerless to stop the tears coursing down her cheeks, she threw herself into Isabel's arms. Clinging to her like a child, she buried her head on Isabel's shoulder and let the tears flow. She knew she was crying for herself; for the sheer unfairness of life; for the loss and the aching void that Isabel would leave that nothing and nobody would ever fill.

CH A PTER 4

Trevor, aghast, looked at Will's unkempt appearance, his scruffy jeans and his open-necked shirt. 'You can't go in and address the committee like that!'

'Why on earth not?'

'Well . . . er . . .' Alarmed by Will's aggressive tone, Trevor backed off. Then, looking at his watch, he tried another tack. 'Anyway, you were s'posed to be here ages ago. The committee won't like it if they miss the bar.'

'That,' said Will, 'would be tragic.'

What the hell, Trevor wondered, had got into Will today? It was almost as if he were spoiling for a fight. And if that were the case, there was nothing he could do about it. 'Well, anyway,' he grinned, 'knock 'em dead.'

'Unfortunate choice of phrase, Trevor.' With that, Will stormed through the reception area and into the hallowed confines of the Conservative Club meeting room.

Trevor had been absolutely right: Will *was* spoiling for a fight. The Alice North episode had troubled him greatly and he was still fizzing at the injustice. It was all very well for the likes of Patrick Hargrave to bang on about how effectively the Conservatives could run the council and improve local services, he fumed, but he now knew that when it came to dipping into their own deeply lined pockets it was a different story. Obviously, their greatest priority was 'looking after their own'.

Hargrave had intimated that Will's interview with the committee would be no more than a formality. After being introduced to the members and ushered to a seat opposite them, Will reflected that the man was in for a shock.

'Doctors,' began Hargrave, with a friendly smile, 'have a reputation for believing that funding is a bottomless bucket, William. As a councillor, would you be tough enough to set a tight budget?'

'The Beeches,' Will snapped, 'is a fundholding practice. I take difficult – not to say critical – decisions every day.'

Hargrave, surprised by Will's confrontational attitude, could only mumble an 'of course'. Will, however, hadn't finished. 'Perhaps that question,' he continued, 'is one that I should be asking the committee.'

'Er . . . in what way?'

'Since moving to Cardale I've observed any number of council decisions that, to be charitable, could only be described as feeble, maybe even grossly inept.'

At that, and at the glowering look that accompanied the words, a frisson of unease rippled through the committee. They were used to people who regarded it as a privilege to be interviewed, not people who threw the gauntlet at them.

'Inept?' Hargrave was stunned.

'As I say, that is being charitable.'

'Perhaps an example might help.'

Will looked squarely at the committee. 'I'm currently treating a young woman for obesity, a condition she's now visiting upon her youngest child. Their treatment is costing . . . what? How many man hours down the drain? And yet it's all just so much wasted effort. Money, as well, down the drain.'

Hargrave was genuinely puzzled by Will's 'example'. 'And the fault rests at our door?'

'In a way, yes. You see, she can't stick to the diet sheets. It's impossible. The only shop she can get to sells tinned everything. Crisps. Pork pies. They don't sell fresh produce because they can't compete with a new supermarket seven miles away. A supermarket,' Will repeated, with an accusatory glare, 'for which you approved planning permission. A supermarket my patient can't reach. The bus route was cut. It was unprofitable.'

'The young lady's plight,' began Hargrave, 'is regrettable, but—'

'It is also avoidable,' Will interrupted. 'Too many of your decisions are taken with total disregard for the *social costs*. I see that in my surgery, day in, day out. It you like, we at The Beeches are footing the bill for your mistakes.' From the expressions on the faces of those opposite him, it was plain they didn't like that. Not one bit. 'To my mind,' continued Will, 'that amounts to false bookkeeping. One might even say, a form of fraud.'

Trevor, sitting quietly in the corner, groaned to himself. This was a nightmare. The man had gone mad. Surely things couldn't get any worse.

Things, however, did get worse. By the end of the session, Will had succeeded in antagonizing every member of the committee – except Patrick Hargrave. To Will's annoyance, Hargrave actually appeared to admire his combative stance and belligerent tone, which was particularly galling for Will as Hargrave was the target of his spleen.

In the bar at the end of the session, Hargrave came up to him. To the latter's irritation, he was grinning wickedly. 'Quite a performance, William. Never hurts to let them see you've got your own mind.'

'Is that what I was doing? Performing? I'm sorry, Mr Hargrave, I meant every word.'

'I don't quite—'

Will stopped him with an angry wave of his hand. 'In fact, to be honest, I don't know what I'm doing here. This place is about *you*. Your ethos. I can't change that.'

Hargrave, astounded and rather hurt by Will's invective, only just managed to keep his temper. 'And what,' he asked in a quiet voice, '*is* my ethos?'

'Money. First and last.'

Hargrave sighed. 'Look, William, what exactly is all this about?'

'About? It's about an old woman called Alice North who's been slowly poisoned by her "ever-so-caring" landlord.' Will almost spat the words at Hargrave. 'And rather than endure the stigma of being a "drain" on resources she very nearly died as a result.' With one last, disgusted look, Will turned on his heel. 'You probably don't know her. She's just a figure in the profit column on Hargrave Holdings.'

Hargrave, speechless, watched Will storm out. Will had been right about many things – but wrong about Alice North. Patrick Hargrave knew perfectly well who she was. He, like Will, was one of her old adversaries.

Will had cooled off by the time he got back to The Beeches. And by the time a rather sullen Trevor appeared, he had simmered down to a state of contrition.

'I . . . er, wanted to apologize.' Looking somewhat sheepish, Will stood on the threshold of Trevor's room. 'If I caused you any embarrassment,' he continued, 'I'm very sorry. All I can say is perhaps next time you'll be less ready to nail your colours to my mast.'

But Trevor appeared to have something else on his mind. 'You were wrong to storm out like that, you know.'

'You're entitled—'

'No.' Trevor, uncharacteristically, cut him off with a forceful denial. 'If half them things you said is what you believe, then more than ever you should stand. I'm not saying that's how I saw things before but I can see you were right.' Trevor nodded in affirmation of his own words. 'I know that much.'

This was the last thing Will had expected. He had been sure Trevor would be gruff, annoyed and ashamed.

Instead it seemed that he had been converted to Will's cause. Unsure of how to reply, he shook his head and walked back to his own room. Did he, he wondered, still have a cause? Was he still interested? Sighing, he tried to concentrate on being a doctor.

Three hours later he went to visit Alice. Now out of hospital, she had made a remarkable and full recovery – so much so that she was back in fighting form, and doing battle with the workmen who were inundating her house.

'What on earth . . .?' Will began.

'Been here since first thing.' Alice glared at one of the men, who retaliated by blowing her a kiss. 'New heating system,' she growled. 'I made sure I was here to keep an eye on 'em, mind. Doctors didn't want to let me go – but I put 'em straight.'

'I'm sure you did, Alice.' Will didn't envy any doctor unaccustomed to Alice North. 'But,' he added as he took in the mess, 'where are you going? You can't stay here. This'll take days.'

'And a load of nonsense it'll be at the finish. Boiling one minute, freezing the next, most like.' Alice was quivering with disapproval. 'I've told 'em enough times.'

Alarm bells suddenly rang in Will's head. 'Told them what, Alice?'

'That I didn't want it. Central heating. They keep going on about it. It's bound to cost the devil to run.'

'Alice, are you telling me that you've turned down your landlord's requests to modernize your central heating?' Will found that he was nearly shouting at her.

Alice, however, was unfazed. 'I was happy with what I knew,' she grumbled.

Will ran a hand wearily through his hair. 'I wish you'd told me this earlier, Alice.'

'You never asked me.'

Will bit back a sharp reply. That was true, he thought. I never even bothered to try to find out the full story. I just rushed in like a bull in a china shop. Yet before he could think of a suitable rejoinder, they were interrupted by a neatly dressed, kindly woman appearing through the back door. 'Hello,' she said with a smile at Will, 'you must be Doctor Preston.' With that she held out her hand and introduced herself. 'Mrs Roberts – the neighbour.' Then she turned to Alice. 'I'm just airing the spare room. You'll be very comfy in there.'

Will couldn't help grinning – Alice was looking hugely embarrassed. 'Well,' she said in a gruff stage whisper, 'it were stay with her, or stay in hospital. Lesser of two evils.'

Mrs Roberts, who already had the measure of Alice, winked at Will.

Beth found herself plodding mechanically through the day. She had cried all over Isabel and she had spent half the weekend crying all over Jack. Like her, he had been horrified and deeply upset by Isabel's revelation: Beth's best friend, surrogate mother and confidante had also become one of Jack's closest friends in Cardale. Yet, understanding that his wife's relationship with Isabel was, in its way, special and sacred, he had let her give free rein to her emotions while keeping his own in check. Throughout the weekend, he had been the proverbial tower of strength.

Now, back at work, Beth was feeling completely washed out – and slightly ashamed. Death, she knew, always brought out a selfishness in those who were to be left, and she was now feeling that her own reaction had been more than usually selfish. If Isabel had managed to avoid the 'why me?' syndrome, then Beth, so she told herself, had no business wallowing in self-pity. Not that being at The

Beeches gave her much time to do that. Especially now that she had the Cardale and District Fire Service to deal with.

As she picked up her coat and medical bag, she thought, not particularly charitably, about David Gilzean. Admittedly, when he had called just now, he had sounded as if he was in urgent need of a doctor, but Beth couldn't help wondering if he now felt that, in Beth and The Beeches, he had his own private medical team. Time, she supposed, would tell. She called to Kim that she would be back within the hour, and made her way to her car.

As she drove, she thought about the other problem with 'her' firemen: George Milton. He had not, as she had insisted, come to visit her the previous evening. No doubt he thought he knew best about his health. She, however, was worried about him. All she could hope was that he had listened to her advice and called in sick.

When she reached the deserted factory to which David Gilzean had called her, she quickly forgot her irritation. It was abundantly clear that she was indeed needed: Casey, the young boy who was stuck high up on the dangerous rafters of the building, was one of her patients.

'I wanted medical cover here as back-up,' said Gilzean without preamble, 'because, from what his brother says, the lad's a bit dodgy all round.'

Not, thought Beth, the most tactful way of putting it. 'He has mild epilepsy,' she countered, with an edge to her voice, 'a few behavioural difficulties, that's all.'

'Hmm.' Gilzean was reflecting why he, a trained firefighter, should have to spend half his time trying to rescue stupid boys who found themselves in desperate straits as the result of a juvenile dare. Then he looked sharply at the other boy, now standing beside him and Beth. 'This,' he said, 'is Jamie. His brother. He were one of the idiots who encouraged the lad to climb up there.'

Jamie, now too frightened and distressed to defend himself from the jibe, looked hopefully up at Beth. She bent towards him. 'Jamie, are your parents being fetched?'

Jamie shook his head. 'Them's in Nottingham. Work.'

'I know you're scared for Casey, but I need to know what medicine your brother's on.'

Jamie wrinkled his brow. 'Dunno. Long words. He doesn't take 'em anyway. Casey always has to know best.'

At that moment, Terri Hellier, the young firewoman who had arrived at the wheel of the fire tender, marched up to Gilzean. 'We can't get to him from inside and he won't move to help himself.'

'How does he look?' asked Beth with a worried frown.

'Like he's not all there.' Terri looked anxious. 'Vacant.'

Gilzean turned back to Beth. 'What does that mean, Doctor?'

'It's probably a staring fit. Possibly a precursor to epileptic convulsions.'

'Christ. That's all we need.' Gilzean gazed up at the precarious structure. 'He'll bring the whole lot down.'

'If you can get me to him I might be able to administer some in vitro diazepam. It'll calm him. If not,' Beth added with a shrug, 'it's just a matter of time.'

Gilzean turned to the fire-fighters. 'Let's get the cradle sorted.' Then, frowning, he said to Beth, 'I hope you're sure about this.'

Beth, looking upwards, wasn't sure at all. She wasn't exactly crazy about heights. The factory wall, with the terrified boy clinging to the outside edge of one of the rafters, suddenly seemed an impossible height. If she didn't go up, though, Casey would simply fall to his death. It was as simple as that.

A minute later she was in the cradle of the fire tender realizing that it wasn't, after all, quite so simple. Her companion – her only companion – was George Milton.

Horrified, she stared at him, disbelieving, and then, in

a quiet, urgent voice, told him that he couldn't go up, that he simply wasn't fit.

There was more than a hint of desperation in George's voice as he pleaded with her. 'Please, Doctor Glover, I'm fine. Really.'

'How can I know that? Unless you're honest with me? Unless you allow yourself to be treated?'

'I just got giddy before,' protested George. 'But I can control it. I *am* controlling it.'

Beth, distinctly sceptical, looked him straight in the eye. They both knew what she, in the space of a few seconds, could do: she could ruin George's career. Suddenly George glared at her. 'Go on, then, tell 'em! It's what you want. That way you'll have covered yourself, won't you?'

For a moment they stood, immobile. Then Gilzean, unnoticed by either of them, came up and closed the cradle lift. 'Set to go?' He smiled.

There was no choice. As he spoke Terri Hellier, inside the tender, began to winch them up towards the dark, forbidding wall of the factory.

Will was feeling distinctly stupid. Standing in the bar of the Conservative Club, he had swallowed his pride and apologised unreservedly to Patrick Hargrave.

Hargrave, as usual, was unperturbed – even slightly amused. 'You're not the first to think the worst of me, William.'

'I didn't know the full story. What I knew fitted—'

Hargrave held up a restraining had. 'I know, I know. You look at me, at this place, it's easy to jump to conclusions.'

'Well, I'm sorry.'

'Don't be. It's good to be hauled over the coals once in a while.' Hargrave, indicating for Will to follow, moved across to the vast window that gave on to the sweeping panorama below them. 'Most of my land's been in the family for centuries. Farming land. The house that Mrs North lives in,' he added with a smile, 'was for crop hands until recently.'

'Times change.'

'Mmm. But for the better? The problem is there are no rules any more,' continued Hargrave. 'We ran around busting up the old social order, sweeping it all away. What were we left with?' Sighing, he glanced at Will. 'Now people are crying out for a bit of order, something to cling to, only there's no one knows how to put the pieces together again.'

'And you do?'

'No.' Hargrave shook his head in sorrow. 'I'm as confused as the rest. That's why I was looking to someone like you, William. Younger. Keener eyes. The offer,' he added with a grin, 'is still on the table. You ruffled a few feathers, but . . .'

'No.' Will, though tremendously flattered, had made up his mind. 'I don't think being a doctor's the best standpoint for taking a dispassionate view. I want to change things.' He gestured back towards the large, plush bar of the Conservative Club and added, 'I thought this might give me a voice. I was wrong. I had one already.'

Beth, too, wanted to change things. Yet her 'voice' as a doctor was putting her in one of the most difficult positions of her life. At least, she thought with relief, she had survived the alarming experience of being hoisted up in the cradle of the fire tender, of succeeding in tranquillizing and rescuing the terrified boy on the rafters, and of being lowered back to safety. But, more importantly, George had also survived without mishap.

'I was always the one out climbing trees as a kid,' he said as they walked away from the mêlée surrounding

Casey, Jamie and the firefighters, 'Out on the roof if they didn't stop me.' He grinned ruefully. 'I had no fear.'

'So when was it you first realized things had changed?'

'Months ago. I were on a shout. Office building.' George winced at the memory. 'I froze. After that, whenever it came on, I learned to bluff.' Suddenly he grabbed Beth's arm. 'Why? Why now?'

Beth shook her head. 'I can't be sure. But I think you've developed Menière's syndrome. Vertigo. There's been an increase of fluids in the inner ear.' She looked up at him. 'That's what causes the giddiness, George. The nausea. It comes on in middle age. It's not unusual.'

George looked horrified. 'Vertigo? But I'm a *fireman!*' Urgent and pleading, he stared at Beth. 'There's a cure, ain't there? Drugs to make it go away?'

'I'm sorry. We can contain it – that's all. A course of Betahistine. A change in your diet.' Seeing George's stricken expression, she ploughed on, determined to make him see the light. 'I know one thing, George. If you don't stop this – now – it'll just get worse. You're already suffering hearing loss. That'll accelerate.'

'But this is what I am.' George gestured to his uniform, to the fire tender and his colleagues. 'A fireman. That's me.'

'Just that? How about George Milton, husband? Father? Grandfather?'

George looked at her in surprise. He had always, he supposed, defined himself by his profession. Seizing the initiative, Beth pressed her case. 'At the christening Pam mentioned something about the Brigade offering retraining—'

'Yeah.' George snorted in derision. 'And where would that leave me? Behind a desk? Going round giving little lectures on fire safety? Can you really see me doing that?'

'That's up to you.' With an odd little smile, Beth turned and retraced her steps towards the old factory. As George caught up with her, she looked at him and smiled again, this time with warmth. 'You know, George, the nicest thing about the christening was the sound of Eamonn and Vicky's baby crying. If you want to carry on as you are you'd best store that in your memory. Because you won't be hearing her Confirmation vows. And you'll be sitting through her wedding with the sound turned off.'

For the first time, George was seriously alarmed. Beth, at last, had hit the right note. George's pride in his granddaughter was even greater than his pride in his job. She looked at him out of the corner of her eye and saw something new in his demeanour that told her he would agree to retrain. Life, after all, was more important than anything else. If George could no longer save other lives, he could at least be at hand to enjoy the life of Vicky's baby.

Suddenly, Beth felt old and weary. It seemed that she was always in the middle of life and death, always saving one and preventing the other. And then she thought of Isabel. Where one life ends, Isabel would say, another always begins. Not for the first time, Beth wished she had Isabel's faith.

CHAPTER 5

Shortly after her encounter with Beth, Isabel noticed her health deteriorate rapidly. It was almost as if, having cleared the final hurdle of telling Beth, both her body and her spirit were indicating to her that there was now nothing more to be done; that her fight against the increasing pain would be short and dignified. For that she was profoundly glad. The pain was something she hated and resented, yet she had been speaking the truth when she had informed Beth that she was not afraid of death. She had made peace with herself, with those around her, and with her Maker. Her strong, unwavering Catholicism was her ultimate solace in life and she knew it would be the same in death. Isabel de Gines had never shirked from tackling anything – however unpleasant or daunting – and she was tackling this final challenge with her customary strength. Yet she was fully aware that others found it difficult to share her stoicism. It was ironic, she thought, as she looked round her dinner table, that those finding it most difficult were doctors.

Isabel had taken on board Jack's comment that she had been avoiding them, and tonight, three weeks after dropping her bombshell on Beth, she hoped she had made up for that. The meal, even if she said it herself, had been magnificent. The wines had been even better. Thinking of the wine, she allowed herself a small smile – and a brief thought of her husband. Seven years ago, Dominic had faced death with even more fatalism then she herself could summon. The only thing, he had joked, that he couldn't face was the thought of leaving his wine cellar behind.

Isabel had said not to worry: she would find plenty of opportunities to raid it, and plenty of people to appreciate it. Will, she noticed with a grin, had done a lot of raiding – and a great deal of appreciating.

'Puligny Montrachet,' he said, with a slight slur, 'then Château Leoville Barton. And now *this*.' He held up his glass of exquisite Sauterne. 'What's the occasion, Isabel?'

Isabel, smiling contentedly, raised her glass and looked from Will to Jack and then Beth. 'Good friends. Isn't that reason enough?'

At that, Jack and Beth exchanged a swift look. Before coming out that evening, Beth had shed a tear and voiced her fears that this might be some sort of 'last supper'. Jack had told her not to be so ridiculous. 'Isabel looks magnificent,' he had said. 'Christ, Beth, you wouldn't even know she was ill.'

But Beth knew. Even if Isabel hadn't told her, she would have been able to tell by now. She stole a quick glance at her friend. Isabel *did* still look magnificent – but the tell-tale signs did not escape Beth: the new lines round her eyes; the sometimes haunted, sometimes pained look; the subtle yet heavy make-up and the expensively tailored new clothes that successfully disguised the loss of weight – all were indications that Isabel was not at all well.

Will sipped the sweet wine and his eyes lit up. 'Well, I just hope you'll consider me a good friend on a regular basis in the future . . .' Then, realizing what he had said, he looked momentarily panic-stricken. 'Er, your wine is truly magnificent.'

'But,' replied Isabel, who had not missed his discomfiture, 'it wasn't made from water. Of that, Will, I can assure you.'

Thank God, thought Beth, for Isabel's quick wit. The awkward moment over, they settled down to enjoy their wine and the gloriously creamy and thoroughly unhealthy pudding that it accompanied.

Twenty minutes later, Beth helped Isabel clear the plates and followed her into the kitchen. Isabel knew perfectly well what was coming: if Beth could tell Isabel's state of mind by her outward appearance, then the same was true of her. Beth had 'concern' written all over her.

'How are you feeling, Isabel?'

Busy with the coffee tray, Isabel grinned to herself. 'Thankful for morphine.'

'Mmm.' Beth lapsed into silence and then, frowning, addressed Isabel once more. 'Have you thought about using a Macmillan nurse? They'd drop by and—'

'Beth.' It was the reproachful voice Beth remembered from her childhood. 'I don't want anyone fussing over me. Not in my own home.'

'No one would be fussing. I just want you to consider the option.'

Isabel, the corners of her mouth twitching, looked at her friend. 'Consider it considered. The answer's no.' Then, registering Beth's look, she added in a gentler tone, 'You know I'd only drive the poor woman to hell and back. I don't want to be a burden to my friends, to you. If it gets to that point, but . . . but I'm coping for now, Beth.'

'Well, all I can say is that you're a stubborn old fool.'

'You wouldn't have me any other way,' countered Isabel. Then, glad that the subject had been dealt with, she turned to the kettle.

Beth was about to take the tray of cups through to the dining-room, but suddenly groaned as she heard the phone ringing. 'Damn! It's not yours, Isabel. I'm afraid it's my mobile. The worst thing about being on call is that—'

'Will and Jack get to drink your share of the wine.'

'You said it.' Beth picked up her phone and moved into the hall to answer it. 'Sorry, I'll just take this. Hopefully I'll be able to deal with it over the phone.'

Yet as she listened to the urgent voice at the other end of the line, her hopes were dashed. Two minutes later she popped her head round the dining-room door and grimaced. 'I'm sorry, Isabel, I've got to go.' Isabel, like Jack and Will, looked bitterly disappointed. Beth noticed they were already tackling the brandy and were obviously settling down for a long, mellow evening. 'Sorry.'

'Not as sorry as I am, Beth,' Isabel said good-naturedly. 'Still, another time . . .'

Once again there was a brief, awkward silence.

'Yes,' said Beth. Then, draping her coat over her shoulders, she stepped forward to kiss Isabel. With a cheery wave at Will and her husband, she grabbed her bag and left the room. Of all nights, she said to herself, it *would* have to be tonight. Rarely did she resent being called out, but now, as she drove away from Isabel's in the direction of the housing estate on the outskirts of Cardale, she could barely contain her irritation.

By the time she reached her destination, she had calmed down. Lisa and Martin Harding were the last people on earth to call out a doctor on a whim, and she was sure their concern about their daughter was both genuine and warranted. Decent and hard-working, both in their mid-thirties, the Hardings were long-standing patients at The Beeches and Beth had always been impressed by their attitude towards their three young children. If eight-year-old Louise appeared to her mother to be ill, then Beth could be sure she *was* ill.

Louise's father, however, was not so sure. As Beth examined the flushed little girl, she was aware of dissent between her parents. 'I told you that it would only be a touch of flu,' said Martin to his wife.

'Yes, but . . .' Lisa, distraught, turned to Beth. 'I'm really sorry for calling you out like this on a Sunday, Dr Glover.'

Beth straightened up and smiled at the couple. 'Always best to be on the safe side. But yes, it *does* look like flu. Louise has a high temperature and pharyngitis and—' She stopped as she felt a tug at her sleeve. It was Tom, a year older than Louise and clearly put out that he was not being examined too. He looked up at Beth cheekily, opened his mouth as wide as he could and made a loud 'aaah' sound. Beth giggled at his antics. 'Actually,' she said as she ruffled the boy's hair, 'it looks like Tom has a touch of pharyngitis as well.'

'Maybe a flu bug going around, eh?'

'Mmm.' That was the only thing puzzling Beth. Everybody in Cardale, it seemed to her, had already had flu. Then she shrugged and reached for her bag. 'Either of them allergic to penicillin?'

'No.'

'Right. I'll prescribe a course for each of them. Just make sure you keep them indoors, with plenty of rest.'

Lisa made a face and looked at her three children. Eddie, the ten-year-old, was bouncing up and down on the other bed in Louise's room, evidently intent on proving that there was nothing wrong with him. But even if he wasn't ill, if she had to keep the other two inside, her hands would be full. 'Do they all turn into monsters at a certain age, or is it just mine?'

Beth grinned. 'You'll be glad to know, it's what passes for normal, Lisa.'

Martin gave Eddie a playful cuff on the head, and said to Beth, 'Well, glad that's sorted out. I'll get off to work, then. Don't want to be late.'

'Still with the security firm, then?'

'Yep. Good job, and the pay's good, too. Mind you,' he added, 'it's a bit difficult to get any kip during the day. Them next door. Always making some bloody racket or other.'

'Oh.' Beth closed her bag and made to leave the room. The last thing she wanted was to get into a discussion about 'them next door'. Half of Cardale was already up in arms about them. She didn't need a Sunday night lecture

71

from Martin as well. 'Well,' she said brightly, 'I'll be off, then. If they don't improve in the next few days, just give me a call.'

Lisa, misinterpreting the cause of Beth's sudden aura of disapproval, looked abashed. 'I'm sure there'll be no problem. And thanks for coming, Doctor. We really appreciate it.'

Driving home, Beth turned her mind to something which the Hardings, in common with most of their neighbours, didn't appreciate: the arrival of their new neighbours. It was ironic that most Cardale residents had prided themselves on their sense of community, until they had been challenged by the concept of 'care in the community'. All four of the Hardings' new neighbours had recently been released from a psychiatric institution. Now in later middle age, they were facing the strange, double-edged sword of independence for the first time in their adult lives.

The decision, of course, had been nothing to do with the doctors at The Beeches, yet Beth was acutely aware that many people expected them to be responsible for Muriel, Freddie, Cissy and Terry, yet such responsibility was held by the district health authority, who provided psychiatric help and other forms of support to aid the four in adjusting to their new circumstances. The Beeches' responsibility, as agreed with the health authority, started and finished with their physical well-being. But, said Beth to herself, try telling that to the people who resented them or who, if truth be told, were afraid of them. None of them were, or had ever been, violent or posed a threat to anyone, yet because they were 'different', because people didn't perceive them as 'normal', they became the targets for every prejudice in what was essentially a very conservative community. While Beth could understand people's reactions, she couldn't forgive them: if nobody gave the four in the group home a chance, then they would not be able to integrate. And while Beth had her private doubts about the motives behind the government's 'care in the community' scheme and its practicality, she could certainly appreciate the theory.

Yet, as she arrived home ten minutes later, she wondered if she would have turned into a Nimby – a 'Not in my back yard' – had the council owned the house next door to her and Jack and turned it into a group home. Martin Harding, after all, was normally the most easygoing and mild-mannered of men. He had even told her that he appreciated the motives behind caring for people in the community – until they had moved next door. Overnight, he had become a Nimby, adamant that he didn't want a bunch of 'nutters' living next door and posing a threat to his kids.

Sighing as she closed the door behind her and headed upstairs, Beth could at least be sure about one thing: there was no way that the residents of the group home were responsible for the Harding children's flu.

'Hi.' Beth stopped at the bedroom door and looked in great amusement at Jack. 'Attacked by a bottle of brandy, were we?'

Jack glared at her. He had only just beaten Beth home and was trying desperately to get undressed and into bed before she returned. He was failing spectacularly. She had caught him in the process of hopping about drunkenly and fighting with a sock. 'Some night,' he mumbled. 'I'll tell you, Will can really talk when he's—'

'Had a few.' Beth, still grinning, walked into the room. 'You look as if a pint or two of water wouldn't go amiss either.'

'Not now. In the morning.' Jack gave up the struggle to undress and flopped on the bed.

'Now.'

'Aw, Beth, there's no way I can get up again.'

Beth joined him on the bed and ruffled his already tousled hair. 'It's only because I love you.'

'That's what I like to hear.'

'And only because I don't want to suffer your sore head in the morning.'

Again Jack glared. 'My little Angel of Mercy.'

But Beth was looking at him in her most doctorly fashion. 'I'd say you were fit enough to get yourself a glass of water – but do you think you're capable of undressing yourself?'

'No. Definitely not. I think, Doctor Glover, I'll have to get someone else to do that for me. . .'

Three miles away on the outskirts of Cardale, Isabel de Gines was also preparing for bed. Yet while Jack reclined in pleasurable anticipation, Isabel waited in trepidation. Night-time was always the worst: the time when the pain would suddenly ambush her. As she lay in bed, she reflected that this evening had taken more out of her than she had expected – and she was heartily glad that none of her guests could see her now. Wearing a warm but unflattering nightgown and with her make-up removed, she looked a shadow of the woman who had sparkled with life throughout the evening.

Then the pain hit. That she had been expecting it made no difference: her face contorted in agony and her body convulsed in spasms, as if dancing to some cruel tune that robbed it of its dignity. Breathless and suddenly afraid, Isabel reached for the bottle of morphine by her bedside. After a brief struggle with the cap, she managed to open it and, with a sigh of relief, took her medicine. Still in pain, she lay back and closed her eyes. Soon, she knew, she would feel better. Soon it would all be over.

CH**A**PTER 6

Jack had a sore head. Beth knew this because when she had asked him how he was feeling he all but bit her head off and snapped that he was 'fine'. That, she knew, was a sure sign of a hangover. She decided, feeling on top of the world and – she had to admit – not a little 'holier than thou' after her abstemious evening, that the best tactic was avoidance. By the time they arrived together at The Beeches not more than ten words had passed between them – and no breakfast had passed Jack's lips. There was only one cure for Jack's hangovers and that was time.

He entered the building and glowered at Laura, The Beeches' capable nurse, standing bright-eyed and smiling in reception. She had a habit of intercepting him with some request or other the moment he came to work, and today he was determined to avoid her. Laura, however, was not to be deflected with anything as feeble as an unfriendly glare. 'Jack?'

'What?'

'I wondered if you could drop in on Terry Alston at the group home . . .' To her annoyance, Laura found herself chasing him down the corridor.

'I've got a heavy round but yes. Of course.' Forcing himself to stop and turn round, Jack smiled. The group home was, after all, a project that had his wholehearted support. 'How have they settled in, do you know?'

'It's all a bit of a new experience at the moment. And the psychiatric services are really stretched, so I said I'd keep an eye on them. But Muriel was saying that Terry hasn't been well and . . . and he won't see me.'

'Oh. It's not something for his psychiatric nurse to deal with?'

Laura shrugged. 'It did sound medical.'

'Right. Well, thanks for letting me know. My first calls are in the area so I'll get over there pronto.' Then, as she walked back to reception, Jack grinned. His hangover, suddenly, had vanished. It wasn't anything to do with Terry Alston but everything to do with Will Preston. Looking thunderous, Will barged past Laura and made for his room.

'How's the head today, Will?'

Will's expression became positively murderous. With a huge effort, he smiled. 'You know, the really wonderful thing about good wine – it limits the after-effects.'

Jack thought, but didn't say, 'Oh, yeah?' That, indisputably, would have been incitement to murder.

Jack had fixed feelings about care in the community. In private, he made it no secret that he reckoned the initiative had been spawned by a government motivated by economic rather than social considerations. Like Beth, he believed the concept to be sound, but the implementation to be far from perfect. And in Cardale, he reflected as he pulled up in front of the group home, they were lucky: they were a small enough community to be able to provide decent care. He was well aware that in London and other large cities there was neither enough care nor any sense of community.

Cissy, at forty-six the youngest of the residents, answered the doorbell. Leading Jack upstairs, she turned apologetically and indicated the closed door of Terry's bedroom. The loud music that had been the basis of Martin Harding's complaint to Beth was clearly audible. 'He won't come out,' she said. 'I've tried everything but . . .'

'Don't worry, Cissy. I'm sure you've done your best.

76

Let's see what I can do.' With that, Jack rapped loudly on the door. 'Terry . . . it's Doctor Kerruish here. Terry?' But Terry clearly wasn't interested. Exasperated, Jack knocked with greater force. 'Terry. Look, I haven't come here for my own amusement. Terry!'

Terry finally replied. His high, reedy voice could easily be heard above the music. 'Bog off!'

Despite himself, Jack grinned. At least I know he's all right, he thought. 'OK,' he yelled back, 'I'm going now, Terry. If you do want help you know where we are. I'll phone your psychiatric nurse.'

Just as Jack was about to leave, the music faded and the door opened a fraction. A pair of sharp, beady eyes looked out and then, still wary, Terry revealed himself. He looked rough, Jack thought. While he appeared younger than his fifty years, his complexion was sallow and he was definitely too thin. Jack's immediate impression was that he hadn't been eating properly.

For a second Terry just gazed at him. 'Can you section me?' he asked then.

Jack, stunned, simply stared back.

'They've dumped me,' continued Terry, sounding pained. 'The hospital, they've dumped me here.'

'Nobody's dumped you, Terry. Now, are you going to let me examine you?'

Without moving or letting Jack into the room, Terry nodded. Jack realized he was going to have to examine Terry as he was – upright on the threshold of his room.

'They think they can just get rid of you,' said Terry as Jack extracted his stethoscope from his bag, 'after thirty years. Just turn me out of the only home I've ever known.'

'Open your mouth, Terry . . . wide. Hmm, you've not been keeping your food down, then?'

Terry shot a venomous look at the opposite door. It was, Jack knew, occupied by Cissy. 'You haven't had Cissy's cooking, have yer?'

Jack refused to be drawn on the subject. 'Well, I suggest you stick to clear fluids for a day or two, drink plenty of water – and no hot milky drinks. If you should feel any worse give me a call.'

'Yer not going to section me, then, Doctor?'

'No, but I'll stand you a pint whenever you're up for it. How's that?' It was clearly not the response Terry had expected but, from the look in his eye, neither was it a wholly unwelcome suggestion.

Jack made his way down the stairs. Cissy had disappeared so he saw himself out. Terry's difficulties in adjusting to life outside a home were only to be expected, he mused. The others seemed to be coping better and, judging by the immaculate state of the house, they were making a good job of keeping the place in order. As long as they got enough psychiatric counselling, he reckoned they would make a success of it.

Driving to his next call, he noted with interest that the couple sitting on a bench in Cardale Square were none other than Muriel and Freddie, the other two occupants of the group home. Alice North, long since recovered both from her poisoning and from the indignity of having to stay with her neighbour, had informed him that Muriel and Freddie were 'sweet' on each other. Jack had been pleased and sceptical: he rated Alice more as a gossipmonger than a fact-finder. Yet had he been able to hear their conversation as they sat together, he would have been forced to alter his view on that issue.

'Freddie,' said Muriel as Jack drove past, 'I've been thinking – why don't we get married? I reckon they'd let us now. I don't see why not. We live in an ordinary house.' As she warmed to her theme, she took Freddie's hand in her lap and smiled dreamily. 'I'd like that. I always fancied a wedding like anyone else.'

Freddie, however, was looking anxious. Muriel, sensing something was amiss, looked at him in alarm. 'What is it?'

Freddie blushed. 'I'd like that, Muriel. A lot. I love you, but it's just . . .'

'Just what?'

'I don't know if . . . if . . .' Embarrassed, he failed to find the words to explain.

Muriel took this as a personal slight. Suddenly irate, she sprang to her feet and started shouting at him. 'Yer bloody bugger, Freddie Cartwright! Yer a bloody bugger!' With that, she stomped off in a rage, leaving Freddie even more crestfallen – and letting the two women who had witnessed the little episode confirm their prejudices: namely, that Muriel and her companions were all 'barmy'.

Several hours after Jack had left the group home, Beth, in a tearing hurry, drew up outside the building. Her destination, however, was the house next door. Lisa Harding, sounding a great deal more panic-stricken than before, had been on the phone again.

Without ceremony, Beth dashed upstairs and into the boys' room. Eddie, she was appalled to see, was lying in bed, his brow damp with fever and his nose dripping blood. 'It's come on so quick,' Lisa wailed. 'He's got terrible headaches and now his nose is bleeding.'

Beth tried to hide her alarm and groped in her bag. 'I'm going to give Eddie a shot of penicillin, Lisa,' she said, with a calm she didn't feel, 'and then Martin can carry him down to my car. He needs to go to hospital for tests.'

A minute later she was back in her car and tapping out a familiar number on her mobile. 'Doctor Glover here, I'm admitting a young boy, query meningitis. I should be there in half an hour.'

Lisa, rushing up to the car, overheard Beth's last words. At the mention of the dreaded illness she felt a twinge of terror run through her: her worst fear had just been confirmed. But Beth, brisk and businesslike, left her no opportunity to speak. 'Martin,' she barked at the frantic husband, 'gently . . . on the back seat.' Martin lowered his whimpering son into the car. The other two children, half excited, half afraid, looked on as he turned to give his wife a desperate hug. 'Don't worry about Lou and Tom,' he said with a slight edge, 'I'll stay with them. I'll take time off.' Then he released her and almost pushed her into the car. 'Go on. Go.'

Beth had already started the car and, as soon as Lisa shut the door behind her, gunned the engine and, tight-lipped, sped down the street. This was precisely the sort of situation she hated: having to drive both as fast and as safely as possible. Concentrating exclusively on the road ahead, she negotiated the steep, narrow streets of Cardale's centre and then, as she left the village, increased her speed. In the back, a silent Lisa cradled her son in her arms.

After a few minutes' silence, Beth caught Lisa's eye in the driver's mirror.

'It's meningitis, isn't it?'

'We don't know what it is at the moment, Lisa.' Lisa opened her mouth to protest but Beth, sounding sharper than she meant to, stalled her. 'We've not far to go now, and the hospital's on standby.' With those words, she pressed the accelerator and gathered yet more speed.

A minute later and cursing inwardly, she was forced to slow down. In front of her on the narrow country road was a set of emergency traffic lights installed in front of a section of roadworks – and the light was showing red. Beth hesitated. It would be madness to crash the light – there was only room for one lane of traffic and the roadworks carried on past a blind corner – but any delay might be fatal. Biting her lip, she opened the window, reached down into the glove compartment and extracted her green emergency light. Then, with a silent prayer, she slapped it on to the roof of the car and tore past the red light. Lisa, she noted with relief, seemed blissfully unaware of the risk she was taking.

It was a risk that paid off: ten minutes and no mishaps later, she screeched to a halt outside the accident and emergency unit of the hospital. On their arrival two paramedics shot through the swing doors with a trolley and, with practised ease, transferred Eddie from the car. Beth, striding ahead, entered the hospital and, after a brief greeting, relayed her story to her old acquaintance Doctor Seema Gupta, the senior house officer. Doctor Gupta went up to Lisa. 'Mrs Harding,' she smiled, 'we're going to take Eddie for tests. It would be better if you could wait here.'

'No!' Lisa was adamant. 'I have to stay with him.'

Beth, sympathetic but firm, put a reassuring hand on Lisa's shoulder. Her implication was clear: let go of your son. Lisa looked from one doctor to the other and then reluctantly let Eddie be wheeled away. With tears in her eyes, she looked helplessly at Beth. 'He's going to be all right, isn't he, Doctor Glover?'

But Beth didn't trust herself to reply. All she could do was nod.

An hour and a half later Beth was still unable to give a firm reply. Lisa, alone in the waiting room, looked up as she returned.

'He's comfortable—' Beth began.

'Is it meningitis?'

Beth shook her head. 'Some of the signs were meningitis but we're convinced now that it isn't.'

'What *is* it, then?'

'He'll have to stay in for observation and wait for the results of the tests before we—'

'Can I see him?'

'Sure.' At least that's one firm answer I can give, thought Beth. 'I'll take you.'

Eddie, in bed in the children's ward, looked marginally better than he had on being admitted. Lisa clung to him, at once tearful and relieved, and stroked a damp strand of hair out of his eyes. Beth drew Doctor Gupta aside and out of earshot. 'Any ideas?'

Seema Gupta shook her head. 'No. None. I'm as baffled as you are.'

By mid-morning the next day the doctors at the hospital were still in the dark. Beth found herself increasingly preoccupied throughout morning surgery and, breaking for coffee, rushed into the kitchen with a pile of textbooks. Forgetting to make herself a drink, she settled down to read. She was so engrossed that she didn't even hear Jack coming in ten minutes later. Determined to make her notice him, Jack began to massage her shoulders as she sat hunched over her book. Even then, she barely registered his presence.

'Nice?' he asked.

No reply.

Sighing, Jack abandoned her for the more rewarding task of making himself a cup of coffee. 'I get the distinct impression,' he said over his shoulder, 'that I didn't marry the sexiest and most eligible woman in Cardale, I married the sexiest and most eligible workaholic.'

'Mmm . . .'

Jack rolled his eyes, walked over to Beth and hugged her. She could hardly fail to notice *that*. 'Any chance of a romantic lunch, Doctor Glover?'

'Ah-huh . . . I mean, no. No, I don't think I'll have time.'

Beth, finally realizing just how unresponsive she was being, suddenly looked up and gave her husband a daz-zling smile. 'Sorry, darling. It's just that I think I'm getting there.'

'What? With the Harding boy?'

'Mmm. Listen to this. Flu-like symptoms to start with.

82

In severe cases, headaches, fever, loss of appetite, nose bleeds. Later, jaundice and kidney damage.'

Jack, somewhat to her surprise, didn't hesitate. 'Weil's Disease?'

'Spot on.'

'There's only one way of getting it, isn't there?'

'Yes. It's spread by rats' urine in water.' With a look of grim determination, Beth snapped the book shut. 'Martin Harding's coming in later . . . I don't really want to alarm him. Not until we're sure, anyway.'

'Hmm.' Jack looked sceptical. 'I think you'll have difficulty with that. Martin's a very determined sort.'

Half an hour later, a distraught-looking Martin was sitting opposite Beth in her room. 'I've been phoning the hospital,' he almost sobbed, 'and they won't tell us anything. 'You *must* know something. If it's not meningitis, then what?'

'They're running tests. We should know fairly soon.'

'You must have *some* idea.'

Beth shook her head – but not vehemently enough. Seeing Martin's expression, she relented. 'It's too early to say . . .'

'But?'

'I was wondering . . . you haven't noticed anything slightly out of the ordinary lately?'

'Like what?'

'Well, that little stream at the back of your houses – has the water changed colour? Or . . . maybe someone's seen rats about?'

'Rats?' Martin looked horrified. Then, as he considered Beth's question, his face darkened. 'Not as such, no, but I wouldn't be surprised. Not since that bunch of loonies moved in next door.'

Beth groaned silently. 'Look, I really wouldn't jump to conclusions, Martin . . .'

But Martin needed to jump no further. 'No, I'm sure of it, Doctor Glover. One of them was out the back the other night, behaving all sort of odd. Calling out to some sort of creature.' Warming to his theme, he leaned forward and banged his fist on the desk. 'These people aren't capable of looking after themselves, Doctor Glover. The house'll be filthy, they shouldn't have been put there. Not next to a family with kids!'

Martin Harding wasn't the only one upset by the antics of the residents of the group home that day. As he sat ranting at Beth, Muriel and Freddie, hand in hand, were making their tentative way round the Mini-Mart in Cardale High Street. Shopping, like most other everyday activities, was still a challenge to them. And it wasn't just the process of buying things that worried them: far more alarming were the unfriendly and wary looks cast at them as they went about their business. Alice North, also in the shop at the time, felt sorry for them. She had elected herself champion of the group home and was more than a little irritated by other people's attitude towards the inhabitants. 'Leave them be' was her motto. She was sure that, given time, they would all get used to each other.

Iris Green, however, was not so understanding. She had lived her sixty-one years without being a bother to anyone (an opinion not shared by anyone else) and she was damned if she was going to let other people bother her. Furthermore, and even though she only minded the till on occasion, she regarded the Mini-Mart as 'hers'. She resented the intrusion of 'those people' in her territory. As Freddie and Muriel, smiling sweetly, deposited their basket in front of her, she set her lips in a grim line and, with several loud bangs, started to tally the goods. Radiating disapproval, she then looked up at the pair. 'Nineteen pounds and ten pence.'

Muriel, always nervous about anything to do with money, became even more flustered at Iris's attitude. Fumbling in her purse, she started spilling coins on the counter. Eventually she gave up, looked to Iris and handed her the purse. 'Just take what it is.'

Iris, tutting as she raked through the purse, announced with something akin to glee that Muriel hadn't enough money. 'You'll have to put a couple of things back.'

Muriel, even more alarmed at this prospect, seemed incapable of making any sort of decison. Both she and Freddie looked bemusedly at their purchases as, behind them, a queue began to form. Glenda Reeves, whose views on the group home were unprintable, stood directly behind Muriel and all but breathed fire over her.

'What don't you need?' asked Iris, relenting somewhat.

'I don't know,' wailed Muriel.

'Well, what about these fancy cakes? You don't really need them, do you?'

Muriel shook her head. Freddie, however, wasn't so sure. 'It's Cissy that wants them.'

'Look,' Iris sighed, 'we've got a queue here – you'll have to make your minds up.'

'If they've got any minds to make up.' Glenda Reeves's stage whisper shocked even Iris, and Alice North, who was also in the queue, was appalled. But Muriel was the only one who reacted. The remark had been the final straw in an already fraught situation. Upset and angry, she rounded on Iris. 'We don't need nothing!' she yelled. 'Yer can bloomin' stuff it!' With that, she grabbed Freddie with one hand and her purse with the other and stormed out of the shop.

There was a moment's uncomfortable silence while Iris, herself upset, gestured helplessly at the pile of abandoned goods. Then Glenda turned to Alice. 'Disgraceful, that's what I call it. They're from the funny farm them two, you know.'

But if Glenda was seeking approval she was looking at the wrong person. Alice glared at her. 'There's more than one kind of funny farm around these parts, Glenda Reeves.'

Outside, Freddie and Muriel made their way home in furious silence. Muriel was angry from the experience but also annoyed at Freddie. He wasn't, she felt, giving her enough support. If he really did love her then he was making a pretty poor job of showing it.

Freddie, for his part, was sinking into an ever deeper depression about their relationship. How, he asked himself, could he possibly tell Muriel what was on his mind? It was too embarrassing. Muriel would laugh.

With neither of them prepared for confidences, they were still edging warily round each other after supper that night. Muriel washed the dishes as Cissy, deep in her own reverie, wiped the table. Terry, who was still refusing food, was in his room. His meal lay untouched on the work surface. Freddie, hovering in the doorway, asked if he could help. 'We can manage.' Muriel, tight-lipped, didn't even look up. Sighing, Freddie slunk out and upstairs to his own room. Looking round to see if there were any more dishes, Muriel spied Terry's plate. She picked it up and, disapproving but undecided, turned to Cissy. 'I can't stand wasting.'

'If Terry don't want to eat,' replied Cissy, 'don't cook him owt.'

'Well, what am I going to do with this piece of fish?'

Cissy, with a sudden glint in her eyes, grabbed the plate. 'Give it here, Muriel. Now just you go and watch telly.'

Muriel did as she was told. If Cissy wanted to eat cold fish then that was her business.

But Cissy had other plans for the fish. Expertly deboning it, she transferred it into an enamel plate and, with one last furtive glance towards the sitting-room, went out of the back door.

Later that evening, Jack and Beth lingered over their own dinner. 'So,' said Jack as he twirled his wine-glass in his fingers, 'you were right about Eddie Harding. It is Weil's?'

Beth nodded. 'We'll need to locate the source, Jack.' She glanced up at her husband. Anticipating what was coming, he was already looking defensive. 'I'll have to ask Laura to get on to the environmental health officer,' she went on, 'get someone round there.'

'And if it *is* the group home?'

'If it's the group home then it's got to be dealt with.' Not wanting yet another conversation about that contentious issue, she stood up and went over to the telephone. 'I haven't had a chance to thank Isabel for that wonderful dinner.' She dialled the familiar number and waited for Isabel to answer. After twelve rings, she sighed and replaced the receiver.

Jack, watching her, realized that a proper 'thank you' was only part of Beth's reason for wanting to contact Isabel: she also wanted to make sure she was all right. 'She knows, Beth,' he began. 'You'll see her at the weekend anyway.'

'Mmm.'

'She's a brave woman.'

'Yes.' Beth, fearing that she was about to become maudlin, forced a smile. 'Too brave for her own good sometimes. A fool to herself – not unlike you at the moment, Jack Kerruish.' She went back to the table and put her arms round him. The issue, she reckoned, was going to have to be tackled. 'Look, Jack, if the council do find that the group home is in some way responsible, one "failure" is not going to mean the end of care in the community. You're taking the whole thing too personally.'

'But it *is* personal. They're my patients.'

'It's more than that. You've got a bee in your bonnet and you know it.'

Jack looked up and grinned. 'Don't think I'd suit a bonnet somehow.'

'Oh, I don't know, those baby features . . .'

But Jack's bee wouldn't go away. 'Seriously, Beth, I just can't help thinking. They're all met with so much fear and ignorance, anyway, without this. And if this instance of Weil's disease *does* come from the group home, I'd like to be the one to deal with it.' Jack cast his mind back to his recent visit there. 'Terry looked as if he might have had a dose of food poisoning. I don't know . . . the incubation period for Weil's can be three weeks. Maybe they've contracted the disease as well.'

'I hope you're wrong. At least,' added Beth with a hint of finality, 'I was able to tell Martin that Tom and Louise are all clear. They obviously had the mild symptoms but the penicillin seems to have done the trick.'

'Yeah.' Jack, too, was happy to close the subject. 'I'll drop in to the group home after morning surgery.'

CHAPTER 7

As soon as his son's illness was confirmed, Martin Harding lost no time in lauching an attack against the group home. That no one yet knew how Eddie had contracted the disease cut little ice with Martin: he was positive that his neighbours were to blame and he determined to stop at nothing until the home was shut down and its residents sent back into hospital.

He had little difficulty in finding supporters. The next morning he went from door to door, distributing a hand-written, photocopied leaflet, announcing that he was going to hold a meeting to discuss the question of shutting down the home. With people like Glenda Reeves living in the neighbourhood, he reckoned he stood every chance of success.

Jack Kerruish's main concern that morning was less hysterical and more practical: as soon as he arrived at The Beeches, he asked Kim to get in touch with the environmental health people. Two hours later, she came into his room looking both despondent and exasperated. 'I've been trying to get through all morning,' she said. 'First off, I got sent to Council Tax 'cos the woman thought I said rates instead of rats. Then, when I did get Environmental Health, they said the man I needed was on his break.'

'God.' Jack put his head in his hands. 'Typical. Bloody bureaucrats.' Then he smiled at her. 'Well, thanks anyway. Keep hassling and let me have a word when you do get through.'

As Kim nodded and turned to leave, Jack buzzed for his next patient. It was Freddie. 'Doctor Kruish . . .'

Breathless and highly nervous, he lapsed into hand-wringing silence.

'Freddie! Sit down, sit down. I was going to call in today and have a word about—'

Freddie, however, wasn't interested. Perching on the edge of the chair, he started blurting out his problems. 'She wants us to get married,' he wailed, 'and I do as well, but I couldn't tell her, could I?' He looked at Jack in wide-eyed desperation. 'I mean, the man's the one supposed to know.'

Jack, baffled, stared back. 'Know what?'

Freddie leaned forward and lowered his voice to a whisper. 'She don't know I'm a virgin. I weren't more than fourteen when I were put in, see . . . I knew when I first saw her. I thought, I like her, but . . . but no one's ever told me proper what you're supposed to do.'

Jack's heart went out to the man opposite him. What a tragedy, he thought. How appalling yet how typical of society to forget that people like Freddie had the same basic urges and needs as everyone else. He tried to disguise his feelings with a stab at humour. 'It's a while,' he said with a grin, 'since I've been through the birds and the bees.'

'Some of them drugs,' said Freddie darkly, 'do things to you.'

Ah, so he was worried he might not be able to perform. 'Don't worry. I'll go through it all with you, Freddie. I'm sure everything's going to be fine. The important thing,' he added, 'is how you and Muriel feel about each other.'

Freddie had no doubts about that one. 'It were the happiest day for me when we got moved here. But now, I don't know if they'll even let us stay.' He looked miserably at his feet. 'I get scared maybe something will happen and we'll get sent different places and I'll never see Muriel again.'

'Look, Freddie, we don't want that to happen. I was going to call in to see you all today. There's – there's been talk of rats in your area, and rats can spread disease.'

Freddie looked confused. Clearly, he was not following Jack's train of thought.

'Have you seen any?' continued Jack. 'Around the house or out in the yard?'

'No.'

Just as Jack was about to explain further, he was interrupted by the buzz of his intercom. 'Hold on a sec, Freddie, I'll be right with you . . . Yep?' he barked into the phone.

'Urgent call for you. One of your group patients. She won't speak to anyone else.' Kim's voice was clear even to Freddie, and at the mention of the home he looked up in alarm.

'I'll take it, Kim . . . Muriel?' He listened, frowning in concentration, to Muriel's frantic voice and then tried to reassure her. 'Right, yeah, OK . . . You did the right thing to call. I'm on my way.' Replacing the receiver, he smiled across the desk at Freddie. 'Don't worry, there's nothing wrong with Muriel.' Then he got to his feet. 'Come on, I'll give you a lift.'

There was indeed nothing wrong with Muriel – but there was a lot wrong with Terry. Thin and yellow with jaundice, he was also feverish and gibbering. Jack, horrified, looked around his bedroom in the group home. It was filthy and in complete disarray. Looking back at Terry, he pulled his mobile phone from his pocket and called for an ambulance. His disappointment was almost as great as his concern: Terry obviously had Weil's disease – and the cause was doubtless to be found among the filth on the floor.

*

Word of Terry's admission to hospital swept like wildfire around the town, adding fuel to Martin Harding's case and causing outrage among the more prejudiced of Cardale's citizens. That Eddie Harding had begun to develop problems with his kidneys didn't help – and next day's episode with Cissy was the final straw. Upset by Terry being taken to hospital, confused by all the comings and going at the group home, she was further upset when, walking along Cardale High Street, she was teased by Glenda Reeves's two young sons. To them, calling her names like 'loony' and 'nutter' was harmless fun, but it was almost enough to push the already distraught Cissy over the edge. She screamed at them that the devil and his angels would come and get them with lightning and fire – yet that only made them laugh. In a fit of rage, Cissy hurled the object she was carrying – a milk carton – at the boys. She missed, but succeeded in splattering them with its contents. She also succeeded in doing herself the ultimate disservice: Glenda Reeves, emerging from the Mini-Mart, saw her throwing the carton.

'Flippin' heck!' she yelled. Genuinely worried that Cissy was intent on damage, she hustled the boys away. 'Come on, you lot, *now*! Can't you see she's off her head?' Then, from a safe distance, she pointed a threatening finger at Cissy. 'We're going to do summat about you lot tonight!'

By now Jack was aware of the meeting organized by Martin Harding: on his rounds he had come across one of the leaflets pinned on to a tree. 'NO TO PSYCHOPATHS IN CARDALE' was its succinct, shocking headline. Shaking his head in anger and frustration, Jack could only hope that the 'rat man', whom he had finally found, would prove everybody wrong about the source of Weil's disease.

When he accompanied Jack to the group home at the

appointed time, the rat man was disappointed by the state of the house. Apart from Terry's room, the place was immaculate. 'A rat wouldn't be seen dead in 'ere,' he said, without the faintest trace of humour. 'Not their scene at all.'

The shed at the bottom of the garden soon restored his spirits. A look of delight spread across his face at the sight of a bundle of material and straw in the corner. 'Eh, now we've summat – been a bit of nest-building going on here.' He looked approvingly at Jack. 'They can make a lovely home, you know, rats can.'

Jack was tempted to say he would employ one as an interior designer but managed to keep quiet. Then, startled by an unfamiliar sound, he looked behind him. Cissy, recovered from her earlier outburst, had been in the garden when he and the rat man came out of the house. She had been looking furtive and had, Jack suspected, just emerged from the shed. She was carrying a large cloth bag. Now, looking even more guilty, she was trying to edge out of the shed into the house. Jack, hearing the noise again, suddenly realized why. He called to her, 'Cissy, I'm not going to tell anyone.' Looking at the bag, he grinned as its occupant wriggled and let out a loud, irate miaow. 'I mean, it's a stray, isn't it? Not really a pet?'

Relief washed over Cissy. 'No, no,' she said, stroking the bag. 'He's not a pet. We're not allowed pets. I only made him a pet because he's a stray.'

'That's what I thought.' Jack nodded and smiled as Cissy, with a spring in her step, walked back towards the house.

The rat man, however, was not at all pleased. Emerging from the shed a moment later, he shook his head in disbelief. 'Funny, I was sure we were on to summat there.'

'You're looking for rats, aren't you?' The voice, high and loud, came from over the low garden wall. Startled, both men looked up to see the interested faces of Tom and Louise Harding. 'That's what made our Eddie sick,' continued Louise. 'Rats. Ugh!' She shuddered eloquently.

'You haven't seen any, though, have you?' asked Jack.

Louise and her brother shook their heads.

'Is there anywhere you've been playing recently,' Jack persisted, 'that's got a pond or . . . or any bit of water?'

Again Tom shook his head. 'No. We've only been playing here. We've not been well either.'

'Ages ago,' offered Louise, who always needed the last word, 'we went fishing with Dad.'

'When?' Jack saw a glimmer of hope.

'More than a week. Didn't catch much, though.'

'Yeah. It were boring so we went in the water, where there was a pool and' – here Tom nudged his sister in the ribs – 'Louise shoved me in.'

'I did not! That were Eddie!'

'Yer did – and we got all wet and Mum gave us a row 'cos we got the flu then, didn't we?'

Jack had heard all he needed to know – except for one thing. 'Where exactly was this place?' he asked the children. 'I need to go there.'

The turnout for the meeting at the village hall was larger than even Martin Harding had expected. Glenda Reeves had broadcast the Cissy episode far and wide and her sons, too young to realize the importance of the affair, had done nothing to disabuse her of the notion that the attack had been unprovoked. Glenda's efforts, combined with Martin's leaflets, had had quite an effect.

Jack, rushing into the hall just before the meeting began, made a bee-line for Martin. 'Martin, can I have a word? It's important.'

Martin, eyes blazing, rounded on him. 'I'm not backing out now, Doctor Kerruish, so you can forget it.'

But Jack was insistent. 'I need to talk to you, Martin. We've located the source of the Weil's disease. The stream where you took the kids fishing—'

'I know all I need to know.' Martin, not even registering what Jack was saying, stalled him in mid-flow. 'Our Eddie's got renal failure. It's their fault – and I'm going to see justice done!' Turning his back on Jack, he made his way to the podium at the end of the room and called for silence.

Jack, angry and frustrated, had no choice but to sit down and listen. On the point of doing so, he was distracted by someone waving at him from the row in front. 'Jack!' It was Laura. Surprised by her presence, Jack went up to her.

'Jack, we've had Terry's results.'

'Don't tell me, obstructing gallstones.' Despite the situation, Jack grinned.

Laura, impressed, raised her eyebrows. 'Yes. How did you know?'

'I worked it out for myself. Once Weil's began to look unlikely . . .' Jack shrugged and sat down beside Laura. The nature of Terry's illness now seemed irrelevant: the damage had been done and Martin Harding, now in full spate, was intent on capitalizing on it.

'Nobody asked us,' he was saying, 'if we wanted these people living next door to us! Nobody was thinking about *our* feelings as a community. Why should we have to put up with this? You can bet,' he continued, 'the value of our properties will go down. Who'd want to live next door to them? But it's our kids I'm most worried about.' Launching into a description of Eddie's suffering, he combined it with a searing invective against the group home. 'My son,' he finished with a flourish, 'will suffer for life because of the Weil's disease. Ex-psychiatrics just aren't fit to live beside ordinary people with family and young kids!'

His words were greeted with shouts of agreement from the floor. Jack, sickened both by the reaction and its sheer unfairness, got to his feet. Walking towards the podium, he went straight up to Martin and, with a steely glint in his eyes, asked to say a few words. 'There are a few facts here that need straightening out,' he insisted. Martin, glowering, could hardly refuse.

Facing the assembly, Jack wasted no time in coming to the point. 'We're all very sorry about young Eddie Harding but this is an isolated case and there are *no* other cases in the village. The source of the Weil's disease has been located. I'd hoped,' he added with a disapproving look at Martin, 'to have an opportunity to pass this on to Martin before this meeting.'

'Where is it, then?' Glenda Reeves, scathing and disbelieving, got to her feet.

'A stream. Not far from here, but not in Cardale.' He looked from Glenda to Martin. 'An environmental health officer is dealing with it now.'

Martin, finally realizing his mistake, frowned and seemed almost to crumble. But Glenda was determined to fight on. 'I still say we can't have psychopaths wandering round the streets,' she shouted. 'One of them nutters attacked my kids only this morning!'

'Aye.' Alice North shot her a look of intense dislike. 'And I saw a couple of your boys thumping a lad from Brompton the other day. Are we going to get rid of them an' all?'

Jack felt like cheering. On the other hand, the last thing he wanted was for the meeting to degenerate into a slanging match. Holding both hands in the air, he made a plea for calm. 'Look, there just aren't any easy answers here. We all know there are grounds for concern—'

'Yeah. If I hadn't seen her Christ knows what she would have done next!' But Glenda was losing her audience. They all wanted to hear what Jack was going to offer.

'We all know,' he continued, 'that there is a need for a better level of aftercare, more money and support for overworked staff – but there also needs to be more done to help people like you and me understand and accept ex-patients into our communities. We have to meet them half-way—'

'Why the heck should we?'

'Because,' persisted Jack with a venomous glare at Glenda, 'this *is* where they belong, not shut away and locked out of sight in some outdated Victorian institution like they weren't somebody's son or cousin or father or the woman you might have married, like they weren't anything to do with us.' With that, he stepped down from the stage. His impassioned words, he was glad to see, had had an effect. The gathering was more subdued now and a steady murmur of agreement began to override the dissenters. Glenda Reeves had lapsed into a mutinous silence; Martin Harding was looking both defeated and thoughtful. If nothing else, Jack thought, I've won this particular battle. But he suspected that the war would continue.

Beth had been in two minds about going to the meeting. She wanted to be able to gauge the tide of feeling for herself, but she was also wary about being seen to take sides. She was a doctor, not a social worker, and her sympathies lay with all her patients. In the end, she decided to leave Jack to it: one of his patients was being blamed for something of which he was innocent, so Jack was directly and justifiably involved. Her presence, Beth felt, would only serve to antagonize people. There was, anyway, something else she wanted to do, something more personal.

She had tried several times that evening to contact Isabel yet her friend hadn't answered the phone. There could be any number of reasons for that. Yet something nagged at the back of her mind, told her that all was not well. Something made her drive hell for leather to Isabel's.

There were lights on in the house, yet there was no

response to the doorbell. Seriously worried, Beth ran round to the kitchen door and, finding it open, let herself in. The first thing that struck her was an unnerving and peculiar silence within the house. Although it was warm in the kitchen, Beth shivered violently and, with a sense of foreboding, went through to the sitting room.

Isabel was lying on the sofa. The light from the nearby table-lamp bathed her features in a soft, warm glow and she looked as if she were enjoying a deep, peaceful sleep. Molly, curled at her feet, looked up at Beth and whined. Beth knew. She didn't even have to check. For a moment she stood, frozen to the spot, and then walked towards the sofa. A stray lock of hair had fallen over Isabel's forehead and, with exquisite gentleness, Beth tucked it back into place, As she did so, she was overwhelmed by an emotion she could scarcely begin to comprehend: she felt removed from her own body, separated from her soul. Only the tears that began to prick at the back of her eyes told her that she was still here, looking down at the best friend she had ever had in the world. 'Goodbye, Isabel,' she whispered. 'Goodbye . . .'

CH**A**PTER 8

Beth found herself operating on automatic pilot for the next few days. Life seemed to become a little blurred around the edges, people appeared slightly out of focus – but apart from that she surprised herself by coping with dignity and aplomb. There was, anyway, so much to do. Isabel had no living relatives and it fell to Beth to make the funeral arrangements. She wouldn't have had it any other way.

The first signs of raw grief appeared, she later realized, at the funeral. Composed and serene, she sat patiently throughout the priest's address and then made her way, as arranged, to the pulpit. Looking at the sea of faces before her, she took a deep breath and, in a strong, low voice, began to read the poem:

'Life means all that it ever meant.
   It is the same as it ever was.
   There is absolute and unbroken continuity.
   What is this death but a negligible accident?
   All is well.
   Nothing is hurt; nothing is lost.
   One brief moment and all shall be as before.
   How we shall laugh at the trouble of parting when
   we meet again!'

Beth found herself smiling as she finished reading. How very Isabel, she thought. How positive. But just as she was about to step down from the pulpit, she noticed the flowers. Pain – real, physical and shocking – shot through her. Isabel, she realized, had done the arrangements. She was staring at something Isabel had created – yet Isabel herself was gone. She faltered and had to grip the mahogany balustrade to support herself. The process of doing so forced her concentration back to herself. Righting herself, her back straight and head held high, she made her way to the front pew, and her place beside Jack.

After that, the blur descended again. She felt as if she were performing in a play. Her role was made easier in that both the service and the subsequent burial had a definite purpose: they were all saying goodbye to Isabel in the correct fashion, following a time-honoured ritual.

At the funeral tea Beth began to feel lost and a little panicked. Suddenly she was required to talk to people and she couldn't think of anything to say. She couldn't even take refuge in her role as hostess: Laura and Chloë White had taken it upon themselves to hand round the food, while Will and Jack were circulating with the drinks. Beth found herself lurking on the edge of conversations rather than taking part in them.

'No relatives turned up at all?' Laura, standing next to Will, fished for something to say.

'No relatives full stop. I'm afraid Isabel was the last of the line.'

'I'd have thought,' said James White, 'one or two of her suitors might have made the effort.'

'Don't know about that.' On the edge of the little group, Trevor grinned mischievously. 'We don't want fights breaking out, do we?'

Everyone duly laughed, but it was a subdued laughter. Isabel, still highly attractive in her widowhood, had been famed for her string of menfriends. Trevor's remark, prompted by admiration and made as a gesture of respect, was nevertheless one of those comments that people at funerals found difficult to cope with. Nobody wanted to be seen to be moping but it seemed inappropriate to be having a good time.

Alice North, Beth noted, was taking refuge in feeding Isabel's – now Beth's – dog. Molly was missing her mistress but the vol-au-vents were proving a delicious consolation. Beth watched the little performance. Funny, she mused, how people choose to seek solace.

'All right, pet?' Jack was at her side with a comforting pat on her shoulder.

Beth smiled and nodded. 'It's . . . it's just hard to tell what's really important any more.'

'It's called grieving, love.'

'I know but . . . it's just that when you come to take stock of your own life . . .'

'Woah, woah!' Jack held up a restraining hand. 'Don't start arranging any mountains to climb just yet, eh?'

'But—'

'As so often in their lives, they were interrupted by the bleep of a mobile phone. Beth shook her head in dismay. Today of all days: could there really be anything more serious than this? Then she checked herself. As Isabel would have said, the merry-go-round doesn't stop just because one person gets off.

Jack pulled his phone out of his pocket, moved into a corner away from the hubbub, and Will took his place at Beth's side. 'You know we can be trusted to hold the fort, don't you? Contrary,' he added with a grin, 'to popular belief.'

Beth gave him a warm, grateful smile. Suddenly she found herself wondering about Will's own grief: not so much at Isabel's loss but at his own personal and different loss of two years ago. He never talked about Sarah any more and he only saw his sons every second weekend. He must be extremely lonely, thought Beth with a pang.

'No need to hurry back to the practice if you don't want to,' he went on.

'Thanks, Will. You're – you've been—'

Seeing that she was becoming distressed, Will swiftly changed the subject. He looked over to Jack and said the first thing that came into his head. 'Superman never stops, does he?'

Beth, more than a little surprised by the remark, was saved from making a reply by Jack's reappearance at her side.

'Accident,' he said with a grimace. 'On the Bakewell Road.'

'Do you want me to take it?' Will was eager both to make amends for his comment and to let Beth and Jack remain at the tea. 'I'm probably a bit more dispensable than you right now.'

'Thanks. That's very good of you.' Beth, for one, appreciated the gesture. She needed Jack at her side.

Jack, however, was pointing at Will's glass. 'You've been drinking.'

'Sherry, not Scotch unfortunately. Alice is standing guard over the strong stuff,' he said with regret.

But Jack was firm. 'It's all the same to the breathalyser. Can't let you risk it.' With an apologetic shrug and a whispered 'sorry' to Beth, he downed the last of his orange juice and headed for the door.

The telephone call had come from the police who, in turn, had been informed by a motorist of an accident on the narrow country road leading from Cardale to Bakewell. The police had told Jack that a car had crashed in trying to avoid a tractor and, while there appeared to be no serious injuries, there was a problem with the ambulance: roadworks meant that the road to the hospital was closed and that it would have to come the long way round.

The accident looked worse than it was. It was not surprising, thought Jack as he pulled up at the scene, that the car had crashed: the tractor, which it had narrowly avoided, appeared to have shed the load from its trailer and was blocking the entire road. What was surprising was that no other vehicles had been involved: the cars lined up behind the crashed vehicle had all seen the devastation in time to avoid it. Taking in the scene in one quick, professional glance, he noticed a young man comforting a toddler, an older man with a dazed expression – and a young woman lying near them, groaning in pain, with a police cape draped over her. Four policemen and women surrounded them: one was trying to shift the fallen debris from the trailer, another was attempting to supervise the build-up of traffic from both directions while the other two were with the injured passengers.

It was WPC Stuart, hunched over the prone woman, who first noticed Jack. Hurrying over to him, she wasted no time with formalities. 'None of them seem hurt too badly,' she began, 'but the young woman,' she added with a hint of panic, 'has gone into labour. Her name's—'

'Amanda Stokes. I know. I'm her doctor.' Jack, in his swift assessment of the situation, had realized that all the occupants of the car now wedged against the telegraph pole at the side of the road were his patients. The older man was Phil Cullam; the younger one was his son-in-law Mark, and Ruby, the little girl, was Mark and Amanda's daughter. Amanda, he knew, was eight months' pregnant with her second child. If the policewoman was right, eight months was as far as she would get.

Mark, his face a mask of anguish, came rushing up with Ruby in his arms. 'I were drivin',' he wailed. 'I didn't see the tractor till the last minute.'

'It's all right,' soothed Jack with a quick glance at Ruby. The child, although distressed, was unhurt, as was her father. 'You just look after her for now, OK?' Then, trying to disguise his alarm, he turned to WPC Stuart. 'No ambulance yet?'

'No. They've had to come by Stourton Lake.' She shrugged. 'Thought they might've been here by now, though.'

Jack rushed towards Amanda. Her concerned father was now hovering over her. 'Doctor Kerruish, thank God for that.'

Would that I had your faith, thought Jack. 'Phil. How're you feeling?'

'I'm fine.' Then, with an impatient gesture, he added, 'Just get to our lass, will you?'

Even before the man had finished speaking, Jack had donned a pair of rubber gloves and was kneeling over the stricken girl. 'Hello, Amanda. How often are the contractions, love?'

'Thick and fast,' she panted. 'I feel like pushing, Doctor. It feels right close.'

'OK, try and relax. I'm just going to take a look.'

Amanda closed her eyes and winced in pain as she was racked by another contraction.

Jack's anxiety increased as he examined her. Amanda wasn't just close – she was almost there. WPC Stuart, kneeling beside him, had gone white. 'Done many home births?' he asked her. 'The head's visible. We're going to have to deliver here.'

The policewoman gave him a wan smile and turned from white to green.

By now the other police officers had ushered the onlookers behind a cordon to restrict their view of the proceedings. WPC Stuart, rising to the occasion and kneeling beside Amanda's husband and father, did her best to soothe all three of them. Only Jack had a clear view of the baby's progress: only he could see that something was wrong. 'Hold off pushing, Amanda, just pant for now.'

Phil, detecting concern in Jack's voice, rounded on him. 'What's goin' on? Is there bother or what, Doctor?'

Jack ignored him. He was too busy trying to unravel the umbilical cord. It was caught round the baby's neck.

'Doctor Kerruish?' Phil was shouting now.

'Just a slight hiccup.' Jack, concentrating on his task, mumbled the words without looking up. 'I'm going to have to cut and clip the cord. Only a few moments now.'

A minute later, Amanda, tearful, exhausted and still reeling from the shock of going into premature labour, gave birth to a baby boy. At exactly the same time, the ambulance, sirens screaming, drew up alongside. Phil, breaking away from his daughter, ran up to the paramedics. 'Over here, lads. Over here!' The first paramedic, taking in Phil's rumpled appearance, rushed towards him. 'Don't bother about me. Go and see to the baby and me daughter. Go on!'

As they arrived, Jack was talking Amanda through what he was doing. Still in a daze, she seemed unaware of what he was saying – and of the concern in his voice. 'He's swallowed a lot of fluid. I'm just going to help him get his breath a bit more easily.' Then he saw the paramedics. 'Accelerated birth after the car Amanda was in had an accident,' he said without preamble. 'Had to deliver straight away. Baby's a bit flat.'

'Fine. Okay. Let's get him into the ambulance.'

Amanda, alarmed by the sight of her baby being wrapped in a green smock and whisked away, looked at Jack, 'Where is he? Where've they taken him?'

Jack patted her shoulder as the paramedics returned with a stretcher. 'We're going to get you both straight to hospital.'

'Is he all right?'

Jack nodded. 'The paramedics are going to get him sucked out, then he'll be fine.'

'But is he all right?'

As his wife was lifted on to the stretcher, Mark bent down to kiss her. 'They'll have it all sorted, love. Course he'll be all right.'

Phil Cullam, now with the wide-eyed Ruby in his arms, beamed at Jack. 'I can't tell you how glad I was when I saw that car of yours. You played a blinder!'

Jack merely smiled in response. Phil, so preoccupied with the events of the past few minutes, didn't notice that it wasn't much of a smile.

Two hours later the baby was in a hospital incubator. Amanda, exhausted and in a wheelchair, sat beside the machine with her husband at her side. They were both looking forlorn: so near to their new baby, yet unable to touch or comfort him. The tubes and wires connected to his frail body only served to emphasize his helplessness and increase their worry. Jack had just been having a quiet word with the paediatric consultant, and was standing a short distance away, looking thoughtful.

It was Phil, returning from the hospital nursery where Ruby was being cared for, who interrupted his reverie. 'He's a bit on the small side, isn't he? What'd the consultant tell you?'

'Well, he's still a little flat. That's why he's got all these tubes – help him to breathe.'

'Stands to reason, I s'pose. He's had a rough ride, born on the road.'

'And they want to keep a very close eye on him,' continued Jack as they walked towards the incubator.

Amanda looked up. "Cos he's premature, like?'

'No. Because the umbilical cord got caught round the

baby's neck. That restricts the oxygen supply so once I saw I couldn't untangle it I had to cut the cord.' Jack, uncharacteristically, was on the defensive.

Mark looked at him. 'Wasn't like this with our Ruby.'

Jack shrugged. 'Well, like I said, it does happen occasionally.' Turning to Amanda, he forced a smile. 'You need plenty of rest, OK? I'll pop back and see you tomorrow.'

Phil escorted him out of the little room. 'Thanks for everything, Doctor. We'll wet the baby's head soon as we can, yeah?'

'I'll hold you to that.' Weary, and suddenly desperate to be out of the hospital, Jack took his leave.

It was getting dark when, deflated and despondent, he arrived home. He supposed he should have been spiritually uplifted because a day that had begun with a funeral had also heralded a new life – yet all he felt was numbness. The birth had happened under less than auspicious circumstances, and the delivery had worried him. It still did. Letting himself into the house, he was surprised to find the sitting room lit only by a small lamp in the corner. His surprise turned to alarm when he saw that the room was still littered with the detritus of the funeral tea – and he had been gone for hours.

Then he noticed Beth. She was sitting on the floor, cradling a cushion and staring vacantly into space.

'Beth? What are you doing sitting in the dark, pet?'

Still expressionless, Beth looked up at him as if he were a total stranger. Her eyes were red-rimmed and swollen. Slowly, she shook her head.

Her look of abject misery pierced Jack's heart. Holding out his arms, he rushed towards her. 'Oh, come here, come on.'

Beth needed no further invitation. Flinging herself into

his arms, she buried her head against his shoulder and burst into tears. Jack, his own eyes stinging, held her close, and gently massaged her back and her tense, heaving shoulders. 'Part of our job, isn't it?' she said, after a few moments. 'Dealing with death, grief, loss. I'd begun to think I was immune to its effects, that I could cope. I . . . I went up to Isabel's while you were away and saw that she was everywhere in that house. Everywhere – but nowhere. Then I knew I was kidding myself. It hit me, the weight of it, the force of it.' Then she sniffed and, fumbling for a handkerchief, gestured towards the mess in the room. 'I came back here, saw all this, and I just . . . dissolved.'

'I know. I know.' Jack lapsed into silence as he followed her gaze. Suddenly he smiled. 'I don't like washing up either.'

Despite herself, Beth laughed. Then, serious again, she said, 'Suddenly there's nothing left to do and, it's stupid, but I find myself wanting to talk to Isabel about the day, to ask her things.'

'That's not stupid.'

'And that's when I don't know which way to turn. I just feel like her death has set me adrift.' Hating the futility of her feelings, angry at her helplessness, she turned to Jack in contrition, and said, 'I'm sorry, Jack. You don't need this.'

Again Jack took her in his arms. 'You're allowed to cry on your husband's shoulder once in a while.' He grinned. 'It's in the marriage contract.'

'I meant, after the day you've had.' Desperate now to tear herself away from her own thoughts, she asked, 'What happened at the accident?'

Jack didn't quite meet her eye. 'It wasn't too bad. Minor injuries.'

'But you've been ages!'

Jack sighed. 'It was just a bit complicated up at the

hospital. That's all.' Now it was he who wanted to change the subject. He gestured towards the still-unwashed dishes. 'Look, why don't you go and have a nice bath and I'll take care of all this.'

Beth sniffed again. 'OK.'

As she headed out of the room, Jack said, grinning, 'You could have protested just a bit, you know.'

Beth didn't reply – but she, too, was grinning as she went upstairs.

CH**A**PTER 9

Beth returned to work two days later. At first, she had thought she was being feeble: the senior partner of The Beeches unable to cope with grief? Surely not. Then she had decided that her protracted absence *was* her way of dealing with grief. 'Letting it all out' was, she knew, impossible in the space of two days, but at least she made no attempt to hide her feelings – especially, and most importantly, from herself. She had spent much of the time on her own, walking the dogs and thinking. She had also made several visits to Isabel's house, and on one of those visits she had found a letter addressed to herself, in Isabel's handwriting. Much of Beth's thinking had revolved round the contents of that letter. Isabel, on paper as in conversation, had not minced her words. And Beth was surprised by just how much those words, and the message they carried, were affecting her.

Now, standing in Trevor's office at The Beeches, she was faced with another and altogether more worrying letter. Although delighted to see her back, Trevor had wasted no time in requesting 'a quick word'.

'You did know about it, didn't you?' he asked as, with a puzzled frown, she finished reading the latter.

'No, we really didn't get a chance to talk,' Beth said. 'I don't think he wanted to worry me. He certainly didn't mention that it was an emergency delivery by the roadside.' Then putting the letter on Trevor's desk with a grimace, she added, 'Poor Jack. They certainly seem pretty serious about it.'

'I'm going to call them,' said Trevor, 'and outline our

complaints procedure. Hopefully they'll be happy to leave it at that.'

'Fine.'

As was his way when broaching delicate subjects, Trevor coughed discreetly. 'Er, Beth, the senior partner would normally oversee any investigation, but in the circumstances if you would rather that Will . . .'

'No, no. I'll take it on.'

'It is Jack you'll be investigating the complaint against.'

More sharply than she meant, Beth cut him short. 'I'm the best qualified to handle complaints. That's all there is to it.' Then, stalking out of the room, she glanced at her watch. Not bad, she thought. Nine o'clock and the day's already ruined.

When he arrived after making an early-morning house-call, Jack also found a letter waiting for him. Laura, handing it to him, looked amused as his face lit up. 'Don't tell me, you've won the *Reader's Digest* raffle?'

'No. It's from an old mate of mine. Francine. We did our voluntary service together in Africa.'

'Oh, right.' Laura looked distinctly envious. 'Something I thought about doing . . .'

'Never too late, Laura.' Jack ripped open the envelope.

'Is your friend still out there?'

'At the moment she's in London fund-raising but most of the time, yeah. Incurable wanderlust, you see.' He looked up at Laura and smiled half-heartedly. Laura got the message. With a sigh, she turned and walked out of reception.

Jack, stood where he was and read the letter. It soon brought a curious smile to his face.

Beth, who appeared a moment later, wasn't smiling. She was so preoccupied that she didn't even ask Jack what he was grinning about. 'Jack? I need a word.'

'Doctor Glover.' Relaxed, happy, and totally unsuspecting, Jack beamed at his wife. 'What can I do for you?'

'We've received a complaint from the Cullam family.'

'What? I don't—'

'About the accident you attended.' Then she passed him the letter. 'The one you forgot to tell me about,' she added tartly.

Jack, still bewildered, started reading the letter. A few seconds later he looked up in a mixture of anger and disbelief. 'I can't understand this! They're saying that I took over a minute to unravel the cord, that I was panicking. This,' he gestured to the damning letter, 'is nothing like what happened.'

'Why didn't you tell me about it?'

'It was the night of the funeral. I reckoned this was the last thing you'd want to hear about.'

Appreciating his reasons, Beth spoke more gently this time. 'But still, you should have told me.'

Jack didn't seem to hear her. 'Can't Trevor clear this up?'

'No. We're going to have to follow the complaints procedure.'

'Beth! We can't treat this as a real complaint! The whole family are in shock – they're going through hell. They've got a two-day-old baby with possible brain damage. This,' he added as he brandished the letter, 'is their way of trying to deal with the pain of it, the unfairness . . .'

'I realize that, Jack, but they've made a written allegation. We have to follow the practice guidelines for dealing with it.'

'I'm aware of the stages, Beth.' He looked at her. 'After all, I drew up the bloody guidelines in the first place.'

Beth, aware of the bitter irony of the situation, didn't reply. Only when Jack turned to leave did she speak. 'Where are you going?'

'I'm going to sort this out. I'm going to the hospital.'
'Jack!'

It had been Mark Stokes, the baby's father, who had decided there was a case against Jack. After the baby started having fits and after Doctor Beattie, under pressure from the family, had admitted that the signs 'were not encouraging', he decided to seek legal help. Jack, who had since made two visits to the hospital, had not been informed of this: Graham Hyde, the solicitor Mark had consulted, told him that he would inform the doctor in question. The doctor, he added, against whom he believed they had a strong case. Hyde, who specialized in medical compensation claims, wasted no time in getting hold of WPC Stuart and she, after much thought, had said that yes, the doctor had taken a long time to cut the umbilical cord. Hyde also told Mark that he had nothing to lose – he was entitled to legal aid – and he might have a great deal to gain. Successful cases of compensation for medical negligence were known to result in enormous awards for damages.

Phil, the baby's grandfather, was behind Mark all the way. While he didn't share the personal animosity that Mark had developed against Jack, he was aware of how difficult the family would find it to cope with a severely handicapped baby. Their only regular source of income was the disability benefit that he received as a result of the dust-related disease he had contracted at work. Since Mark's decorating business had collapsed, he could only find occasional part-time employment and Amanda had her work cut out looking after Ruby and trying to feed and clothe her family on their meagre income. An irreversibly brain-damaged baby would be the last straw: the tensions that already existed through the family being obliged to live in Phil's house would – sooner rather than later – lead to an almighty falling-out. Phil knew that his son-in-law hated being dependent on him.

Amanda, though, was concerned only for the baby. Still distressed and exhausted from the birth, she was concentrating her thoughts on the minute chance that the baby was not damaged. She had only half listened to Mark's talk about solicitors and compensation. She was, however, aware that Jack was *persona non grata* in the hospital and it was with a strained smile that she greeted him as he came charging into the ward. 'Hello, Doctor.'

'Hi.' Jack looked around. They were all here: Amanda and Ruby beside the incubator; Phil and Mark sitting a little way off. 'Look,' he added, 'I realize none of this can be easy for you—'

'Do you?' Mark, aggressive and unimpressed, was already spoiling for a fight. Phil, anxious to preserve some sort of dignity, steered Jack to one side of the room. 'I'm sorry, Doctor Kerruish, but this solicitor bloke reckons you should have done summat about that cord round the baby's neck sooner than you did.'

'I had to try to untangle it first, Phil. It was only a matter of seconds.'

Phil's response was quiet – but definite. 'We figure it were more like minutes.'

'I can certainly understand how it *seemed* like minutes—'

'Because it was!' Mark, joining them, was having none of Jack's excuses.

Jack exhaled deeply. It was useless. The man's mind was already made up. He walked over to Amanda. 'How is the baby? Any news this morning?'

But it was Mark, brushing angrily past him and placing himself between Jack and the incubator, who replied, 'He's lying in an incubator with some sort of brain damage. We're still to sit and wait till we find out how bad.' The implication was clear. It was all Jack's fault.

115

'I'm sorry. I want you to know that any help or support you need . . . well, that's what I'm here for.'

Mark jabbed him so hard in the chest that he was forced to take a step back. 'So why've you come round? To warn us off complaining?'

'Mark!' Amanda, shocked by her husband's attitude, feared that the two men might come to blows.

'Eh, eh, come on, son.' Phil took him by the arm. 'This isn't the way.'

Jack took a deep breath. 'I've come because I've known you all since I moved to Cardale. I think of you as friends as well as patients. I'd hoped,' he added, with a hint of regret, 'we could resolve this without any bad feeling between us.'

Phil looked genuinely contrite. 'I'm sorry it were you, Doctor, but we've taken good advice and we've been told we've got a case.' Then, with more than a hint of his son-in-law's resolve, he added, 'You know we have. You'll not put us off.'

Jack was shocked. What had happened to the jovial, proud father and grandfather who had been so effusive in his congratulations only two days before? As Jack looked him in the eye he realized that it was useless to protest: the family was determined. Disappointed and humiliated, Jack turned and walked out of the room.

'You shouldn't have done that, Mark,' said Amanda.

'Mandy, *listen*. You can't work. I get a job once in a blue moon. We've got a kid who needs help.' He held out his hands. 'We need some money from *somewhere*.'

Amanda felt like screaming. I don't care about the money, she thought. What about the baby? Instead, with great self-control, she asked Mark if he'd thought about a name yet.

'What?'

'A name. For the baby.'

Mark stared, open-mouthed, at his wife. 'You do my 'ead in sometimes, you know that!'

'He needs a name.' Amanda was adamant.

'He might never be able to say his own name. Don't you see? He's in trouble, love. How's a name gonna' help him?'

'He's still our son.'

'That's right.' Mark nodded and looked towards the incubator. 'And Jack Kerruish damaged him. And I want something back for that. We deserve something back.'

'You went to see the Cullams?'

'I did.'

'But, Jack, that could be interpreted as improper press-ure on the complainant.'

The last thing Jack wanted was another argument – especially with his own wife. 'They were my friends before they were "complainants", Beth.'

'Well . . . I'm afraid they've sent their complaint to the FHSA. Their solicitor has been in contact. There's going to be a hearing.'

Jack, weary and upset, ran a hand through his hair and looked bleakly at Beth. 'I'll get on to my medical defence organization. Play it by the book.' With that, he handed her a file. 'You'll need these. My case notes.'

'Thanks.'

'Beth, I did everything I could.'

'I know. And you know as well as I do that these things happen. Every doctor faces complaints in their career.'

'I did my job well and now I'm getting hounded for it.'

'And that'll all come out. At the hearing.' Beth, trying to hide her anxiety under a businesslike veneer, nodded and left the room. Alone in the kitchen of The Beeches, Jack looked more than doubtful.

*

If Jack needed any reminder that he was in trouble and that the whole of Cardale knew it, the next day's newspaper carried, in a blazing headline, the latest on the 'Roadside Birth Drama'. Alongside a particularly unflattering picture of Jack ran the legend 'Family to Take Action Against Local Doctor.' Jack groaned when he picked up the newspaper. Again the downside of living in a tiny community had come to haunt him: it seemed like only yesterday when he had been battling against local prejudice to save the group home. Perhaps people still harboured a grudge against him for his strong stance, yet the fuss about the home had died down. Terry, who had never wanted to be released into the community in the first place, had been sent to a psychiatric home. Freddie and Muriel, so Alice North had informed him, were getting married and – this was especially pleasing to Jack – the Harding children had made friends with both Cissy and her cat. Perhaps it was inevitable that, with no more mileage to be made out of that story, the press had pounced with glee on the latest development at The Beeches.

The public, too, reacted swiftly to the story. By ten o'clock that morning, Kim had received six phone calls from the nearby health centre informing her of patients wishing to transfer to them from The Beeches. Laura tried to assuage her panic by telling her that people had notoriously short memories and that the whole affair would 'settle down', but Kim was not so sure: if Jack was found guilty of negligence she knew she could expect an even greater exodus.

At the same time as Kim and Laura were discussing the situation at The Beeches, Beth was looking at the headline for the second time that day. Perched on the edge of the sofa in Phil Cullam's house, she could hardly fail to notice it: it was lying face-up on the table in front of her. She looked towards the kitchen where Phil was making tea. She had always enjoyed her visits to this house: Jack had not been exaggerating when he had cited the Cullam family as friends. But on this occasion the friendship was looking distinctly strained. The small-talk between herself and Phil had rapidly dried up. 'Look,' she said as he returned with the tea, 'I might as well get on with it. I'm here to take you through the procedure for the hearing.'

Phil had the grace to look slightly abashed. 'Our solicitor's been through it with us.' Lapsing into an embarrassed silence, he looked down and sipped his tea.

'Why couldn't you have come to the surgery first,' continued Beth after a pause, 'and we could have talked this through?'

Phil took a deep breath. 'Look. I know what you're trying to do. I respect it. I'm not enjoying this.'

'It's not exactly a bed of roses for Jack.'

Phil looked up, half apologetic, half imploring. 'I'll always be grateful to all of you at The Beeches for the way you battled for me when I were laid off with me chest. But I know I'm not getting any better and in the time I've got left I want to enjoy me grandkids. I won't hide it – I wanted a grandson. Some lad I could look at and say, "He's got something of me in 'im, carrying on the genes, like."'

Beth was unimpressed. 'You *have* got a grandson.'

'Yeah, who might never be able to walk, talk, play with other kids. We don't know how bad he is. We won't know for months.' Phil looked Beth straight in the eye. 'Now, your husband might be going through a lot, but I don't think it matches that, do you?'

Beth didn't know how to reply. She hadn't been prepared for such strength of feeling on Phil's part. 'I know that this is all very painful—'

'I know that I owe Doctor Kerruish for what he's done in the past. But if I let that stop me going through with this hearing, well, what sort of a father would that make me?'

This time Beth didn't even try to reply. Like Jack, she was experiencing – and regretting – the claustrophobic element of living in a small community. Friends one minute, she thought sadly as she got up to leave, and adversaries the next.

By the evening, she was even beginning to fear that the affair was souring her own relationship with Jack. He wanted her to look at the defence statement he had prepared for the hearing. 'I can't edit it for you,' she remonstrated. 'You know that.'

'Course you can.'

'All right then, I *won't*. I don't think it's ethical.'

Jack waved the paper in the air. 'This is ridiculous! You're my *wife*!'

'I'm also responsible for the practice, and to the village. You shouldn't be asking me to do this, Jack. It isn't fair.'

Jack's exasperation suddenly gave way to anger. 'My God!' he yelled. 'This place really knows how to bring down the shutters, doesn't it?'

'Please don't make this any more difficult—'

'I know I thought I had friends in Cardale. Even kidded myself I'd started to fit in.' Again Jack waved the paper in the air. 'But this place is so bloody close sometimes I could suffocate!' With that, he threw the paper on to the desk and stormed towards the door.

'And that's how you deal with it? By walking out on it?'

Angrily, Jack turned back to her. 'I'm meeting Francine. You know that. I told you about her letter.'

As he marched out, slamming the front door behind him, Beth slumped back on the sofa. Picking up her glass of wine, she stared moodily over its rim into space. Francine. Jack had indeed told her about Francine and, with all the dramas of the day, she had forgotten that he had arranged to meet her for a drink tonight. Beth frowned and took a sip. She was not, she told herself, jealous of Francine: she was jealous of the part of Jack that she had shared and that she, Beth, knew little about. And now she was worried. She had never doubted Jack's commitment to her or his love for her, but she had always, at the back of her mind, harboured the feeling that Jack would begin to find Cardale stifling and that his wanderlust would re-emerge. Francine's letter had alerted Beth to that possibility – and it couldn't have come at a more appropriate time: the actions of the Cullam family and the inevitable reper-cussions were suffocating him.

Beth sat back, closed her eyes, and thought of another letter. Isabel's letter. In death, Isabel had reached out to Beth and said the things she had intimated, but never dared to voice while she was alive. She had confirmed Beth's suspicion that she had been able to read her mind: that she knew there was one thing Beth now needed to make her life perfect. Beth sighed and took another sip of her wine. How could she tell Jack? How, with his current restlessness and with the trauma of the forthcoming hear-ing, could she possibly tell him that she was desperate to have a baby?

'Francine Sinclair.' Jack's voice startled the woman stand-ing at the bar. 'Still searching for talent in seedy dives?'

Francine grinned widely. 'Jack Kerruish. Still hanging around in them, I see.'

For a moment the two old friends studied each other. Jack, thought Francine, hadn't changed at all: perhaps he had put on a little weight, but the twinkling blue eyes were the same as ever.

Francine looked radiant, mused Jack. Deeply tanned from the African sun, she was relaxed, happy, and carried with her a vibrancy that spoke of a woman fulfilled, of a life enjoyed to the full. As he leaned forward to clasp her in a bear-hug he felt suddenly gripped by an unfamiliar emotion: it took him a good few seconds to identify it as envy.

Then they both started talking at once. How long had it been? Four years? No, Jack said, more like six. Francine threw back her head and laughed. That, she said, would make them both in their early forties. Jack gave her an old-fashioned look.

For half an hour and over several drinks, they talked of their time together in Africa, of hopes both realized and dashed, and of the sense of adventure that had lured them there in the first place. A sense of adventure, thought Jack, that Francine still had. He looked at the leaflets and photographs she had spread over the table. 'So, the old clinic's still standing.' He hoped Francine couldn't detect the wistfulness he felt.

'Thriving.' Francine beamed at him. 'You'd be proud of us. That,' she said, indicating a *Volunteer Africa!* brochure, 'is how we got the backing for the outreach programme.'

Jack's eyes sparkled as he flicked through it and digested the scale of the project. 'You're going to have your work cut out, aren't you?'

'It'll be worth it. It always is, isn't it? Front-line medicine.'

'Yeah.' Jack leaned back and laughed at the memory of his first taste of Africa. 'My first few days out there I thought I was going to die of exhaustion.'

'Yes. I remember you were ready to get the next plane home.'

Jack grinned at her. 'I would have done if you hadn't hidden my suitcase.'

For a moment they were silent, content and reflective in their shared memories. 'I always seemed to be knee deep in screaming kids,' said Jack. 'We never finished till the last patient went home.' Then, recapturing the enthusiasm of those days, he leaned forward and gazed intently at his companion. 'But when I saw the impact of my work, when I saw what medicine could *do* – well, there was no way you could leave then, was there?'

'I always thought you only stuck it 'cos you got a taste for bottled beer.'

'That,' Jack laughed, 'probably had something to do with it too.' Then with another glance at the brochure, he added, 'So, how long are you giving yourself to get these outreach clinics set up?'

'Two years. But I need the first one up and running within the first two months.'

'Well, wouldn't mind volunteering myself. Be nice to see the old place.'

'You serious?' The nostalgia, the wistfulness in his voice and his expression told Francine that he was, at least, tempted.

'Nah . . . Come on. I think my safari days are well behind me.'

'I do need experienced people.'

Jack met her eyes. 'I'm a married man.'

Francine brushed that one aside with a sweep of the hand. 'I'm sure Beth would understand.'

'She might but my patients wouldn't. I'm a country GP, Francine. Wellies, anorak and varicose veins. This is where I belong now.' Even as he said the words he heard how feeble they sounded – how feeble *he* sounded.

Francine smiled. 'But you are tempted, aren't you?'

'Let's just say I'm flattered you'd consider me. But time's moved on.'

Realizing that she had whetted his appetite, Francine was not going to give up. 'Would it be difficult for you to get cover at the practice?'

'Well . . . no. That'd be easy enough.' Then, seeing where the conversation was heading, he added, 'But I'm settled here. With Beth.'

'Look.' Brimming with enthusiasm, Francine leaned

forward and gripped her old friend by the arm. 'How about coming out for just the first two months? Surely Beth wouldn't begrudge you that?' She made it sound like she was asking for two days. She made it sound irresistible. Jack didn't trust himself to reply. He leaned back and sipped his pint. Over the rim of the glass he caught Francine's eye. Earlier that day he had cursed Cardale for swamping him; now he felt like cursing Francine for the breathing space she was offering him.

When he got home hours later, he didn't mention Africa to Beth. It was neither the right place nor the right time: not after Beth mentioned what was on *her* mind.

CHAPTER 10

The following morning the kitchen of The Beeches was converted into a temporary conference room. Even though he was in his own domain Jack, for once wearing a jacket and tie, felt distinctly ill at ease. On the other side of the table, Phil Cullam and Mark and Amanda Stokes were also looking uncomfortable, and were doing their best to avoid meeting Jack's eye. Only Ann Grainger, the conciliator representing the FHSA, looked calm and in control. A friendly woman in her mid-fifties, she sat at the head of the table and addressed Jack in a polite, enquiring tone. 'Mr Cullam and Mr Stokes insist that you were trying to unravel the cord for nearly two minutes, Doctor Kerruish.'

Jack, still uneasy, wasn't sure to whom to address his reply. He had already stated that he had spent no more than twenty seconds unravelling the cord. What was he supposed to say now? That Phil was a liar? After a moment's hesitation, he turned to Phil. 'Well, Phil, with respect, time always drags in a crisis. When you've waited for ambulances as often as I have . . .' Seeing the expressions on the faces of the others present, he lapsed into silence.

'We've also heard from PC Helen Stuart,' continued Ann Grainger, 'the officer who assisted with the birth?'

'Oh, yes.'

'She also puts the time at a lot longer than twenty seconds. How do you feel about that?'

Jack would have thought his expression was answer enough. Yet, knowing how much was at stake, he leaned forward and, with total conviction, began to plead his case.

'The thing is,' he said, 'in some ways the amount of time I spent trying to unravel the cord is irrelevant.'

'Oh?' Ann Grainger looked unconvinced. 'Could you explain what you mean by that?'

'Yes. The cord may well have been caught round the baby's neck for some time in the birth canal.'

'So,' interrupted Phil, 'you're saying the time doesn't matter at all?'

'No!' Fighting the impulse to argue, Jack clasped his hands in front of him. 'I'm saying it might be less important than we think.'

'Are you saying it might 'ave been longer than twenty seconds now, or what?' asked Mark with a sneer.

'I *know* it was twenty seconds. I'm sorry, but I think you and Phil were too emotionally involved to give a rational assessment.'

'What about the policewoman?'

Jack, remembering the look on Helen Stuart's face when she realized she was going to have to play midwife, looked evenly at Phil. 'I think it was a stressful situation for her as well.'

Mark was unimpressed. 'So you were the only one there with his head screwed on? That it?'

'I'm not saying that.'

'But do you feel,' interjected Ann Grainger, 'that your prior experience of such events perhaps made you calmer than those around you?'

'That's right. Exactly.'

'And consequently better equipped to recall the events accurately?'

'Well, yes. If you want to put it like that.' Again, Jack began to feel distinctly uneasy. Ann Grainger seemed to be phrasing her questions in a way that invited arrogance in his responses.

She looked down at her notes briefly and then addressed Jack once more. 'Could you explain to Mr

Cullam why you went to see his family at the hospital *after* their complaint had been made?'

'As the family doctor I was concerned for their welfare.'

'But you did talk about the hearing when you went to see them?'

Jack glanced over at the family. 'I thought the hearing would just add to Amanda and Mark's problems. Obviously it was a very difficult and emotional time. I needed to make sure that was what they wanted.'

'Are you still happy that you did the right thing in visiting Phil and Mark?'

Jack sighed. 'With hindsight I can see how it could be misinterpreted.' And with foresight, he felt like adding, I can predict the outcome of this meeting: Jack Kerruish being accused of medical negligence; Jack Kerruish being taken to court.

There was a silence as Ann Grainger stopped to take notes – a silence interrupted by a loud, brisk knock at the door. Before anyone had a chance to react, Beth walked in. Her expression was inscrutable as she nodded to Ann and then looked towards Amanda. 'Sorry to interrupt. I need to talk to Amanda in private. I have some news.'

A frisson of both fear and excitement visited everyone round the table. Beth could only be bringing news about one thing: the scan which the baby had been undergoing that morning. Dr Beattie, they all knew, had promised to phone in with the results.

In a daze, Amanda stood up and followed Beth into her consulting room. 'I'm afraid,' began the latter after they were both seated, 'that the scan did show your baby has a problem called calcification of the brain.'

'What?'

'It's a condition that would account for his poor response patterns. It seems that the foetus suffered some damage while it was in the womb.' Amanda continued to look blank. After a pause, Beth looked her in the eye and added, 'It isn't the sort of thing that could happen during the birth.'

Realization began to dawn on Amanda. Suddenly she had to face the possibility that it was her fault, that she had done something to harm her baby. 'When? But how has it happened? Do they know?'

'A second blood test has to be done but it's almost certainly toxoplasmosis. The infection can cross the placenta and damage the foetus.'

'An infection? But I didn't have any infection. I didn't have *anything*.'

'The symptoms,' said Beth gently, 'are like flu. Can you remember suffering from a flu-like illness at all? A heavy cold?'

Amanda looked up at Beth with tears in her eyes. 'Yes. Yes, I did. I were about five months gone. I were in bed for a couple of days, that were all.'

After a brief silence but without a hint of reproach, Beth asked her if she had gone to see Doctor Kerruish about it.

'No.' Amanda's voice barely rose above a whisper. 'I didn't think it was important enough.'

Five minutes later Beth was sitting opposite Ann Grainger. On her left, the Cullam family was reeling with shock. On her other side, Jack had also had the wind knocked out of him. Relieved and upset, angry yet vindicated, he chose to remain silent as Beth, by necessity brisk and efficient in the face of such raw emotion, did her best to establish the facts. 'Toxoplasmosis is most commonly caught through cat faeces and uncooked meat,' she explained, 'but sheep are also highly infectious carriers.' Mark, she noticed out of the corner of her eye, was looking stricken. 'If Amanda was on a farm during lambing season . . .'

'No.' Mark shook his head.

'Or was in contact with anybody who was, she may have contracted the infection from them—'

Suddenly Mark, with an anguished howl, buried his

head in his hands. 'Oh, God! It were me! I were there.' His face was bleak as he looked up at Beth. 'Up at the farm on lambing. It were *my* fault.'

'Mark, it was nobody's fault. But it is possible some infected matter passed from your clothes or hands into Amanda's bloodstream.'

'It's my fault. It was me.'

'Mark.' It was Jack who spoke. 'It was an accident.'

'What,' asked Amanda in a quiet, controlled voice, 'is going to happen to the baby? He'll have problems, won't he?'

'Yes.' Beth looked her straight in the eye. 'It's likely he'll have problems.'

A silence descended on the little room. It seemed as if there was no more to say: too many words had been spoken already; too much anger and resentment had been spilled out in the two short days since the baby had been delivered.

The silence was broken by the sound of Mark sobbing. Again, broken and inconsolable, he held his head in his hands. For a moment nobody did anything and then Phil, with a determined smile, put his arms round his son-in-law. 'Come on, lad. Come on, we've got my grandson to look after.'

Jack and Beth sat over the remains of dinner that evening. The flickering candles cast a mellow light over the room – a light that did not match their mood. Even though Jack had been vindicated, he – and Beth – felt a sense of defeat, of hollowness. Neither had yet admitted that their sombre mood was not entirely due to the day's events.

Beth, cupping her wineglass in her hands, smiled at Jack. 'Not exactly been the easiest few days, has it?'

'No. I'm sorry.'

'What about?' Beth's voice was almost a whisper.

'You needed some time, space to cope with Isabel dying. The hearing – well, it took that away from you, didn't it? Pushed everything to one side.'

'Nonsense. It helped, if anything.'

Jack sounded doubtful: 'Don't know about that.'

Beth leaned over and touched her husband's arm. 'Let's put it behind us, Jack. All of it.'

But Jack, still morose, didn't even look up.

'You're allowed to lighten up a little,' said Beth, with a determined grin.

He changed the subject. 'It was good to see Francine again,' he said. 'She's pretty fired up with these new clinics she's setting up in Africa.'

'Yes. It all sounds very exciting.'

'Yes, it is.'

Again they were silent.

'More exciting than Cardale?' At last Beth raised the issue.

'Well . . . different, that's all.'

Not trusting herself to speak, Beth merely nodded in response.

Jack began to fiddle distractedly with his knife. 'Francine's always seemed able to get her priorities sorted, you know. Laid out in straight lines.'

'Not everybody can live like that.' Beth's tone was controlled, deliberately flat.

'I know. But when your own life feels muddied, complicated . . . and I look at her. Clear, decisive.'

This time Beth couldn't disguise the hurt in her voice. 'So starting a family with me isn't clear or decisive enough for you?'

'It isn't that at all . . . It's just . . .' Jack was unable to articulate his thoughts.

'Do you wish you were going to Africa instead?'

Jack didn't reply.

'Jack? Is that what it is?'

At last he looked up. A sheepish, tentative smile played on his lips. 'Francine did say she needed someone experienced just to help while she gets these outreach clinics up and running.'

Beth saw that her knuckles had gone white around her glass. 'And what did you tell her?'

Jack avoided her eye.

'Well, thanks.' Suddenly Beth let fly. 'Sticking my neck out, putting the reputation of the whole practice on the line. *Hurting* for you and all the time you're getting ready to cut and run!'

'Beth! It isn't like that!'

'Oh? Isn't it? Isn't this all about Jack Kerruish at the centre of the universe again? Only him that matters, *his* feelings, *his* career?'

'I haven't even said I'll go!'

'But,' Beth's voice was dangerously quiet, 'you haven't said you won't, have you?'

Jack's silence was answer enough. 'Why don't you come out with me?' he said eventually. 'Just for the first month.'

'Ha! And leave Will to cope with the practice single-handed? Jack,' she added, forcing herself to remain calm, 'don't you think you might just be overreacting to the hearing – that on top of the group home business?'

'Maybe, but it's made me cynical, Beth, and I don't want to end up like that. Perhaps I need to restore my faith in medicine.'

Again, this was too much for Beth. 'You can sit there and talk all night,' she snapped. 'You might even convince yourself. But why dress it up? Be honest, Jack. You're running away. That's all there is to it.'

There was genuine pain in Jack's eyes as he looked over at her. 'This community turned its back on me, Beth. At least out there I'd know I was wanted!'

Beth reacted as if he had hit her. She blanched and felt herself going rigid with shock. Then she reached out for him. Later she hated herself for doing what she thought she would never do: for begging. 'You're wanted here, Jack. By *me*.' There were tears in her eyes as she gripped his arm with a force that surprised them both. 'Please stay.' But even as she said the words she knew she had lost him. They may have been sitting together, but in reality they were miles apart. Thousands of miles apart.

CH**A**PTER 11

'This is outrageous!' Beth looked in exasperation at Kim. 'How can a locum just not turn up?'

Equally put out, Kim reached once again for the telephone. 'I've called and called – I just don't get a reply.'

Beth sighed and glanced towards the waiting room. She knew, from the muted buzz of conversation – and from the bulging appointment-book – that the place was packed. How the hell, she wondered, are the two of us going to cope?

'Anyway,' Kim continued, 'I'm chasing the recommendation that the health centre gave us.'

'At this rate Jack'll be back before we get a replacement.' Thoroughly irritated, Beth stalked off towards her room. She failed to return Will's smile as he passed her in the corridor.

'What the hell is the matter with Beth?' asked the latter, as he approached reception.

'Still furious about the locum not turning up.'

'Well, I'm not exactly chuffed about it either.'

'Ah.' Kim looked up at him and smiled. 'But Beth also got out of bed the wrong side this morning. Slept in.'

Will grinned. 'None of Jack's snoring to keep her awake, I s'pose.'

'Don't mention Jack,' whispered Kim. 'Bad word around these parts.'

'Oh? I thought they'd got over all that?'

'Ah.' Kim arched an eyebrow knowingly. 'You never get over it when they don't call.'

'Wouldn't have thought there were many telephones in

the bush,' Will replied as he rummaged in the filing cabinet.

'Try telling that to Beth.'

Will found what he was after and shut the cabinet. 'Later, perhaps.' He inclined his head towards the waiting room. 'When we've dealt with the marauding hordes.'

'I've been called many things,' said a bright, cheerful voice that startled both of them, 'but never a marauding horde.'

Will and Kim looked up in surprise. Before them was a pretty, smartly dressed blonde woman carrying an expensive-looking briefcase. She herself looked expensive, thought Will.

Carefully, though not elaborately, made-up, she carried herself with great confidence and was smiling broadly at both of them. Will suddenly realized they were both staring at her: he with interest, Kim with something approaching dislike.

'Er . . . have you made an appointment?' Will returned her smile. 'We're rather busy.'

'No. I thought I'd just drop in on the off-chance.'

'Are you registered with us?' Kim already knew the answer: she'd never seen this woman before.

'No. I'm not a patient.' After a fleeting smile at Kim, the woman held out her hand to Will. 'Janey Cooper, Amachem Pharmaceuticals.'

'Will Preston. Hello.'

'I've really just come to introduce myself,' she continued, 'but if you can spare me half an hour, I thought we might have a talk about—'

'Hang on, hang on!' With a rueful smile, Will gestured towards the waiting room. 'We're up to our eyes this morning. I'm afraid it's out of the question.'

'Then perhaps we could talk over lunch?'

'Oh.' Will was nonplussed by her forthright manner. 'Well . . . yes, that would be nice.'

It was just as well Janey and Will were looking at each other. Kim, who had been watching them with amusement, now looked thunderous. She felt like saying, What about that oh-so-generous prawn sandwich you were going to treat me to as a reward for working overtime on your bloody statistics? But as she caught the look that passed from Will to Janey, she knew that the sandwich was well and truly forgotten. Will had better fish to fry.

'I'll come back, then,' said Janey, 'at about one. Is that OK?'

'Fine.' Will, grinning, walked back towards his room. Kim, like her sandwich, was forgotten.

Beth soon forgot her rage about the vanishing locum. She and Will would cope on their own. Hadn't they done just that before Jack had appeared on the scene nearly four years before? Conveniently forgetting just how much the practice had grown since Jack had joined them, she transferred her annoyance, in between patients, to what was, anyway, its original cause: Jack's departure.

After her initial horror, when she had realized that he was in earnest about going, Beth had tried to rationalize her feelings. Jack, too, had become rational instead of wistful and moody and, after a week of intermittent discussion, they had agreed that he should go – for a month. Beth had pointed out, reasonably, she thought, that if he were away for longer then he might begin to lose his patients. He had already, she reminded him, lost six to the health centre after the headlines about the Cullam inquiry. Jack had been about to protest that a month was hardly anything and that it wouldn't give him long enough to have any effect on the outreach programme. Just in time, he had stopped himself. Beth, he saw, was being more than reasonable. She was prepared to give him the breathing-space he needed: she was letting him exercise his wanderlust and – it went unspoken – sort out his priorities. Cardale and Beth – or a life on the wing? It was, he knew, a hell of a decision for her.

He had tried his best to reassure her that his commitment to her was unwavering. Beth wasn't so certain; yet one thing she did know was that it was now or never. Better, she reasoned, for Jack to battle with his demons now, rather than when they had a family. That, although again it went unspoken, was Beth's ultimatum. Isabel's letter had touched her deeply and served to confirm what she had never really admitted to herself: that she was desperate to start a family. Jack had assured her that he wanted that too. After Africa.

What, Beth had asked herself, would Isabel have counselled?

She didn't even have to think about it for long. Isabel would have told her to let him go. Men (and Isabel, Beth remembered with a grin, had had a lot of experience with men) hated feeling trapped. The most important thing he'll discover, Isabel would have said, is just how much he misses you. Let him go. Trust him.

But Beth thought as she escorted her last patient of the morning to the door, if he was missing her so much, then why the hell hadn't he phoned? It was Isabel, again, who answered. Beth grinned again as the voice in her ear told her he'd only been gone three days and that the African bush wasn't exactly awash with telephones.

Just as she had sat down again to busy herself with paperwork, there was a hesitant knock and Laura popped her head round the door. 'Beth?' Laura had been warned about Beth's earlier bad mood and, testing the water, left her question hanging in the air.

'Yes?' Smiling brightly, Beth asked her in.

Laura sighed in relief and, without preamble, told Beth what was troubling her. 'I've just come from a visit to Edna Sturgess.'

'Mmm? The hip operation?'

'Yes. You know that sore from her operation wound? It's just that I'm not very happy with it. She's been on antibiotics for ten days.' Laura frowned. 'There should be some response by now, but it seems to be getting worse, if anything.'

'Oh. Damn. I wanted that completely cleared before she goes back into hospital.' After a moment's consideration, Beth said, 'Look, I'll pop over while I'm on my rounds this afternoon.'

'Great. Thanks, Beth. Probably just on account of her age, but I *was* worried.'

Edna Sturgess, thought Beth as she drove towards her house, was not the sort of woman to take a hip operation lying down. The only problem was, of course, that she *had* to take it lying down. An active woman in her seventies, she was also the sort of person who hated being reminded of her mortality. 'Mark my words,' Alice North had informed her with a knowing look, 'she's going to make life hell for that husband of hers. She won't like being laid up. Frank'll have his work cut out. Just you wait and see.'

But Frank, Beth noted as she surveyed Edna's makeshift downstairs bedroom, seemed to be doing a sterling job, especially for an eighty-year-old. The house looked clean and Edna, despite her lack of mobility and the wound that caused it, was in good spirits. 'You shouldn't be wasting your time on me, Doctor Glover,' she remarked as Beth took a swab from the sore on her hip. 'It's only a bed sore.'

'I'm sure it is.' Beth looked up at her and smiled. 'I'd just like it gone, that's all. And this swab will tell us if there's a more effective antibiotic we should be using.'

As she rearranged Edna's nightdress and bedclothes Frank, on cue, tapped at the glass partition leading to the kitchen. In deference to both his wife and the doctor, he had absented himself during the examination. 'Is she decent?' he asked.

Beth suppressed a giggle as Edna shouted back, 'Who's she? The cat's mother?'

'I'm finished, Frank.' Snapping her briefcase shut, Beth rose to her feet as Frank, looking anxious, stuck his head round the door and offered her a cup of tea. 'I'd love one, but I've got a million calls to make. Thanks all the same.'

'How's the patient?' Frank cast a hesitant look in his wife's direction.

'Doing fine, all things considered. We'll get this sore cleared in no time. I'll have the results back in a day or two, then we'll see what's to be done.' As she walked to the door, Beth turned and added, 'I'll let myself out – you stay and look after Edna. I'll be in touch as soon as I can. Bye!'

As soon as Beth had gone, a tension developed in the room. Frank, aware of it and anxious to dispel it, smiled at his wife and ambled forward to sit on her bed. As soon as he had done so, Edna yelped in pain. 'Don't do that!' she screamed. 'Have you got no consideration? You know it's agony for me, any movement like that.'

Frank, getting to his feet with alacrity, couldn't help remembering that there had been no shouts of agony when Beth had sat on the bed. Yet any remark in that direction would, he knew, just make matters worse. 'Sorry. Is there anything else you'd like?'

Edna glared at him. 'Dancing at the Ritz? A nice long walk in the park, perhaps?'

Frank sighed, and looked down at his bed-ridden wife. 'Don't go on, Edna, love. It's not my fault you're like this. I know it's miserable for you, but I *am* doing my best.'

Edna grudgingly acknowledged the truth of that statement. 'Aye. Aye, I know you are. It's just . . . it's just . . .'

'Aye. I know, love, I know.'

But he doesn't know, thought Edna as he left the room.

He hasn't a clue. A lifetime of frenetic activity, nearly fifty years of keeping house for Frank, and now I can't even boil an egg. She looked down at her injured hip and her face, the brave face that she was trying so hard to sustain, crumpled into a silent sob.

Frank, slowly climbing the stairs, also dropped his mask. I'm eighty, he thought. I can't go on like this, helping Edna to the loo, catering to her every whim, supporting her both physically and mentally. I've got problems of my own. And then, as he reached the top of the stairs, his problem hit him with a vengeance: a sharp, searing pain in his chest that reduced him to clutching the banisters, bent double and fighting for breath.

Will was having an altogether better time than Beth or Frank and Edna Sturgess. Janey Cooper, as promised, arrived at The Beeches at one o'clock. Will raised an eyebrow as he saw her car – a bright red sports model with, it was obvious, 'all the trimmings'.

'No recession in the drugs trade, I see.'

Janey, opening the door for him, was momentarily disconcerted. Not sure if he was joking or not, she pointed to the Range Rover parked beside her. 'That yours?'

'Well . . . yes.'

'Thought so. You look the type.' Now it was Will's turn to look bemused. Janey Cooper, he thought, was not someone to be messed with.

They went to the Manor, as Will always did if he was going out to lunch. Apart from being the only pub in the centre of Cardale, it was run by James and Chloë White, a couple who were practically family to all three doctors at The Beeches. They had also lived through more than their fair share of medical traumas, the latest of which had been Chloë's Hodgkin's disease, a form of cancer. The illness had been discovered at a relatively late stage and Chloë, against all the odds, was pulling through. As he approached the bar, Will recollected that Beth was seeing Chloë tomorrow for the results of her final test. He looked at Chloë, talking animatedly to a young farmer. She looked radiant. Will mentally crossed his fingers for her: surely she would be given the all-clear.

James, with a pointed glance in Janey's direction, greeted Will and took his order. Will was equally pointed about not elaborating on his lunch-date. He knew perfectly well that his love-life – or lack of it – was a regular talking-point in Cardale. Since Sarah's departure, there had been several attempts by well-wishers to matchmake the born-again bachelor. Will, everybody agreed, had an awful lot going for him: he was good-looking, well-spoken, charming, amusing and moderately well off. That he also had two young boys at boarding-school was, admittedly, a complication – but, then, the boys spent most of their time with 'that woman'.

'That woman' – or Sarah, as people had called her before she bolted – had never fitted into Cardale. Will knew it; Sarah knew it; and the less charitable among Cardale's population had made a point of demonstrating it. The irony was that, now that she was filing for divorce and would therefore be staying permanently in Nottingham, people were inclined to look more favourably upon her. Will was well aware of that. But Beth had been unable to disguise her delight when he had announced that he and Sarah were finally calling it a day. Sarah had been famously difficult, their marriage notoriously rocky.

As Will walked up to the table Janey had appropriated for them, he found himself examining her with a critical but not disapproving eye. When she suddenly met his gaze, he felt himself blushing.

After he sat down, neither knew what to say. Janey, who rarely lost her composure, took a gulp of her drink and looked around. 'Nice pub. Quiet.'

'You should see it in the evening. Heaving.' Will inclined his head towards James, now with Chloë and Tim Shardlow, the young farmer. 'Run by friends of mine.'

Janey looked over to the bar. 'Yes. He,' indicating Tim Shardlow, 'obviously thinks so as well,' she said.

Will followed her gaze. Tim, relaxed and clearly enjoying himself, was laughing at some remark of Chloë's. 'Mmm. Good to see him laughing, I must say.'

'Oh?' Janey shot him a quizzical look.

'Poor man's wife died a month ago.'

'Oh, my God.' Janey looked back at Tim with a mixture of guilt and curiosity. 'How awful. She must have been so *young.*'

'Yeah.' Will shook his head. 'Twenty-five.' He sipped his drink. 'But I'm sure you haven't asked me to lunch just to sit here and discuss local tragedies.'

Janey had already decided that she was quite happy to sit and discuss absolutely anything with Will Preston. He was gorgeous, good company and evidently not a little interested in her. But he was also a doctor and she had asked him here to discuss medicine. With some reluctance, she turned to him and began her sales pitch. She was new to the job at Amachem, but she had done her homework about which medical practices were worth targeting. The Beeches in Cardale, she had discovered, was definitely worth while: that The Beeches contained Will was a bonus.

Will, however, was not an easy man to impress. He was well aware that drug companies were primarily motivated by money and not by the well-being of individuals they had never met. They might have manufactured the latest wonder drugs, with all manner of statistics from trials to back them up, but the bottom line was: would his patients be better off with expensive new drugs from Amachem? Despite Janey's impressive sales patter, Will was sceptical – and unmoving.

But Janey rarely took no for an answer. An hour later,

when they got up to leave, she turned to him. 'Give me your address.'

'What?'

Janey smiled. 'I'll get the trials literature and promotional video sent to you. Read, watch – and if you're still not interested, I'll take no for an answer. How's that for a deal?'

Will, amused by her gall and not entirely convinced that her motives were pure, gave her his address. Businesslike, she thanked him. When they parted he found himself wondering just how impure her motives were. Very, he hoped.

CH APTER 12

'Good morning!' Kim looked up as Beth came into reception. Although she had been back to her normal cheerful self by the end of the previous day's surgery, Beth was evidently not enjoying her nights alone. She looked much the same as she had yesterday – only worse. 'What on earth have you been doing? Kim continued. 'You look like something the cat dragged in.'

'Thank you, Kim.' Beth gave her a wan smile. 'Next time I want my ego boosted I'll know where to come. I was up till one with a vomiting baby,' she said as she leafed through her post. 'Then I was so anxious not to sleep through the alarm again that I woke up at half-hour intervals throughout the night.' Finding nothing of interest in her letters, she looked up. 'Any joy on the locum front?'

"Fraid not. The one the health centre put me on to is off to work for someone else in Wales and they can't give me any other names.'

'Damn! This is impossible. Look, find out how long it'd take to get an ad in the press, and see if we can get someone that way.' Without much enthusiasm, she scanned the appointment-book to see who she would be treating that day.

'Oh . . . Beth?'

'Mmm?'

'Frank Sturgess is in the waiting room in a bit of a state. I know he's not got an appointment but—'

'Frank?' Beth looked up, a worried frown creasing her features. 'Give me five minutes and send him through.

Poor old chap's got enough on his plate without being turned away from here.'

The 'poor old chap' shuffled in five minutes later and, with an apologetic smile, thanked Beth for seeing him at such short notice. 'Hate to bother you,' he said, 'but it's my heart. I think . . . well, I think there's something wrong.' Frank's smile failed to disguise the worry in his voice.

'Well, there's an easy way to find out.' Beth, brisk and upbeat, told him to strip to the waist and lie on the couch. As he did so she fetched her stethoscope. She hoped to God there was nothing wrong with Frank's heart. Who would care for Edna? Who would care for *him*?

After another five minutes she removed the stethoscope from his chest and gave him a reassuring smile. 'You haven't had a heart attack, Frank, just a touch of angina. I can give you a spray to sort that out. Just pop a bit under your tongue whenever you get a twinge. You'll need plenty of fresh air as well.' Leaving him to get dressed, she walked to her desk to fetch her prescription pad. 'A spot of fishing wouldn't go amiss,' she added casually. Fishing was Frank's passion. It was also something he was quite unable to do with Edna in her present state. She looked at him in concern. 'I know it must be difficult at home, but . . .'

'Well, it won't be for much longer, will it?' Frank, relieved about his own health, was now confident for Edna's.

'No.' Beth smiled back. There was no reason, after all, to suppose that Edna would be laid up for much longer. 'Her test results should be in today,' she remarked.

'That's good.'

'But, Frank, do try to ease up a little.'

He just looked at her.

As he left, Laura came breezing into Beth's room,

holding a slip of paper. 'Edna Sturgess's test results,' she said, as soon as Frank was out of earshot.

'Thanks.' Beth took the paper and began to read. Then she looked up at Laura. From the latter's expression, it was clear that she had already read the result. 'MRSA.' She grimaced. 'Which is why,' she said, 'Edna's sore didn't respond to the penicillin.'

'They'll have to cancel her operation.' Laura shook her head in disappointment. 'The hospital won't take her if she's got an infection, will they?'

'No. Oh, *poor* old Edna,' said Beth, with feeling, as she handed back the paper.

'Poor old Frank.' From her brief glimpse of him, Laura had seen that he was looking even more run down than before.

'Oh, I'm sorry,' said a voice behind them. 'I didn't know . . . Kim said . . .'

Beth, startled out of her reverie, looked up. Chloë White was standing, looking apprehensive and apologetic, at the half-open door. James was hovering behind her in the corridor. Laura pulled the door wide open and smiled. 'It's all right, come on in. I was just having a quick word.' Then she turned to Beth. 'I'll talk to you later.'

Beth ushered James and Chloë into the room. They, too, were coming for test results: it was no wonder they were looking a tad worried. 'Come in and sit down. No need to be nervous.' She sat down and beamed at them. 'I just wish Jack was here to give you the good news himself.' Her grin widened. 'Clean bill of health, Chloë. Congratulations. Not a malignant cell in sight.'

For a second or two Chloë stared at Beth. Then she burst into tears and buried her face in James's chest. Beth wasn't surprised by her reaction, by the sudden release of pent-up tension. Still smiling, she turned to James, who was looking happy yet bewildered – and rather ill. 'You, on the other hand, look like you've been in a fight,' she said.

'You should see the other bloke.'

'Fighting over a bottle of whisky, were you?' Beth knew a hangover when she saw one.

'He was up drinking with Tim Shardlow all night,' said Chloë, raising a tear-stained but smiling face.

'Oh?' Beth was delighted. She had been seriously worried about Tim since Maggie's death. He was so isolated on his farm and, she suspected, even more isolated in his emotions. 'In that case I'll let you off. He could do with some good company.'

'Boozy company, you mean.' Chloë fumbled for a handkerchief. 'I went to bed and left them to it. Still,' she went on, 'I'm glad he came. He popped in at lunchtime and, I don't know why, but I just invited him for dinner, didn't I, James?'

'Glad you did.' Then James frowned at Beth. 'He did *stay* a while, but I couldn't exactly turf him out, could I? Not when he was so . . .'

'So what, James?'

'Well, I dunno really. He said he was fine, but . . .' James couldn't find the right words.

'Don't worry,' said Beth. 'He's got an appointment with me. I'll talk to him. As for you two,' she added, 'I don't normally say this, but I'm hopeful that I won't be seeing you for a long, long time.'

They all laughed and Chloë, still slightly shell-shocked, looked reprovingly across the table. 'Are you saying there's something wrong with our hospitality? And there we were, thinking we were the best publicans in Derbyshire.'

Beth chortled. 'No. I'll still be dropping in to the Manor. Your hospitality's as perfect as your health.'

*

Two hours later Beth had little to smile about. She was standing outside the hospital in Derby, slightly flushed and thinking just how much she disliked the man opposite her. 'It's completely out of the question, Doctor Glover,' he finished. Then, with a patronizing nod, he strode off down the path towards the car park.

Beth, angry at being dismissed in such a cavalier fashion, went haring after him. The best orthopaedic consultant in England or not, Adam Kitchener had no right to be so bloody superior. 'Mr Kitchener,' she said, trying not to betray the anger she felt, 'it is imperative that Mrs Sturgess has this revision op as soon as possible, both for her own sake and for the sake of her husband who is her primary carer, and who is eighty. He simply can't cope much longer.' Swallowing her pride, she added, 'I'm not asking lightly, Mr Kitchener, this is urgent—'

'Do you know what is involved in an operation on someone who is MRSA positive, Doctor Glover?' interrupted Kitchener as he stopped and turned abruptly to face her.

'I—'

'We are talking about a bacterium that is resistant to virtually all antibiotics. The risk of infection to other patients – the risk of septicaemia is enormous. It would mean total theatre scrub-down and sterilization before and after, patient in sterile isolation for at least a week. I simply can't afford the resources.' With that, he stalked off again, leaving a speechless Beth in his wake.

Again, she charged after him. 'But she picked up the infection during her operation at this hospital!'

'We don't have MRSA at this hospital,' said Kitchener through thin lips.

'Yes, you—'

'Look, Doctor Glover, I'm sorry for Mrs . . . er . . . for your patient, but there is really nothing I can do.'

This time Beth knew it would be useless to follow him.

Frustrated and furious, she stood and looked in distaste at the back of his well-groomed head and his expensive, beautifully cut suit. 'Sturgess,' she whispered to herself. 'Her name is Edna Sturgess.'

'So what you're saying,' said a disbelieving Edna, 'is that I went in with one illness and came out with another?'

'In a nutshell, yes.'

Edna looked thunderous. 'I'll sue.'

At least this hasn't destroyed the woman's spirit, thought Beth. With a sad smile, she sat down on the edge of Edna's bed. Frank, sitting opposite, noticed that Edna, again, neither squirmed nor screamed as Beth did so.

'The point is, Edna, that this particular infection may take some while to clear up.'

'How long?' It was Frank who asked.

'Impossible to say. As long as it takes. But I have to warn you, Edna's hip revision is almost certainly out of the question till it does clear up.'

Both women looked on in concern as Frank leaned his elbows on his knees and lowered his head into his hands in the ultimate gesture of defeat.

'The risk of spreading the infection is so great,' continued Beth in sympathetic explanation, 'that the hospitals are simply refusing to admit you until it's completely cleared up.'

'But can't they do what you said? Put her in some sort of isolation?'

'It's not just that, Frank. To make sure the infection is contained they'd have to shut down the operating theatre for a week or so afterwards. Nobody can afford to do that.'

Frank looked close to tears. 'But she must have her operation!'

Beth sighed and stood up. There was no more she could

do – and staying with Frank and Edna would just prolong their agony. 'I know how important it is to you both. Believe me, I will keep trying.'

Frank escorted her out to her car. 'Look, Doctor, I can see why the National Health don't want her, but . . . well, I've got a bit put by. Don't you think we could . . .'

Beth touched his shoulder. 'I'm sorry, Frank. No private hospital would take her either. Money just won't buy Edna this operation.' That, she knew, wasn't strictly true, but the last thing Frank needed was a lecture on the preferences of pig-headed consultants.

'Oh, well,' Frank gave her a defeated smile, 'no harm in asking?'

'No. No harm in asking. 'Bye, Frank.' To her shame, Beth was relieved to get away from him. She couldn't bear his pain or the brave face with which he was trying to disguise it.

Neither could Edna. She couldn't bear her own disappointment either. 'Oh, well,' she sighed as her husband returned to the living room, 'I daresay I can put up with it a while longer.'

'And just how long,' replied Frank, 'd'you think I can put up with it?'

'You? I'm the one in constant pain.'

'And I'm the one that's working my fingers to the bone. Cleaning, shopping, cooking . . . and the cups of tea, the visits to the bathroom—'

'And how d'you think I feel about that, eh?' shouted Edna. It was the visits to the bathroom – the ultimate indignity – that touched a raw nerve. 'D'you think I like having to beg to be taken to the toilet?'

'Beg? You don't beg, Edna, you demand. You nag. You're always on at me for something. You're making my life a misery.'

They both knew he was right, but Edna was too stubborn to admit it. 'Well, pardon me,' she said. 'I mean, I only did this hip in on purpose to get at you. I enjoy lying here day after day in bloody agony. Wonderful knowing I might be here till kingdom come and getting no better. Life of Riley I've got!'

Frank was upset by her outburst. 'I'm sorry Edna. I didn't mean—'

'Oh, get out of my sight! If I'm making your life such a misery, then get out of it. I don't need you – me and that nurse who visits can manage perfectly well by ourselves.' Frank looked at her. 'Go on!' she screamed. 'Clear off!'

After looking both appalled and undecided, Frank was suddenly resolute. 'Fine,' he said. 'Right. I will.' And he did.

Half an hour later, Edna heard her husband leave the house. She also heard the familiar scrape of his fishing rod against the hall radiator and was seized by panic: Frank always stayed the night with their nephew when he went fishing. She closed her eyes and lay back against the pillow in the fearful knowledge that this time she had gone too far.

Three unexpected things happened in Cardale that night, two of which made people very happy indeed. The first was that Jack phoned Beth. They had a long, loving conversation after which Beth lay in the bath in blissful contentment, savouring both a glass of expensive wine and the delightful words that Jack had repeated over the phone: 'I love you and I miss you.' Isabel, as ever, had been right. For the first time in days, Beth slept like a log.

Will, on the other hand, didn't get much sleep at all. At eight o'clock he was disturbed from his dinner – a Chinese takeaway – by the doorbell. Hoping that his unexpected caller wasn't a patient, he flicked the TV on to standby and, making vague attempts to tuck his shirt in and look more presentable, went to answer the door.

Janey Cooper, looking both expansive and expensive, was standing on the doorstep holding a bottle of champagne in one hand and a video in the other. Will was too startled to say anything other than 'Hello.'

Janey laughed in response and flourished the video at him. 'I've brought it round for you. I thought,' she added as she gestured towards the champagne, 'we might watch it together?'

Will thought that was an extremely good idea.

The third thing that happened took place in the kitchen of the Sturgess household. Edna, bored, irritated, and thirsty, had managed to get there on her own. Leaning on her stick and grabbing any surface that could support her, she struggled to make herself a cup of cocoa. Her face set like iron and her jaws clenched in painful determination, she spooned powder into a mug, then poured boiling water on top. Sighing with the effort, she then moved to the fridge and bent slowly to open it. Extracting a bottle of milk, she closed the door and, with a huge effort, retraced her steps. Then she lost her balance. The milk bottle fell to the floor and smashed, her stick skidded in the spilled milk and Edna, open-mouthed in horror, fell heavily to the floor.

CH APTER 13

Will was late for work the next day.

'You're looking extremely pleased with yourself. What've you been up to?' If I didn't know better, thought Kim, I would think he'd been having . . .

'Nothing, Kim,' said Will, with a huge and rather smug grin. 'I'm sorry about yesterday lunchtime,' he added, as visions of Janey sprawled in his bed sprang before him.

Kim was unimpressed. 'And you're late. I'm going to buy you and Beth new alarm clocks for Christmas.'

'Oh? She late as well?'

'Not today,' replied Kim pointedly. 'In fact, she was early. Just as well, really.'

'Why?'

'Laura paid an early visit to the Sturgesses – found poor old Edna face down in the kitchen. Broken femur.'

'Oh, God, poor old thing.' Will had heard about Edna Sturgess, and Beth's contretemps with Adam Kitchener. 'Well, they'll have to let her into hospital now.'

'Won't they just. In fact that's where she is – with Beth.'

'I shouldn't have said it, Doctor. I should never have said any of it.' Edna, lying in her hospital bed, was the picture of misery. It was all her own fault, she told Beth: if she hadn't been so nasty to poor Frank he wouldn't have disappeared and she wouldn't have been in the kitchen and . . .

'Don't upset yourself, Edna. It'll all be all right now.' Beth smiled down at the old lady and patted her shoulder.

'But it's too late! He's gone!' Then Edna came the closest she'd ever been to pleading. 'Try and find him for me. Please.'

Beth, who only knew that Frank had 'gone fishing', concealed her doubt from Edna about her ability to track him down. As she took her leave she reflected that, anyway, she had a rather more important person to find.

She discovered him at the first try – in his consulting room. 'Mr Kitchener?'

Adam Kitchener looked up in annoyance. When he saw that his visitor was Beth, he was even more irritated.

'May I assume,' Beth continued when she realized that a greeting wasn't going to be forthcoming, 'that you'll do Mrs Sturgess's hip revision in the same op as resetting her femur?'

Kitchener put the notes down on his desk. They were Edna's notes, Beth noticed. Then he looked coldly at her. 'I really have no choice, do I?'

Beth couldn't stop herself smiling. She decided to make her exit as suddenly as she had entered. Adam Kitchener obviously wasn't in the mood for small-talk.

Before she left the hospital she decided to look in again on Edna. Much to her surprise and relief, she found an agitated Frank standing by her bedside. 'Frank! How did—'

'Oh, Doctor Glover! I came back first thing this morning and when – well, when I saw that Edna wasn't there—'

'He came rushing up to The Beeches.' Edna was clearly chuffed to bits that her husband had come back so quickly and had acted so promptly.

'Yes. And Laura told me what had happened so . . .' He turned and looked fondly at his wife, 'so I came here.'

Beth was delighted. She also had some good news for Frank – for both of them. 'Look, I've already discussed this with Laura. We're arranging some home help for when you come out of hospital. That,' she added as she turned to Frank, 'should take some of the strain off you.'

Frank looked like all his Christmases had come at once. 'Aye, that'd be fine.'

Edna, however, wasn't so sure. 'I hope,' she grumbled, 'that she'll be able to make a decent poached egg. Not like that muck you've been giving me.' But from the look she gave her husband it was clear that after the scare of his disappearance she'd be prepared to take anything he gave her – even his next words.

'Shut up, you silly old bat.'

Beth giggled at his mock-reproving tone. The Sturgesses, she reckoned, would be fine.

An hour later and back at The Beeches, Beth herself began to feel less than fine. Two doctors, no matter how hard they worked, could not take the place of three. Will, rather surprisingly, seemed unfazed by the extra workload. He was behaving in an altogether uncharacteristic fashion, reflected Beth, after they had met over coffee in the kitchen. She had asked him how he was and had given him a 'look' – but to no avail. He just gave her a cryptic grin in reply. But better, she conceded, to have a happy Will than a truculent one. His moods and his attitude to being lumbered with extra work had led to more than a few confrontations in the past. Yet Beth felt rather annoyed that she rather than Will seemed to be the one affected most by the extra work.

'What's happened about the ad?' she asked Kim.

'Oh, God. Beth, it'll take an age by the time we run an ad, interview applicants and—'

'Oh, well, then, let's just forget it.' Realizing how abrupt she sounded, she smiled and gave a resigned shrug. 'We've managed this far without a locum. Can't get much worse.'

'True.' Kim was secretly relieved. As practice manager, she knew perfectly well that she would be the one deputed to organize and look after the locum. Practice manager *and* receptionist, she corrected herself. And *she* wasn't complaining.

'You all right, Kim?' Beth was looking at her in a most peculiar fashion.

'Yes, fine.'

'Mmm. When am I seeing Tim Shardlow?'

'I don't know. I didn't think he'd made an appointment.' Kim quickly checked the book. 'No. Nothing.'

'How very odd. Oh, well, only three more appointments and then it's off for my exciting evening out.'

'Oh?' Kim was riveted. 'Where're you going?'

'The supermarket.'

'Some girls,' said Kim, as Beth turned to leave, 'have all the fun.'

Her words stuck in Beth's mind as she wheeled her trolley down the aisles that evening. Fun. Yes, I'm really having fun. Snickering to herself, she looked at the items in the trolley. She hoped none of her patients would come in and catch her. 'Comfort food' was the phrase that sprang to mind: steak, red wine, crisps, biscuits and chocolates looked accusingly – and appealingly – up at her. A large lettuce caught her eye as she turned into the next aisle: she grabbed it and arranged it so that it covered the worst of the offenders. Then it struck her: she was behaving exactly like a naughty schoolgirl.

A loud crash from the next aisle interrupted her thoughts. Instinctively, Beth abandoned her trolley and ran round towards the source of the disturbance. Surrounded by fallen tins and jars, a woman was lying flat on the floor. She looked up in anguish as Beth approached. 'I slipped with the trolley. This lot came down on me.' Then, flinching, she dabbed ineffectually at her ankle. Blood was slowly oozing from what looked like a deep gash.

Other customers gathered round in trance-like fascination. None offered assistance. Irritated by their proximity, Beth asked them to clear some space. Taking a handkerchief from her bag, she knelt beside the woman. 'Keep that pressed against the wound . . . that's right. It's not as serious as it looks.' Then, asking one of the staff to keep an eye on her, she rushed outside to her car to get her doctor's bag. As she returned to the supermarket, she was dimly aware of a young girl loitering a few cars away, following her progress with a seemingly all-consuming interest.

Five minutes later she knew why the girl had been staring at her. The woman, whose name was Barbara Sykes, had allowed her to dress the wound which, as she had predicted, looked worse than it was. As Beth helped her out of the supermarket and offered her a lift home, Barbara suddenly noticed the girl. Both her face and her tone hardened. 'Joanne!' she shouted. 'Come here! This minute!'

Beth watched in surprise as the girl reluctantly stepped forward. 'My daughter,' said Barbara in explanation. Beth found it odd that the woman should make her daughter wait outside while she did her shopping – and said so.

'No, no. She didn't like the fuss. She got frightened. Ran off. Who wouldn't, eh?' Barbara gave a forced little laugh. 'With their mum flat out on the supermarket floor.'

Joanne glared at Beth. Beth said hello.

'Joanne! The lady's talking to you!' But Barbara, too, failed to elicit a response from her daughter.

Beth just smiled. Kids, she thought: this girl looked as if she were about eight. No doubt she was going through whatever stage girls went through at that age. Then she shrugged and, lugging Barbara's shopping as well as her own, opened her car door. 'Well, here we are.'

'No, really. It's OK. We always get the bus.' Barbara, as

she had in the supermarket, made a feeble attempt at protesting.

Beth looked at her ankle. 'Don't be silly. I live in Cardale as well. It's absolutely no problem. Hop in.'

Hop, Barbara realized, was the operative word. She was in no state even to walk to the bus stop. She gave her daughter a warning look and told her to get into the back seat.

Joanne, still silent and mutinous, reluctantly climbed in. Barbara said little during the journey, Joanne nothing at all. Beth, exhausted after a long day, was happy to be able to concentrate on her driving, yet she was acutely aware that the atmosphere in the car was less than merry. She was relieved when, twenty minutes later, they pulled up in front of the house to which Barbara had directed her.

Once out of the car, Barbara insisted on carrying one of the shopping bags up the garden path. Beth carried the rest and Joanne, bounding ahead of them, carried nothing. She also refused to take the key and open the door. Barbara, with a pleading look at Beth, told her they could manage.

'Are you sure?'

'Yes.' After a struggle, Barbara managed to open the door. 'Thanks for the lift home.'

'No problem. But remember to come for that tetanus tomorrow morning.'

'I'll see. I'll try.'

'You must get one done . . .'

But Barbara had already shut the door. Feeling both foolish and annoyed, Beth stood on the step for a moment then turned away. She was half-way down the garden path when she heard Barbara's raised voice from inside the house. She paused and then, frowning, continued on her way. It was none of her business – and she really couldn't blame Barbara for shouting at Joanne. Beth had rarely encountered a less appealing child.

As she drove home, she found she was grinning to herself: the prospect of yet another evening on her own suddenly seemed rather attractive.

Will was also contemplating another evening on his own. When she had left his flat that morning, Janey had said that, no, she wouldn't be able to see him that night. But she had also said that, yes, she most definitely wanted to see him again – and that was why Will, like Beth, was grinning to himself as he drew up in front of his flat. Parking and locking the car, he looked up as he heard his name called from the other side of the square. Janey, waving a paper bag and a bottle of champagne, was standing beside her own car.

Will was delighted. 'You should have told me you were coming!'

'I wanted to surprise you.' Janey crossed the road and walked up to him. 'Wanted to catch you sneaking home with a nubile patient, so I could report you to the BMA.'

'Hmm.' Will, however, was more interested in the contents of the paper bag than in the British Medical Association. 'What on earth have you got in here?'

'Provisions. I need a free place to kip, so I can save my expenses.'

'Charming.'

'So I've brought sardines, apricots, chocolate and champagne.' Looking up and catching Will's puzzled expression, she added, with a wicked grin and in a voice loud enough for the whole of Cardale to hear, 'They're supposed to be aphrodisiacs!'

'For God's sake, Janey.' Will grabbed her by the elbow and hustled her towards his flat. 'Most of my neighbours are on our register.' Suddenly he was desperate to get Janey indoors – and not just because she was embarrassing him. He had a sneaking feeling he was going to be late for work again the next morning.

In the event, he was early. He was also accompanied by Janey. Although they had found better things to do during the evening than discuss work, he had, teasingly, informed Janey that she was wasting her time if she thought that seducing him was a way to get The Beeches to prescribe her company's new antibiotic. 'It's up to Beth to decide that sort of thing,' he had said. 'She's the senior partner. Maybe you should sleep with *her*.' Janey had responded by hitting him with a pillow – and said that she would come in with him in the morning to talk to Beth.

Kim looked deeply disapproving as Will and Janey walked into reception. Janey, she felt, was moving in on Will rather too quickly: she was what her mother would call a 'fast piece'. There was certainly something about her that Kim didn't like. 'Oh, Kim, could you tell Beth that Miss Cooper's here to see her?'

Kim smiled up at Will. 'Miss Cooper? Straight away, Doctor Preston.'

Will, not sure how to handle the heavy sarcasm of her tone, looked bemused. Behind him, Janey looked pensive. So, she thought, that's the way the land lies. Although Kim was trying her best to be jokey, it was clear – to Janey at least – that she was annoyed.

Beth, when Kim buzzed her on the intercom, was also annoyed – but for professional rather than personal reasons.

'Patients,' she said crisply, as she buzzed back, 'come first. Tell Miss Cooper I'll see her later.'

Embarrassed because Beth's voice had been loud enough for Janey to hear, Kim looked up with an apologetic smile.

'Sorry.'

'Not a problem.' Janey smiled back. She had heard a lot worse from doctors in her time as a drugs rep. 'I'll wait.'

She had to wait more than an hour. Beth, as well as seeing the patients who had appointments, had received a call from Barbara Sykes about her tetanus injection, and had agreed to fit her in. She arrived at ten o'clock, accompanied by a truculent-looking Joanne.

Sitting quietly in reception, Janey found herself next to Joanne while the girl's mother went down the corridor to Beth's room. A strange child, she thought. Joanne was sitting, staring straight ahead with her hands clasped tightly in her lap. For some reason she made Janey feel uneasy.

Five minutes later the unease had given way to outright alarm. Suddenly, and seemingly without provocation, the girl got to her feet and started screaming. Janey, Kim and the other patients looked on in horror as she stamped her feet, waved her arms in the air, and let out piercing, ear-splitting yells. Laura, rushing out of the surgery, was the only one not shocked into immobility by the child's behaviour. Yet there was no way she could calm her, and when Beth and Barbara, closely followed by Will, came rushing into reception, Joanne's screams became even louder and she began to run in a manic circle round the room.

It was Beth who finally stopped her by running forward, catching her and enfolding her in a cross between an embrace and an arm-lock. 'Stop it, Joanne,' she urged. 'Stop it, stop it, stop it.'

Gradually the screams subsided, leaving the child limp and panting in Beth's arms. Concerned, Beth looked at Barbara. 'Has this ever happened before?'

Barbara hesitated before replying. When she did it was with a mixture of guilt and fear. 'Yes.'

'Hmm. Let's go back to my room. Come on, Joanne.'

The threesome departed, leaving an admiring Laura – and an embarrassed silence. It was Janey who broke it.

'Could I interest you,' she asked Will, in a voice loud enough for the others to hear, 'in our new arsenic compound? It's specially suitable for children.'

Will smiled uncertainly. It was neither the right time nor the right place for levity, and Kim's expression revealed that she was thinking along the same lines. Belatedly realizing her mistake, Janey meekly retreated to her seat and opened a magazine.

In Beth's room, Joanne wandered around, irritably picking up papers, pulling the cord of the blinds and opening drawers. Beth, watching her out of the corner of one eye, was trying to hazard a guess as to what had brought on her strange behaviour. 'Has she always been this irritable?' she asked Barbara.

'Well . . . no. A bit. Got worse since her dad left. What kid wouldn't?'

'And she's only got you to take it out on?'

Before Barbara could reply, Joanne went up to the filing cabinet and started to kick the drawers with all the force she could muster. Barbara sprang to her feet. 'Joanne! Behave! Joanne!' Then she looked back at Beth. 'See what I mean? There's no telling her. Joanne!'

Joanne, finally registering her mother's protests, glared at her for a second and then went for her with a violent kick. Barbara dodged out of the way in time and then, just as suddenly as she had erupted, Joanne lapsed into morose inactivity. Yet something about the sheer violence of her actions alerted Beth. 'Did she take it out on you in the supermarket the other day?'

Although clearly reluctant, Barbara nodded her assent. 'With the trolley. I tell her again and again but . . . she just . . .'

'Do you think it'd be any help if I had a chat with her?'

Barbara, immediately on the defensive, glowered at Beth. 'She's not ill.'

'I'm not saying she is. But sometimes . . . somebody neutral. It *can* help, Barbara.'

Still doubtful, Barbara pursed her lips and looked over at her daughter. Joanne was now standing demurely beside the filing cabinet against which she had just been venting her fury. 'Well . . . all right. When?'

'Now?' Beth smiled pleasantly. The last thing she wanted to do was antagonize Barbara, but she was worried about Joanne. Something was going on here and she was determined to get to the bottom of it. And, furthermore, her next appointment was with Janey Cooper. Beth disliked drugs reps at the best of times – and there was something about Janey that she particularly disliked. Janey could wait.

'Well, OK, then. D'you want me to wait outside?'

'Yes. It won't take long.'

Beth watched for Joanne's reaction to her mother leaving the room. There was none. She stood, looking slightly dazed.

'Joanne? Would you like to come and sit down over here?'

The child considered the invitation and, without any change of expression, sat down on the chair beside Beth.

'Now, I want you to cross one leg over the other.'

'Don't want to.'

'It's only to test your reflexes.' Beth reached over for the little hammer on the side of her desk. 'See, I'll give your knee a little tap with this hammer. Like this . . .'

Joanne's leg, now crossed as instructed, suddenly jerked in reaction to the hammer. Intrigued, she smiled for the first time since she had been in the room.

'Good. Now the other one. Good.' Now that she had at least some sort of rapport going with the girl, Beth asked her, in an almost offhand fashion, how she was getting on at school.

'It's boring. They sit me on my own.'

'Oh? Why's that?'

Joanne merely shrugged in reply. Beth made a quick note and, much to Joanne's surprise, sprang to her feet and on to her tiptoes. 'Can you do this, Joanne?'

'Course.'

Beth smiled encouragingly. 'Go on, then.'

'No. It's stupid.'

'So you can't do it?' Still smiling, Beth came down on to her heels.

Joanne, riled by the implied insult and rising to the challenge, immediately got up and on to tiptoe. 'See?'

'Good. Very good.'

But Joanne was suddenly manic again. Still on tiptoe, she started jumping round the room. 'See! See! See!' Getting more frenzied by the second, she raised her voice with each jump until she was shouting almost as loudly as she had in reception.

Beth, deeply troubled, asked her to tiptoe back towards her. 'Your balance is fine,' she said. But Joanne, now teetering out of control, lurched towards the desk and, in one fluid movement, swept all Beth's notes on to the floor.

'Joanne.' Beth was commanding, firm. 'Come over here, please.'

But Joanne was looking for more things to sweep to the floor. Giggling now, she tried to grab the telephone.

'No!' Moving towards her, Beth again had physically to restrain her. She grabbed her by the wrists and, as she did so, saw a flicker of alarm cross Joanne's features. Puzzled, Beth looked down. She had inadvertently pushed up the sleeves of the child's cardigan – revealing a mass of bruises on her forearms and elbows.

'Did you find anything wrong, Doctor?'

'No.' After taking Joanne back to reception, Beth was

164

careful to keep the open and friendly manner she had earlier adopted with Barbara. 'But I was wondering if it'd be all right to visit you,' she added with a smile, 'just to see how Joanne is at home.'

'What for? Why do you want to come if there's nothing wrong with her?'

'It would help,' said Beth with quiet determination, 'if I could see her there – in her own environment.' She fixed Barbara with a look that indicated she would brook no argument.

'Well, if you want to come tomorrow. Before school.' Barbara reached out for her daughter's hand. 'But I don't know what you think you'll find.' Then, unable to disguise her anger, she flounced out of reception with a reluctant Joanne in tow.

Kim, who had witnessed the little scenario, raised her eyebrows at Beth, who sighed.

Then Beth caught Janey Cooper's eye. 'Doctor Glover, if you have a moment . . . I *have* been waiting for . . .'

'Oh, all right, then.' With an uncharacteristic lack of grace, Beth motioned for Janey to follow her down the corridor. Janey wasted no time in getting into her sales pitch. Immediately upon sitting down, she delved into her briefcase and extracted a drug sample with an accompanying leaflet. 'As you can see, it's a broad-spectrum antibiotic. Five-day course, and, as you can tell from this graph, the trials were pretty spectacular.'

'Where were they carried out?'

'University of Oregon.' Janey gave Beth the benefit of her most dazzling smile. 'Here is a reprint from a medical journal in Portland,' she added as she produced more literature, handing it to Beth.

After a perfunctory examination, Beth looked up. 'We've chosen our drugs for next year.' She knew she was being rude. She found that she didn't care.

Janey, undeterred, ploughed on. 'Always room for one

more, surely? Specially as it's ten per cent cheaper than its competitors—'

'The price,' Beth interrupted, 'is the least of our considerations. What matters is whether it's clinically effective.'

'There's absolutely no doubt about its effectiveness. It's an all-purpose, all-American wonder drug.'

'Beats as it sweeps as it cleans?' Beth didn't even attempt to hide her sarcasm.

'No doctor can afford to be without it.' Janey, replying calmly and still smiling, wanted to hit her. Will had said that Beth could be a tough customer, but she had never expected something like this.

Beth picked up the sample again. 'Are any of the local hospitals using it?'

'Not yet. But by the end of the—'

But Beth had had enough. 'Well, why don't you come back when they do? Oregon's six thousand miles away.'

Janey gave up. There was no way she was going to make any headway with this woman and she would be better off – as Beth was so clearly intimating – retreating to Oregon herself.

CH**A**PTER 14

'Kids fall over all the time, Beth. Especially kids like Joanne.' Will flashed Beth what he hoped was a reassuring grin. 'She was practically climbing up the curtains when I saw her yesterday.'

'Mmm.' Beth was unconvinced. She had spent nearly twenty-four hours being unconvinced. Last night her sleep had been disturbed by visions of what might or might not be happening in the Sykes household. Finally, she voiced the fears that had been plaguing her since her examination of Joanne. 'She was showing classic behaviour patterns of an abused child.'

'It could be anything.' Will's tone was surprisingly firm. 'Don't jump to conclusions, Beth. Junk food, not enough exercise . . . anxiety.'

'The fact that her mum and dad have split up?' Too late, Beth recognized the tactlessness of her remark.

'Gee, Beth, thanks for those kind words of reassurance for divorced parents everywhere.'

'I'm sorry.' Then, with a rueful smile, she added, 'And I'm sorry if I've messed up your love life.' That had been another overnight worry – her rudeness to Janey. There were polite ways to give someone the brush-off – and Beth's way hadn't been one of them.

Will, thankfully, was amused. 'Janey? Yes, she told me. Well, at least I'll find out if I'll still see her now that Cardale isn't on her rounds.' With a distracted wave at Beth, he walked down towards his room, leaving her to prepare for her early-morning call to the Sykes house. But as soon as he turned his back on Beth, his smile disappeared. Last night, Janey had sown seeds of doubt in his mind about their relationship. Knowing that she had a busy week on the road, Will had asked her round next week, same place, same time.

Janey had been a touch evasive. 'Can't promise, Will,' she had said. 'Depends on my diary.'

'Depends if you write it in. Thursday night, eight o'clock. Dinner with Will.'

'I'll do my best.'

'Right.' Will had tried to hide his disappointment.

Realizing she had hurt him, Janey tried to make amends. 'You know me, spur of the moment, take life as it comes. I'll just appear on your doorstep.'

The point is, Will had thought, that I don't know you. 'No definite arrangements?' he had asked. 'Just sporadic house calls?'

Janey had smiled up at him and pecked him on the cheek. 'Better to live in suspense than die of boredom.'

Did that mean, thought Will as he closed the door behind him, that he was boring? Her remark had been troubling him all night. He wasn't entirely sure if he had liked it – it reminded him of some of Sarah's more barbed comments. 'Golf and work,' she had said on umpteen occasions. 'It's all you're interested in.' Still, their marriage had lasted for fourteen years. He hadn't even known Janey for fourteen days. Surely she couldn't walk out on him already?

Beth didn't notice the police car until she drew up behind it. Even then, she didn't pay it much attention: it was only when she noticed a uniformed policeman standing at Barbara Sykes's front door that she began to get alarmed. Jumping out of her car, she ran up the garden path and addressed the impassive officer. 'What's wrong? Has something happened?'

'And who might you be, love?'

'I'm Mrs Sykes's doctor – and Joanne's.'

The policeman gave her an odd look. 'Oh, well, you'd best go in, then. Joanne's done a runner.'

Oh, God, that's all we need, thought Beth as she rushed into the hall and through the open door of the sitting room. A red-eyed Barbara was sitting on the sofa, wringing her hands in her lap and staring vacantly at the wall.

'Oh, Barbara . . .' Beth ran up to her, sat beside her and clasped her hands. 'When?'

'About six o'clock.' Although she was still staring straight ahead, Barbara appeared to welcome Beth's comforting presence. 'I heard the front door slam, but I didn't think . . . I never thought she'd do anything like this.'

'Did she take anything with her?'

'Not as far as I can tell.' At last she looked at Beth. More tears were brimming as she added, 'We'd had one of our spats, you know. I said some terrible things. Joanne isn't a bad kid but she just – she just—'

Beth patted Barbara's hand. 'I'm sure it'll be all right. The police will find her. If you like,' she added after a moment, 'I could prescribe you something, to help you stay calm.'

Barbara smiled for a second and then dissolved into tears. 'No. No. I don't need anything. I just . . .' she sniffed into her handkerchief '. . . I just want Joanne back.'

'Wouldn't you like a cup of tea?' said a voice that startled both of them. Beth and Barbara looked up. Another policeman was standing above them, proffering a cup and saucer. Barbara automatically reached for it and then, holding it on her lap, subsided into a pensive silence. The policeman then turned to Beth. 'WPC Benson is upstairs,' he said. 'Maybe you'd like a word with her?'

Beth smiled in acknowledgement and got up. Police officers, in her experience, were prone to jumping to swift conclusions. She would be interested to know what WPC Benson was doing upstairs.

She was rummaging around in Joanne's bedroom. It was difficult to tell if she had found anything that may have interested her because the room, as Beth discovered to her horror, looked as if it had been vandalized. Dolls and teddy bears – some of them mutilated – were lying around on the floor; one curtain was hanging off the rail; a broken lamp was leaning drunkenly over the bedside table and the walls, floor and bedspread were splattered with paint. Beth, open-mouthed in surprise, must have said something without being aware of it, for a policewoman, half hidden in the wardrobe, turned round. 'Ah, Doctor Glover? Joanne's mum said you were coming.'

'Yes. I'd arranged to call.' Beth, still shocked by the state of the room, fell silent.

WPC Benson, taking in the room with a sweep of her hand, smiled grimly at Beth. 'Was Joanne ill?'

'She had some behavioural problems. I wanted to see how she was at home.' Again she looked at the mess. 'Clearly not a great deal better.'

'Awful, isn't it? We've been called out by the neighbours because of the noise three times in the last fortnight.'

'The noise?' Alarm bells started clanging in Beth's head.

'Yes. Stand-up rows. Screaming and shouting in the middle of the night.' Then the policewoman fixed Beth with a piercing gaze. 'Do you . . . er, have any reason to suppose that Joanne Sykes was being physically abused?'

Even though Beth had anticipated the question, she didn't want to answer. The truth would only serve to confirm the policewoman's suspicions. 'There was some bruising,' she said, 'on her arms, but that's hardly conclusive.'

But it was enough for WPC Benson. 'I'd better give the social services a call, then.'

'No!' The vehemence of Beth's response surprised even

herself. 'If we call them in now,' she added in a more moderate tone, 'it'll be taken out of Barbara's hands. I really don't think we should escalate this until we're sure we know what we're dealing with.'

'An eight-year-old child is missing. Don't you think it's already escalated?'

But Beth held her ground. 'We're all assuming Barbara's involved. Say you bring social services in and you're wrong. What effect will that have on Joanne's future?'

WPC Benson looked distinctly piqued. Not used to having her decisions countermanded by a civilian, she gave Beth a rather lofty, supercilious look. 'I'll have to talk to my superiors about this. I'll make sure your reservations are reported.' I'm sure you will, thought Beth.

'And then,' continued the policewoman, 'it'll be out of my hands.'

Beth nodded, bowing to the inevitable. If the social services were alerted then the situation would be out of her hands as well, and the dreaded words 'child abuse' would gather their own momentum. Unless Joanne turned up of her own volition, Beth doubted that she would ever be reunited with her mother. Suspected child abusers, in her experience, were always treated contrary to the law of the land: they were presumed guilty – and nobody wanted to find them innocent.

'Any news on Joanne Sykes yet?'

Beth looked up from the cup of coffee she was making after surgery that afternoon. 'No, Will. Not a word.' At lunchtime she had confided her fears to Will. Now, with no report on Joanne's whereabouts, her fears had increased. 'Do you think I should have agreed to let the police call social services in?'

It was most unlike Beth, thought Will, to ask him for advice. She must be really worried. 'I think,' he said, 'that you're an experienced doctor and that you should trust your own judgement.'

Beth smiled at him in gratitude. He couldn't have made a more apt – or flattering – remark. She couldn't help wondering what Jack would have said. It was funny, she mused as she watched Will make himself some coffee, being just the two of them again: it was actually rather nice. Jack's arrival in Cardale had ruffled feathers far and wide and had changed the complexion of the practice – and of Beth's life – for good. It was most disconcerting to find that she wasn't missing him as much as she thought she would. Sure, she had felt sorry for herself when he had decided to go to Africa on his self-styled sabbatical, but that had been due to the reasons for his departure, not the departure itself.

'Penny for them?' Will jolted her out of her pondering.

'Oh . . . I was just thinking. Actually, I was just thinking what Jack would have said about the social services.' Beth hadn't meant to articulate her thoughts: was she sounding disloyal?

'D'you mean, would he have rushed in and called them before establishing the truth of the situation?'

'Yes, I suppose I do.'

'Beth, your husband may behave like a bull in a china shop sometimes, but his heart is in the right place.'

'Yes. Africa.'

So, she *is* missing him more than she's letting on. 'Er . . . how's he getting on?'

Beth looked him straight in the eye. 'I don't know, Will. He's – he's only called once.'

'There aren't many telephones in the bush.' Will hoped he didn't sound too flippant.

'Well,' replied Beth as she stood up, 'we wouldn't know, would we? Neither of us has been to Jack's spiritual home.' With that, she gave a tight little smile and walked out of the room. Damn, she thought, it's no use pretending: I really am missing him. And I really *am* annoyed that he went.

Feeling rather foolish, she walked out to the car park to fetch the files she had left in her car that morning. With no more patients that day, she was planning to spend the rest of the afternoon catching up with her paperwork. Her plans, however, were thwarted. Crouching by the passenger door of her car, looking half frightened and half pleased, was Joanne Sykes.

Beth, more than a little startled, caught her breath. Then she bent down to the child and held out her arms. 'Joanne?'

The little girl made no move to approach her. 'Joanne. I'm glad you've come here. You've done the right thing – and I think you're very brave. Would you like to come in and have a chat?'

Still without speaking, the child nodded and followed Beth into The Beeches. As they walked past a stunned Kim, Beth hesitated and looked round. 'Kim? Could you ring Joanne's mum and the police and tell them she's here and she's safe – and that I'll drop her off at home?' As she said the last words, she looked at Joanne out of the corner of her eye, and was glad to see she looked relieved.

With a gentle hand on Joanne's shoulder, she steered her into her room.

'Now. Where've you been all day?' Joanne bowed her head but didn't reply. 'You know that your mum's very worried about you?' Still no response. 'Why did you run away?' persisted Beth. 'Did you and your mum have an argument?'

'Yes,' answered Joanne in a small, scared voice. 'She shouts at me.'

'When you've done something wrong?'

'Yes. And I can't go to sleep.'

'Why don't you like to go to sleep?'

'I can't.'

'Don't you ever get tired?'

'Yes. Mummy gives me some pills.'

Beth did her best to disguise her horror. 'Your mum gives you pills to help you sleep?'

'Yes.'

'And do they help?'

'No. They used to, but not now.'

A glimmer of comprehension dawned at the back of Beth's mind. 'Would you like,' she asked, 'to go home now?'

For the first time, Joanne smiled. 'Yes. I'd like that.'

During the journey, Joanne opened up to Beth. A clearer picture began to appear in Beth's mind about what was happening at Barbara's. Visions of social workers began to fade and, when they arrived at their destination, Barbara herself, after a tearful reunion with her daughter, confirmed Beth's suspicions. 'I bought them at the chemists,' she said as, at Beth's request, she showed her the tablets she had been giving Joanne. 'Over the counter, like. Thought they couldn't be too strong.'

Beth, frowning, read the label. 'Antihistamine.'

Embarrassed and mindful of WPC Benson's presence, Barabara tried to explain her actions. 'I got them for my sinuses. They made me drowsy so I thought they might help Joanne to sleep.' She looked to Beth for approval. 'They worked at first.'

But Beth wasn't going to condone such irresponsible behaviour. 'Some antihistamine tablets,' she said crossly, 'contain a chemical that certain children react badly to.'

Barbara looked completely astonished. 'You mean the *tablets* were causing her behaviour?'

'Yes. Obviously Joanne was reacting badly to her dad going in the first place, but I think the tablets explain why it is so extreme. They kept her awake, made her clumsy, running around knocking into things, falling over. They made her,' she finished with a sympathetic smile at Joanne, 'permanently hyperactive.'

In a mixture of relief, confusion and guilt, Barbara reached out and hugged her daughter. 'Oh, Joanne, I'm so sorry. I didn't think . . . I didn't know . . .'

'I think,' interrupted Beth, 'if you stop giving her these she should be a lot calmer.'

Barbara looked up in gratitude. She tried to thank Beth, but the tears streaming down her face and the lump in her throat precluded anything more than a smile.

'Social services,' said WPC Benson as she and Beth walked to their respective cars, 'will want to interview her as a formality. Nothing too heavy.'

'Good. They don't need it.'

'The mess in her room, the bruising – she did all that herself?'

'Yes. Poor child. Hurling herself against things, hitting any object in sight.' Beth sighed. 'And, anyway, the poor kid has a lot of genuine grief and anger against her father. Those wretched pills just compounded the whole issue.'

The policewoman, rather to Beth's surprise, smiled broadly. 'You know, I really am glad that you were right. I just hate having to involve the social services, but,' she gestured apologetically, 'it's my job.'

'I know. Tell me about it. My job's not exactly a bed of roses either.' Feeling pleased with herself, Beth gave WPC Benson a cheerful wave and walked off to her own car.

CH**A**PTER 15

Over the next weeks, Beth continued to miss Jack, yet she began to feel much more sanguine about the situation: he was doing his thing; she was doing hers and it was, she realized, A Good Thing. When they had married, both had been insistent that they would not relinquish their respective independence, that they would not live in each other's pockets. Yet in the first year of their marriage, they had rarely spent more than a night apart. This, the first real separation, was bound to be difficult.

As she got more used to being without him, Beth went out with friends that she and Jack had not seen for ages: she spent several evenings with Annie and Dominic Kent, old friends of hers whom Jack, rather inconveniently, didn't like, and she also spent time on her own, not feeling sorry for herself. Yet on her evenings alone she found her thoughts straying to Isabel. Now that the agony, the anger and the grief of Isabel's death had diminished, Beth found that she could think of her, always with sadness, but now with affection and gratitude. She also found herself reading Isabel's last letter over and over again and recognising just how well Isabel had known her: Beth's longing for a child, now that Isabel had forced her to acknowledge it, was becoming ever greater, ever stronger. It was, however, a yearning that she kept quiet about. It was hardly the sort of thing she could mention to Kim, Laura or Trevor, and as for Will . . . well, he already had two children, a soon-to-be-ex-wife and a steady girlfriend. Janey. Rather to Beth's surprise – and much to Will's delight – Janey hadn't done a disappearing act after Beth had refused to become a client of Amachem. It seemed, if anything, to be the reverse: Will was forever appearing late for work looking happy and exhausted – and the rest of The Beeches staff knew that he hadn't taken up early-morning jogging. Although she still had reservations about Janey, Beth was pleased for Will. With her happy-go-lucky attitude to life, Janey seemed to be doing him a great deal of good. Beth wondered what Sarah would think of that. Knowing Sarah, she would be eaten up with jealousy.

On the Saturday before Jack was due back from Africa, Will also found himself wondering what Sarah would make of Janey and, more to the point, what his sons would think of her. Today he was going to introduce her to them. Nudging the bedroom door with his foot, he grinned as he looked at Janey, dead to the world under the duvet. Kicking the door shut, he approached the bed, concentrating hard on not spilling the contents of the tray he was holding. 'Wakey, wakey! Time to get up.'

Janey's mumbled response was short and to the point. 'Piss off!'

'Freshly squeezed orange juice, coffee, toast, honey, peaches . . .' Will stopped, hoping to elicit an enthusiastic response. None was forthcoming. 'Come on,' he continued, 'you know how long it takes you to get dressed.'

At last, Janey raised her head. 'Do we have to go?'

This wasn't quite the response Will had been hoping for. He deposited the laden tray on the bedside table and sat down beside Janey. ''Fraid so. It's the school's two thousandth anniversary or something. I'm a family man, Janey, at least at weekends.'

Janey rubbed her eyes and reached over for a peach. She looked, he thought, slightly apprehensive. 'Won't your sons feel uncomfortable being introduced to their father's lover?'

'No, of course not. Anyway,' Will ruffled her hair, 'I need you to be there.'

'Why?'

'To wake me up when I nod off during prize-giving.'

'Beast.' Janey threw the peach at him.

Royston School was in a picturesque part of Derbyshire and, as Will and Sarah had agreed when they had sent Tony and Julian there, the perfect environment for the boys to board on a weekly basis. The school had a good academic record and also laid great emphasis on sport; as Tony showed promise as a rugby player while Julian was more scholarly, this seemed the perfect combination. Will had been to public school and could conceive of no other way to educate his own children. Sarah, initially reluctant to part with them during the week, had eventually let snobbery win her over: she was only too aware that she was not of the same social class as her husband, and had felt that her objections to boarding-school would only show her up further. She had, anyway, been keen to join the county set – and that clique all sent their sons to Royston.

Since their separation, Will and Sarah had taken pains to show a united front at any of the school's open or sports days. Today, however, Sarah had been compromised by a long-standing arrangement with her mother and was unable to attend. Hence Janey. Will, warmly wrapped in Barbour and scarf, looked at her as she stood beside him on the touch-line. They had, as he had predicted, arrived late and – despite travelling in Janey's sports car – only just in time for the start of Tony's rugby match. As soon as she had stepped out of the car in front of the imposing Georgian mansion that was Royston House, Janey immediately seemed at home. Dressed in chic tweeds and a stylish coat, she could easily have been one of the boys' mothers. She looked, thought Will, much more at ease than Sarah had ever managed to appear.

But Janey, watching the play with an interested if slightly baffled expression, was feeling anything but comfortable. She had, she knew, dressed the part – and, anyway, it wasn't the adults who worried her. It was Tony and Julian. How would they react to her, their father's girlfriend? Thus far, she had escaped their attention. Julian hadn't yet appeared and Tony was too busy playing rugby even to glance at the spectators.

Janey scanned the pitch, looking for a small boy bearing a resemblance to Will, but they all looked the same. She asked, 'Which one's Tony?' Will, transfixed by the game, pointed excitedly towards the scrum. 'There! In the blue shirt.'

Janey laughed. 'Very helpful.' Fifteen of the boys were wearing identical blue shirts – and none looked like Will. It was only when the ball was won by the boys in blue and swiftly passed out to the backs that she could identify Tony. 'There! That's him!' Will nudged her as the boy at the end of the line caught the ball and flew off down the pitch. Janey, who understood only the rudiments of rugby, realized that he stood a chance of scoring a try. Sure enough, after ducking and weaving past potential tacklers, Tony flung himself over the try-line and, with a triumphant roar, brought the ball to the ground. Will, cheering like mad, was beside himself with pride. Only when the applause had died down did he hear the shrill voice behind him. 'Dad! Dad!'

Janey, like Will, turned round. So this, she realized, is Julian. Delighted to see his father, he flung himself into his arms. Will, equally ecstatic, hugged him, and then said, in a slightly stilted manner, 'This is Janey.'

'Hello.' Julian, curious but a little wary, held out his hand.

Janey, feeling horribly self-conscious, managed a smile. Visions of wicked stepmothers swam before her eyes as she shook Julian's hand. 'Hello.' Then she nodded in the direction of the playing-field. 'That's some brother you've got. I'm impressed.' Evidently she had said the right thing. Julian, who hero-worshipped Tony, looked at her in appreciation.

As play resumed after a failed conversion from one of Tony's team-mates, the little group on the touch-line turned to follow Tony's progress. Five minutes into play, the game deteriorated into a untidy ruck over the ball and the referee, running round the bunched-up players, blew his whistle to call a scrum. Gradually, the players unpeeled themselves from the mass of bodies and moved away. One player, however, remained where he was, prone on the ground. Janey, worried, said to Will, 'What's happened?'

'Looks like someone's taken a knock. It's all right . . .' But, as he said the words, he knew it wasn't. The ref, kneeling down beside the boy, took one look and shouted for a doctor. Will didn't hesitate for a second: he ran on to the pitch as if his life depended on it. As he sprinted towards the boy, his worst fears were confirmed. At that moment he didn't care a damn about his own life – only for that of the boy: his son.

Fighting back panic, he pushed through the huddle and knelt beside the ref. Tony was unconscious; lying perfectly still with his head at an odd angle. Will, shocked into inaction, stared down at him. Then, willing himself to behave normally, he opened Tony's mouth to check his air passage. Although the boy was breathing, there was no movement, no response. Janey, who had followed him on to the pitch, stood behind him with her hand over her mouth. 'What is it?'

'His neck.' Will heard his own voice: it seemed to come from a distance, from someone else. He reached into his pocket and pulled out his phone. As the ref ushered the boys off the pitch, he dialled the emergency services. Janey, choking back tears, saw that his hands were shaking so badly he nearly dropped the phone.

It was answered within seconds. 'I have a severe injury at Royston School, Tipton,' Will barked. 'He requires immediate evacuation.' Then, distraught, close to tears, and irritated by the voice at the other end, he lost his temper. 'Just get something, will you! We need a helicopter here! Now. *Now!*'

The helicopter didn't come 'now', but even Will was impressed by the speed of its arrival: Tony was in hospital within the hour. Will, who, to his distress, hadn't been allowed into the helicopter with him, made the journey by car. For the second time that day, Janey's sports car flew across the Derbyshire Dales. She insisted on driving: Will, she said, was in no condition to take the wheel. Julian, gaunt and pale, sat in the back.

Will spent much of the journey trying to contact Sarah on his mobile. Eventually, he succeeded. Sarah, as he had expected, took the news badly. Loath to give her too many details or to confide his worst fears over the phone, he arranged to meet her at the hospital as soon as possible.

When they arrived, Janey tried to keep out of the way. At Will's suggestion, she took a subdued Julian off to the hospital cafeteria while Will rushed to Tony in intensive care.

It was there that Sarah found him. Haring down the corridor, hair flying and with a haunted, desperate expression, she burst into the room and stopped dead. Will was bent over Tony, holding his hand and staring intently at him, as if willing him back into consciousness. But Tony just lay there, eyes closed, breathing gently but as pale as death.

'Oh, Tony . . .' Sarah's voice cracked as she approached her son's side. She stood, immobile, her hand over her mouth, gazing in mute horror at her son.

At the sound of her voice, Tony's eyes flickered open. They were, Will noted, unfocused: he looked disorientated and was evidently in some pain. 'Mum . . .' But he could summon no more words: with a small sigh, he lapsed back into unconsciousness.

Will walked over to his estranged wife and hugged her. For a moment she stood rigid in his arms. Then she laid her head on his shoulder and burst into tears. Will, also crying, held her even more tightly.

'I should have been there,' she sobbed, 'at the match. I should . . .'

Will put a tender finger to her mouth. 'It wouldn't have made any difference, Sarah.'

Sarah withdrew from his embrace and wiped her eyes. 'I saw the doctor outside. He said, he said—'

'I know. His neck.'

Sarah looked Will in the eye. 'What if . . . what if he can't walk again, Will?'

But Will chose not to answer. Taking Sarah by the arm, he ushered her out into the corridor. 'Calm down, please, Sarah. You mustn't let Tony know you're frightened.'

Meekly subsiding into silence, Sarah let Will lead her down the corridor – and straight into Janey and Julian. For a moment there was a stunned silence as Sarah registered this stranger holding her other son's hand. On seeing his mother, Julian ran straight into her arms. Distracted and confused, Sarah hugged him, at the same time throwing Will a 'who's she?' look.

Will, embarrassed and awkward, introduced the two women. 'Er . . . Sarah, this is Janey. She was at the match. She's been looking after Julian.'

Sarah twigged immediately. The body language, the stilted introduction, and that Janey had been with Will at the match all suggested 'girlfriend'. It hadn't occurred to Sarah that Will might be dating someone. Then she realized she was looking suspiciously at Janey, sizing her up and eyeing her as a rival. She forced a smile. 'Thanks.'

Janey, feeling ill at ease, smiled in response. I shouldn't be here, she thought. This is the place for parents: I'm invading their space.

'Mum?' Julian tugged Sarah's coat. 'Where's Tony?'

Sarah sniffed, and smiled down at her son. 'I'll take you to see him, darling, but you must promise to be quiet.' Reaching for his hand, she smiled briefly at Will and Janey and then walked back into intensive care.

'How is he?' asked Janey.

Will shrugged. 'There's no change. It's going to be a long day – and night.'

Before Janey could respond, they were interrupted by a discreet cough from behind. The consultant had arrived. 'We're ready to X-ray your son now, Doctor Preston.'

'Right.'

Janey, desperate to be useful but equally anxious not to intrude, stopped him in his tracks as he prepared to follow the doctor. 'Will, would you like me to take Julian home? I can stay the night with him, if you like – you and Sarah will both want to stay here, won't you?'

'Would you, Janey?' Will beamed at her. 'That would be brilliant. Thanks.'

Several hours later, when Tony began to stir, both his parents were sitting by his bedside. He noticed Sarah first. 'Mum . . . Mum . . .'

'Yes?' Sarah leaned close and stroked his forehead.

'When can I get up?'

Sarah looked over to Will. He clenched his fists then forced a smile. 'You'll have to stay put for the time being, Tony. You hurt your neck in the match.'

Tony, digesting that information, stirred in tbe bed. After a moment he turned, puzzled, to his father. 'Dad, why can't I feel my legs?'

Will felt like crying. Instead, squirming and trying

desperately to think of a fitting response, he evaded the issue. 'You'll just have to be a bit patient . . . get lots of rest.' Then he smiled proudly. 'That was a terrific try you scored.'

Tony momentarily forgot his legs. 'D'you think they'll make me captain?'

'Well, if I had any say in the matter, I most certainly would.'

'But how long will it be before I can play rugby again?'

Neither Will nor Sarah could muster a reply. Over the supine body of their son, they exchanged a silent, yet eloquent glance.

It was Sarah who eventually replied. 'We don't know yet, darling. They'll have to do more tests before we know for sure.' Before we know for sure, she thought bitterly, that you'll be in a wheelchair for the rest of your life.

CH**A**PTER 16

Jack came back two days later. He was desperately excited about seeing Beth again: he was also glad to be returning to Cardale. The wanderlust that had sent him back to the southern hemisphere had evaporated. While Africa had been challenging and rewarding, it had also been – although he would never admit it – less satisfactory than his previous spell there. Something within him had changed since he had first arrived in Cardale and now he knew what it was: he had grown up, found the place he now considered home, and found the person with whom he wanted to spend the rest of his life. Ironically, it had been the separation from both Cardale and Beth that had brought him to that realization. Now he was back. For good.

At least, that's what he thought until he rang the doorbell of his marital home. He had expected a delighted Beth to come rushing into his arms: indeed, a delighted Beth had promised on the phone that she *would* come rushing out to greet him. Puzzled, he looked at his watch. It was eight in the morning: she must have overslept. Miffed that Beth could sleep through his return of the conquering hero, he sighed and fished for his keys. In the process, he dropped the African mask and the bongo drums he had brought back. Somehow they looked even more ridiculous now than when he had got them off the plane at Heathrow. Then he grinned. He would put on the mask and beat the drums as he charged into the bedroom. That would shock Beth into consciousness.

A minute later he realized he wasn't going to be charging anywhere: his keys wouldn't open the door. Increasingly irritated, he went round to the back and tried the kitchen door. But that key, too, didn't seem to fit any more. The only reason for that, he concluded with mounting unease, was that Beth had changed the locks. Suddenly the warm welcome home he had envisaged was turning into a frosty 'keep out'. Eventually, he got in through the small window of the utility room which had been left slightly ajar. That served only to increase his foreboding: most people changed their locks because they had been burgled. Beth, evidently, was still worryingly casual in her attitude to security.

The minute he entered the house he knew it was empty: his cursory glance into the bedroom confirmed Beth's absence. With a weary sigh, he deposited his belongings, found his car keys – at least she hadn't changed *that* lock – and drove to The Beeches.

Kim was on the phone when he waltzed into reception with a broad 'look at me' smirk on his face. She smiled briefly at him, interrupted her conversation long enough to shout, 'Hi there!' and to raise her eyebrows at the African mask. Then, frowning, she resumed what was apparently an argument with a difficult patient.

Jack shrugged and poked his head round the door of the waiting room. There were only two patients, neither of whom he knew. They both looked up and smiled politely at this tanned stranger. Feeling increasingly like a spare part, Jack wandered down the corridor to his room. The door of Will's room, he noticed with interest as he passed, was open and the room itself was empty. Trevor, he knew, was away on a conference. Beth, judging by her closed door, was seeing a patient. Some welcoming committee. He went into his own room, dumped the mask on the floor and shuddered at the mass of paperwork on his desk. Then he resumed his search for company, for someone who would, at the very least, acknowledge his presence.

He found it in Laura. 'Jack! Welcome home!' She

bounded up to him and pecked him on the cheek. 'What's it feel like to be back?'

'Odd.' Suddenly Jack didn't know what to say.

'What was Africa like?'

'Brilliant.'

'Good.' Evidently feeling that they had 'done' Africa, Laura addressed herself to the stack of syringes and kidney-bowls in front of her. Realizing from Jack's silence that she was being rude, she looked up in apology. 'Sorry. Got to get on – busy day and with Will not here—'

'Not here?'

'No. Oh, God, of course, you don't know. Tony's had an accident. He's broken his neck playing rugby.'

'Oh, my God. Bad?'

'Paralysed, they think. From the waist.'

'Jesus.' Again Jack couldn't think of anything to say. Africa, suddenly, seemed trivial. 'So he's in hospital, then?'

'Yes. Nottingham General. Beth's manning the fort.'

'Oh. Well, at least she's still working here.'

'What on earth do you mean?' Laura, astonished both by the words and by Jack's bitter tone, looked up at him.

'Well, I thought she might have done a runner, sold the house. I couldn't get in. She's changed the locks.'

Laura laughed at his forlorn expression. 'Oh, you poor thing – didn't she tell you? She lost her keys last week. Frightful fuss.' She wrinkled her nose in disapproval. 'Had the whole wretched building turned upside down. Had to change the locks in the end.'

Jack laughed in relief. 'Well, thank God for that. I thought she didn't want me back.'

'Oh she does, Jack, she does.'

But Beth, when she emerged from her room half an hour later, found herself curiously unable to welcome Jack with

189

the open arms he – and she – had anticipated. It felt, when she walked to reception and bumped into her husband, as if they were strangers again. They hugged then drew apart, looking at each other, sizing each other up. A stilted 'how are you?' from Jack elicited 'Fine' from Beth. Like-wise, her enquiry about Africa was greeted with a mono-syllabic response. Both felt strained, shy and not sure how to react. Finally, Beth asked him if he was tired. Jack replied that yes, he was, and that the best thing to do would be to go home and sleep off his jet-lag. The only laughter that passed between them was when he men-tioned the change of locks. 'No,' replied Beth, 'I wasn't planning to keep you out. Quite the opposite.'

Yet it was only over dinner that the atmosphere between them began to thaw. A delicious meal and a bottle of good wine followed by brandy melted the ice. Late in the evening, they sat together on the sofa and exchanged stories about the different, separate lives they had been leading. Even then, Beth felt conscious that her conver-sation about Cardale was small-town gossip; that her interests were parochial and her outlook narrow. Jack, in turn, felt that his tales of Africa were irrelevant, meaning-less snippets of information about far-flung places and faraway people. Only when he started regaling Beth with anecdotes did they recapture a sense of real camaraderie. As Beth laughed at his story about a kleptomaniac ele-phant, Jack suddenly sprang up from the sofa and went over to a bag in the corner of the room.

'I've brought us,' he said as he rummaged in the bag, 'a little present each.'

'More bongo drums?'

'No.' Finding what he was looking for, he turned and beamed at Beth. 'Look. Paw-paw fruit.'

Beth looked. Dubiously.

'You can eat them,' Jack said, as he came back to the sofa, 'seeds and all! They're meant to encourage fertility!'

Beth wished he hadn't said that – or, at least, that he hadn't treated such a serious subject so flippantly. But Jack, unaware of her mood change, carried blithely on. 'I visited a witch doctor out there. Traditional healers they call them now. I fixed his hernia, he gave me a piece of wisdom in return.'

'Which was?'

Jack grinned. 'Very roughly translated – "If you're thinking of having kids at your age, my boy, you should stop messing around and just get on with it"!'

Beth wasn't amused. 'Having children isn't something you just get on with, Jack.'

Jack could have kicked himself. Things had been going so well. Now he appeared to have ruined the atmosphere. 'I know, I know.' Sighing, he sat down again and looked Beth straight in the eye. 'Look, I really did miss you and I know I shouldn't have just cleared off like that—'

'Let's not go into all that now.'

But Jack was already into it. 'Beth, I want to stay put, here with you, for the rest of my life—'

'Well, forgive me for not leaping up and down with joy, but I thought all that had been decided when you married me.' Thoroughly irritated, Beth sprang to her feet and ran towards the door. Before she reached it, she turned on him once again: her eyes blazed, her words stung. 'Do you have to take a safari every year to remind yourself?'

The consultant looked at Will. There was no point in trying to pull the wool over his eyes. 'He's still in spinal shock, Doctor Preston. The latest X-rays show we aren't getting a correct realignment of the vertebrae. It, er . . . may be necessary to operate and do a surgical reduction.'

Will, eyes bleary with lack of sleep, ran a hand through his hair and felt defeated. 'So, the outlook's pretty bleak, isn't it?'

The consultant didn't have to say yes. His expression said it all. Skirting the issue, he added, 'We can't yet say how much function he'll recover.'

Will didn't reply. There was nothing to say: the news was exactly as he had anticiapted.

The consultant looked at his watch. 'Now, if you'll excuse me, I have to get on.' With a brief smile, he strode off down the corridor. Will, dejected and exhausted, fished in his pocket for some change and walked over to the coffee machine. He didn't notice Janey sweeping down the corridor behind him. Only when she kissed the back of his neck, startling him and making him spill some coffee, did he turn. 'Janey!'

She held up a huge fluffy bear. 'Something for Tony.'

'Oh.' Will looked doubtfully at the animal. How old did she think Tony was? 'It's rather splendid,' he said flatly.

'How is he?'

'Not brilliant, I'm afraid.'

Janey put a hand to his cheek. 'And how are you?'

'Bearing up, I suppose. Just about.'

'Can I see him?'

Will coughed apologetically. 'Er . . . Sarah's with him at the moment.'

'Ah.' Janey pushed the bear into Will's arms. 'Well, I'd better run along then, hadn't I?' Then she pecked him on the cheek and went back the way she had come. She knew the tone of her last remark had been unpleasant – and unfair to Will. He had quite enough to worry about without Janey implying that she was feeling neglected. And it was, she supposed, only natural that Will and Sarah should be drawn together in their time of crisis. Nevertheless, she was irritated by Sarah's attitude to her. When Will and Sarah had returned from the hospital on Sunday morning, it had been to find Janey asleep on the sofa. True to her word, she had spent the night at Will's with Julian. And – tactfully, she thought – she had refrained from sleeping in

Will's bed. Will had been greatly appreciative of her efforts. Sarah had been brusque.

'Thanks,' she had said. 'I'll take over now.' Janey had felt – and still did – like the newly dismissed hired help.

Will watched her walk down the corridor, and set off back in the direction of the intensive care unit. He felt for Janey: it must be difficult for her, trying to be supportive yet mindful of whose territory she was on. Wearily, he trudged on down the corridor.

Sarah was just emerging from Tony's room as he entered. She looked askance at the toy he was carrying. 'Who's that from?'

'Janey.'

'Good God. How old does she think Tony is?'

Will didn't reply. Then he put the bear on the chair beside them and looked at his wife. 'Mr Rhodes says they might need to operate.'

'But he said that traction would fix it!'

'I know, I know, but Tony's neck still isn't in a good position.'

Sarah, with a strength and an urgency that surprised him, grabbed the lapels of his jacket. 'Tell me – honestly – do you think he'll be able to walk again?'

Will was unable to meet her eyes. 'We'll have to be prepared,' he mumbled, 'for the worst.'

Sarah started to cry. The fact that she cried silently made her distress seem more acute to Will, more touching. He reached out for her and enveloped her in a protective hug.

'Will,' she said at last, 'what are we going to do?'

'We'll work something out.'

'But what sort of a life is he going to have, stuck in a wheelchair?'

Will straightened up and tried to sound positive. 'We'll just have to make sure it's a happy one.'

Sarah mulled over that one. 'He's going to take a lot of looking after.'

'Let's not worry about that now. There's a good chance—'

'But if the worst comes to the worst, do you think we should move back together? It would make sense, wouldn't it?'

Will hadn't been expecting that. He hoped Sarah didn't notice the sudden tension in his body. Unsure of what to say, anxious not to hurt her further, he suggested they talk about it later.

But Sarah was keen to talk about it now. 'I know we've been through some horrible times in the last couple of years.'

'So have the boys.' Visions of the raging arguments of the past came back to him. He did not want any action replays. 'Look, Sarah, you left me. You took the boys with you.'

Sarah, looking and sounding helpless, wrung her hands in misery. 'I know . . . it just . . . it just seemed the right thing at the time.'

Will just looked at her. 'We've started divorce proceedings, for God's sake!'

'I know.' Sarah's voice changed again. This time her tone was pleading. 'But we could try and make it work for them, couldn't we?'

It had been a long time since Will had been under Sarah's spell. Suddenly he remembered how entrancing it was: memories of their good times together came flooding back to him. Yet a voice in his head urged him to recall the bad times. Torn, confused and exhausted, he squeezed Sarah's hands. 'We'll see,' he said. 'We'll see . . .'

Jack and Beth came to the hospital that evening. Their argument of the previous day had been if not forgotten at least forgiven. Beth, on going upstairs to bed, had decided that she had overreacted due to a combination of tiredness and too much alcohol. Jack, for his part, had acknowledged that he had been too flippant. As a doctor, he should have taken on board that Beth – his own wife – was worried about his commitment to having children, about her ability to conceive – and about her age. Thirty-eight wasn't exactly geriatric but Jack conceded that the ticking of the biological clock was a subject that only a woman could fully understand. Feeling chastened, he had followed Beth upstairs and had apologised profusely. She, in turn, had said she was sorry for getting so riled. Then, in bed, Jack had practised his seduction techniques, or rather, he had informed Beth that it was so much nicer sharing a bed with her than with a family of cockroaches. Beth, naturally, had been ecstatic about that. Then Jack had fallen asleep.

In the morning they had laughed about it – and made up for it. Now, after Jack's first day back at The Beeches, he was desperate to see Will. Beth, who had only seen him once since Tony's accident, was also keen to come and offer whatever help she could.

Neither, somehow, had expected to see Sarah. 'Silly of me,' said Beth later, 'but I suppose I'd rather forgotten about her.' But if Sarah's presence came as a surprise, Will's news was a shock.

'Sarah seems to be getting some comfort from the thought of us being together again,' he said to Jack after they had been to see Tony, 'I don't want to take that away from her.'

Jack, who couldn't seriously believe that Will and Sarah being together again could possibly be of any comfort to anyone, nodded. 'Well, Tony's only been here since Saturday. Give it a few more days, Will. He could well pick up.' Then, taking in Will's exhaustion and confusion, he added, 'If there's anything you'd like me to do . . .'

Will offered him a tired smile. 'Thanks. I'm sorry – I haven't even asked you about Africa yet. How did it go?' Jack knew that the last thing Will needed – or wanted –

was a blow-by-blow account of his travels. Still, it was decent of him to ask. He clapped him on the back and steered him down the corridor towards Beth and Sarah. 'I'll tell you about it over a pint sometime.'

Beth was finding it difficult to hide her disapproval of Sarah's desire to return to Will. Sarah, aware of Beth's reaction, was becoming defensive and bolshie. 'We've made up our minds,' she said firmly. 'It's what's best for Tony.'

'Well, obviously it'll be great to have you back here again.' As soon as she had uttered the words, Beth regretted them. She'd always been hopeless at lying.

Clearly, she hadn't improved: Sarah was staring suspiciously at her. 'You think so?'

Beth decided to change the subject. 'But what about the life you've built for yourself in Nottingham?'

'What life? I don't have any life outside the children, and they're at boarding school . . .'

'Hasn't it been a bit less fraught than it used to be?' persisted Beth. 'When you were with Will?'

Sarah was starting to get annoyed. 'You just don't understand, do you? You haven't got children.'

'We're thinking about it, though.'

'Well . . .' As Sarah spoke, the men reached them. Grabbing Will's hand in a defiant, proprietorial manner, Sarah glared at Beth. 'When you and Jack do get around to it, don't go thinking kids are going to mean "happily ever after" – because they don't.' Then she looked up at Will and smiled. 'But once you've had them, you have to put them first.'

What a pity, thought Beth, that it takes a horrific accident for Sarah to start practising what she preaches. 'I don't think,' she said to Jack as they left the hospital, 'that it would work. Will and Sarah getting back together again.'

'Mmm. They're sellotaping over the cracks in their

relationship for the sake of the children.' Then he took her hand and squeezed it. 'We wouldn't do that, Beth.'

Ah, she thought, but we don't have any children. Yet.

Will returned to work the next day. Beth informed him that there were several messages for him, most of which were from Janey. Although she would never admit it, Beth was warming to Janey now that Sarah's reappearance on the scene appeared to be a distinct possibility. Will, thanking her for relaying the information, confirmed her worst fears. 'I think it's only fair to let her know,' he said, 'that Sarah and I might have to get back together.'

Beth, pouncing on the use of 'have to' as opposed to 'want to', did her gentle best to dissuade him from burning his bridges. 'Tread water for a while,' she urged. 'You know how it is in times of crisis. We all need to cling to what we know, what's familiar.'

But Will admitted that he felt responsible for Sarah's happiness – or rather, her unhappiness. 'She is, after all, the mother of my children.'

Beth gave up. She was getting rather sick of conversations along the lines of 'you don't know what it's like to have children'. So she didn't have children: that didn't make her a lesser being, did it? She went back to her room to prepare for morning surgery. Will, who had at last had a decent night's sleep, did the same.

The phone call came in the middle of the afternoon. Will, who just seen out his last patient of the day, picked up the receiver with a weary 'Yes?'

'Will.' Kim's voice was urgent. 'I've got Sarah on the line.'

'Oh. Good. Put her through.'

'Will?' From the way she said his name he could tell that Sarah was fighting back tears. He tensed in his chair.

Was this it? Was she going to tell him that Tony was paralysed for life? 'Will . . . it's Tony . . .'

'What, Sarah, for God's sake, *what*?'

Sarah's sobs were now audible. 'His legs! His legs, Will. He's just told me they're all itchy, like pins and needles.'

Suddenly excited, Will hunched over the phone. 'Have you told the doctor? Is he with him now?'

'Yes.' Sarah was almost incoherent, crying and laughing at the same time. 'He says . . . he says it's going to be all right.'

'A toast to Tony!' Carrying drinks from the bar, Beth walked over to Will and Sarah at the corner table. So recent, she thought, yet it all seemed so long ago.

As soon as Will had put the phone down on Sarah earlier in the afternoon, he had rushed into Beth's room. His eyes, she had noted, were moist, but his expression radiant. Now, three hours later and in the bar of the Manor, he was looking positively ecstatic. So was Sarah. The consultant had confirmed that Tony was likely to make a full recovery. 'He won't be able to play rugby for quite some time,' he had added with a twinkle in his eye, 'but, yes, he'll soon be walking again.'

'What a relief, eh?' Will smiled at Beth and lifted his glass.

Sarah raised hers as well. 'He certainly had us worried this time.' Then she gave Will's hand an affectionate squeeze.

Beth, sitting opposite them, had to force herself to smile. She was experiencing an alarming sense of *déjà vu*.

Will took a great gulp of his pint and then looked over Beth's shoulder. 'Where's Jack?'

Beth shrugged. 'You tell me. He's done another disappearing act.'

'Probably gone back to Africa.' Sarah meant it as a joke

– or did she? Either way, Beth was distinctly unamused. She asked, 'How long till Tony'll be up and about?'

'He'll be off school for at least a term. And then he'll be driving us all mad again. Thank God.' As Will spoke, some sort of sixth sense made him look towards the door.

Janey was standing there. For a fleeting moment their eyes met – and then she was gone. Without looking at Sarah, Will stood up, muttered a brusque 'excuse me' and rushed out after her. He caught up with her just as she was getting into her car. 'Janey! I've been trying to get hold of you. Tony's picked up at last.'

Janey, delighted, grinned up at him. 'Brilliant. I knew he would.'

'Why don't you come in and have a drink? We're celebrating.'

For a split second Janey looked sad. Then, with a glassy smile, she turned the key in the ignition. 'I won't, thanks, Will. I'm driving up to Manchester for a conference.'

'Oh. Well, can we talk soon?'

Janey paused. There was warmth, but also a hint of something else, something lost, in her face. 'Will, I just popped in to say goodbye.'

But Will didn't click. 'So when are you back from Manchester?'

Janey clasped the steering wheel with both hands. 'Look, I've been thinking this thing through. It isn't just that we haven't been seeing each other. I know the pressure you've been under and, well, I suppose it's made me realize that you're still a family man at heart. You know, with all those responsibilities and I, well, I'm just not ready for all that.' She looked helplessly, regretfully, up at Will. He was stunned: so surprised he couldn't speak.

Janey took the opportunity to close the door and put the car into gear. With a smile conveying a brightness she didn't feel, she waved and drove off.

Will stood for a full minute and watched as her car disappeared into the distance. Then, shoulders slumped, he turned and walked back into the Manor – and back into Sarah's life.

CH**A**PTER 17

The storm came a month after Jack returned. He had, during that time, made several quips about how the weather in Derbyshire was not nearly as dramatic as in Africa. On the night of the storm he was obliged to eat his words.

After evening surgery, the entire staff of The Beeches gathered in the kitchen for a council of war. Beth, as usual, sat at the head of the table. 'Apparently the whole of the Midlands is going to be hit hard, so we can expect the emergency services to be even further stretched than usual. The latest forecast,' she added as she looked down at her notes, 'is for winds at seventy miles an hour and flooding in river valleys in the Peak District. Kim's volunteered to man the phones—'

'Woman the phones, please, Beth.'

'Thank you, Kim. And I'm the lucky one on call.'

'But,' said Jack with a grin, 'we've got to look on the brighter side. It's the semi-final tonight.' As he spoke, Will got up and headed for the door. 'You not coming, Will?'

'Sorry.' Will shook his head. 'Needed at home. Sarah's arranged a family dinner for Julian's birthday.'

'His birthday was four weeks ago,' said Kim indignantly. 'I sent him a card.'

'Yeah. We couldn't do much with Tony laid up, but now that he's back on his feet . . . Well, you know Sarah – never misses a good party.'

'Oh.' Beth was surprised. 'I thought she was going back to Nottingham?'

'No.' Will refused to meet her eye. 'So it's happy

families for me tonight. See you tomorrow.' As he left, Jack and Beth exchanged a look. The last report on the Sarah situation had indeed been that she was going back to Nottingham.

For the past few weeks Will had been insisting that they were not back together: he had even gone as far as to say that he was sleeping on the sofa while Sarah slept in the bedroom. They were only in the same house because of Tony. Nobody, however, had been entirely convinced. Laura, who hadn't been at The Beeches before Will and Sarah's separation, had met Sarah for the first time three days previously. She had confided to Kim that Sarah struck her as a 'scheming minx'. Laura was not one to mince her words.

As soon as Will left, the meeting broke up and they all repaired to the Manor. Kim, whose leg was in plaster following a riding accident, had to be helped into and out of Jack's car. 'I might as well answer the phones when the weather gets worse,' she had said to Beth when the first storm warnings had come through. 'Not much use for anything else.'

'Serves you right for trying to jump a five-bar gate on an untrained two-year-old,' replied Beth.

'You should thank your lucky stars I didn't fall on my head.' Kim, mock-indignant, looked down her nose at Beth. 'Then The Beeches wouldn't stand a chance in hell of winning the semis.'

The semi-final that Jack had referred to was an important event in the Cardale calendar, mainly because it involved a lot of fun and a lot of alcohol. It was the Cardale Trivial Pursuit Team Competition and The Beeches team of Jack, Kim and Trevor had – rather to their surprise – won every round thus far. But tonight they were up against it: they were pitted against the Farmers team. Jack, initially, had been scathing. 'Since when,' he had enquired loftily, 'were farmers intellectuals?'

'Since when,' his wife had replied, 'were doctors regarded as intellectuals?'

Yet half an hour into the competition it became clear that one of the farmers, a rotund, red-faced chap called Fred Murray, was intimidatingly well informed. He answered every question in a flash and left The Beeches team feeling distinctly second rate. Worse, their humiliation was being witnessed by half of Cardale: the Manor was packed to the gunwales that night, partly because of the competition and partly because of the storm. The community spirit, in more ways than one, was in full spate, and the ranks of the regular drinkers were swelled by some of the people who had been evacuated from the houses that backed on to the river. Earlier in the evening, the emergency services had been warned that the river was likely to burst its banks and, to the consternation of some of the inhabitants – Alice North among them – the little row of houses had been declared a danger area. To the consternation of the Vicar (although he kept his doubts to himself), the church had been converted into a temporary dormitory for the evacuees. The younger contingent, not especially enamoured of the situation, was determined to spend as much of the evening as possible in the pub. James and Chloë were delighted: trade hadn't been this brisk for years. So crowded was the pub that they had taken on an extra barmaid for the night. Marion Daley, a pleasant but slightly hard-looking woman in her late thirties and a relative newcomer to Cardale, had asked them several times if they could use a helping hand. Tonight, for the first time, they could, not least because James was stepping into the role of question master.

'What,' he asked the hapless Beeches team, as he read from a card, 'is the derivation of dandelion?'

Jack, Kim and Trevor exchanged desperate looks. Opposite them, the Farmers looked smug.

'Come on, Trev!' Trevor's wife Leanda, acting as scorer, was, inevitably, biased in favour of The Beeches – and they needed all the encouragement they could get. 'You can do it!' But neither Trevor nor his colleagues could answer. Around them, the grinning spectators started a slow hand-clap, and a minute later James threw the question over to the Farmers team.

Fred Murray answered immediately. 'Dandelion. *Dente di leone*. Lion's teeth.'

'Correct!' James turned to Leanda. 'And at the end of that round, if my lovely assistant will give me the score . . .?'

Leanda, preening, turning to her chart. In imitation of a vacuous game-show hostess, she smiled broadly and wriggled seductively, showing off her outrageously short skirt, tight Lycra top and impossibly high heels. Those who didn't know Leanda assumed that her attire was a deliberate send-up of her role: those who did know her didn't even bat an eyelid. Leanda *always* dressed like that. Her personality, as Will had once said with mordant accuracy, saved her from being a bimbo.

Yet, in fairness to her, she was deliberately camping it up this evening. 'In second place,' she said, flashing a smile at the imaginary television camera, 'with sixteen points, The Beeches!' After muted cheers from the crowd, she announced, 'And the winners at this stage, with thirty-three points: The Farmers!' Loud cheers – and some equally loud boos – greeted the result. When the noise had died down James announced a five-minute break before the next round. 'Unless,' he added, with a smirk at Jack, 'the medics want to throw in the towel now?'

'Certainly not.' Jack and his team-mates were incensed. As he said to Marion at the bar, they were just beginning to warm up.

Beth, who had been chatting to Chloë, came up to her team and, dripping irony, said how proud of them she was. Trevor, sulking, cast an annoyed glance in Fred Murray's direction. 'It's not fair. If Murray's a farmer, I'm a bloody astronaut.'

'Well,' Beth followed his glance, 'he owns Hildred Farm.'

'He owns Hildred Farm*house*.'

'Well, Trevor,' said Jack over the rim of his pint, 'if one of us hadn't insisted that the capital of Brazil was Buenos Aires, we might still be in with a chance.'

But Leanda wasn't going to stand for that. 'And who was it who thought that Andrew Lloyd Webber wrote that Shakespeare line?'

Jack, looking sheepish, took refuge in his drink.

Leaving the highly competent Marion to look after the bar, Chloë looked on contentedly. She was enjoying herself this evening: firstly because it was good to see the Manor so busy, and secondly because Sarah-Jane, her two-year-old, was staying with her sister in Northumberland. Much as she loved her only child, Chloë was glad of the break. It meant, as she had said to Beth, that she only had one child to look after. James, at that point, had been mercifully out of hearing.

As the teams prepared for the final round, the door opened, letting in a strong gust of wind and, to Chloë's eyes, a complete stranger. A sulky-looking youth of about seventeen wove his way through the throng and to the bar. Chloë watched with interest as he exchanged a greeting with Marion: evidently they knew each other. It was only after watching them together that she noticed the resemblance: of course, Marion had said she had a son. This must be him. Chloë decided she didn't envy Marion. The boy looked decidedly shifty. Also, she thought as she peered at him, he looked rather unwell: pale and wheezy. Just as she was debating whether or not to go over and ask if everything was all right, the decision was taken out of her hands. Without so much as a flicker of warning, every light in the place went out.

For a split second the pub was plunged into silence as well as darkness. Then the room erupted into a good-natured chaos; mild screams of alarm being drowned out by weak jokes, cries of 'sexual harassment!' and a barrage of shouts. 'Will everyone,' yelled James above the din, 'just keep still.'

'Game's postponed!' shouted Jack.

Trevor was delighted. 'Re-match! Re-match!'

Fred Murray was scathing. 'Re-match, my backside!'

'Mr White,' called Marion from the bar, 'the till won't open.'

'Oh, sod it. No. Of course it won't.' Guided by the flames from the lighters and matches struck by the more enterprising smokers, James made his way back to the bar. Grabbing the ice bucket, he emptied its contents down the sink and called out to his customers, 'OK, folks, we'll have to close early, I'm afraid, so it'll be one last drink. Use this,' he added to Marion, 'as a money-box.'

Everybody, it seemed, wanted a last drink. The power cut had killed the music as well as the lights and, in the lulls in conversation, the sound of the pelting rain and howling wind could be heard. It was, as Trevor remarked to Jack, 'one hell of a night'.

Ten minutes later, clad in wellies, hats, Barbours and raincoats, The Beeches staff made their way outside. The near-torrential rain whipped at their faces and the dark-ened street lent a funereal aspect to the already dismal night. 'We'd better go to the church,' said Beth, 'to see what's happening. Looks like the entire village is without power.'

Without much enthusiasm, Jack agreed to go with her. Trevor and Leanda slunk off home. Kim, aided by Laura, went back to The Beeches to attend to the phones in case of emergency.

Beth was pleased to see that the council electricians had been quick off the mark. As she pulled up outside the church, she saw that they were already rigging up a portable generator. Alice North, however, was not pleased: as Jack and Beth approached, they saw her standing in the porch, clutching her crate of hens and glaring belligerently at the vicar, Mr Kelly. 'They're frightened outside,' she said, nodding at the clucking creatures. 'Where's your Christian charity?'

'It's reserved for Christians.'

'If they stay outside,' countered Alice, 'then so do I. And if we all die, it'll be on your head.'

'I'm sorry, Alice, I can't—'

Beth, grinning, interrupted him. 'Hello, vicar. Everything OK?'

'Fine, Beth, fine.' The last thing Mr Kelly wanted was a witness to his lack of charity. 'Why don't you go in and have a cup of tea?'

But now Jack was also beside them, and looking with interest at the hens. 'Hello, Alice. Spending the night?'

Alice saw her chance. 'I am, yes, if you'll give me a hand with my chickens, Doctor Kerruish.'

Without further ado, Jack took the crate and walked into the church. Alice, head held high and looking smug, followed him.

Beth was engaged in conversation with Sergeant Eddie Williams, the heavy-set, rather lugubrious local bobby. He was always forecasting disaster: this time he appeared to have found it. 'No real emergencies yet, Doctor Glover, but we've lost power and phone, so—'

'The phone lines are down as well?'

'Fraid so. River's rising as well. Trees going down like ninepins. Apart from the radio and a few mobiles we're completely cut off. Exciting, isn't it?'

Beth, as always, wasn't sure how to take his humour. Was it even humour? She smiled vaguely and turned to Jack. 'I suppose I'd better hang around here. Do you want to go home?'

Jack looked around. There was something strangely comforting about the 'wartime spirit' of the scene in the church. Many of the pews had been pushed to one side to allow space for rows of camp beds while at trestle tables in front of the altar, volunteers were serving soup and rolls. Alice, he noted with amusement, had grabbed a bed next to one of the portable gas heaters: her hens had the one beside her. Then Jack grinned at Beth. 'No, I'll stay. As long as the vicar doesn't get us singing hymns.'

Beth walked with him towards the trestle tables. 'Nobody in their right minds would be out and about on a night like this,' she said. 'I can't imagine we'll be needed anywhere other than here.'

James and Chloë, very much in their right minds, decided to lock up and retire to bed. With no electricity and no source of light beyond a few candles, there was little point in attempting to clear up the evening's debris. The only effort James made was in the direction of the ice-bucket-cum-makeshift-till. Rather to his surprise, he found it contained eighty pounds. 'Not bad,' he muttered, 'for five minutes' drinking.' With the till out of action and no safe on the premises, he emptied the money on to a bar-towel, tied it up and, after a moment's consideration, put it into the fridge. Then, going slowly so that his candle wouldn't blow out, he left the bar and climbed the stairs to their flat above.

Chloë was already in bed, sitting up and looking somewhat apprehensive. 'What's the matter, love?' he asked.

She gestured towards the window. 'Storms. Hate 'em.'

James gave her a wicked grin. 'Well, I can think of something we could do to take your mind off the weather.'

'James White, you saucy—' Suddenly Chloë frowned and cocked her head. 'What's that?'

'What's what?'

'That noise.'

'I didn't hear anything.'

But Chloë was looking suspiciously at her husband. 'Did you check all the windows downstairs?'

'Yes – well, I think so.'

Chloë fixed him with one of her looks. She knew all about his 'I think so's. 'Don't you think you'd better go and check?'

'Aw . . . Chloë! Do I have to?'

She looked at him again, teasingly this time. 'Oh, I think so. I won't be able to . . . you know, *relax* until you do.'

James got the message. Wearily, he trudged back down the stairs.

If the layout of the pub had been different he might have stood a chance. As it was, the stairs gave almost immediately into the bar itself, and as soon as James entered he was cornered. Crouching by the open fridge and illuminated by the beam from the torch in his hands was a scruffily dressed youth. James entered his vision just as he was reaching for the bar-towel with the money.

'Oi!' James was so astonished that he didn't even think of backing off. 'What the hell—'

The youth, fired up by the adrenalin born of fear, grabbed the nearest object and took a swipe at James. The object was a full bottle of brandy and his aim was true.

The glass smacked against James's head, knocking him sideways. With his mouth open in a mute 'O', James fell to the floor. As he collapsed, he hit his head – even harder this time – against the counter. His eyes flickered and then, losing consciousness, he crumpled to the floor.

His attacker, breathing heavily and with difficulty, looked in terror at the prone body. Then, regaining his wits, he grabbed the towel with its stash of money, scrambled over the counter – and fled into the night.

At first Chloë thought James was playing 'silly buggers'

– deliberately trying to annoy her for bullying him to go back downstairs. The unfamiliar noises, she reckoned, were just James's way of trying to spook her. But the last of those noises – the repeated banging of the front door – began to frighten her. The wind, howling through the bar and whistling up the stairs to the bedroom, seriously unnerved her. Clambering out of bed and not bothering to put anything over her night-dress, she went downstairs.

She didn't see James until she stumbled over his inert body. Then she stared at him in silent horror. She knelt beside him and, mumbling to herself, to him, to anyone, she ran feverish hands over his body. When she got used to the darkness she saw the cut on his head: it didn't look serious and there wasn't much blood. As she stood up, she saw the brandy bottle lying beside the open door of the fridge and knew what had happened. Her panic mounting, she reached up for the wall-phone. 'Please, God,' she whispered as she dialled, 'don't be . . .'

But God wasn't playing. The phone was dead. With a little scream of anguish, she slammed the receiver down on the counter. After only a brief hesitation, she ran towards the open door and hurried out into darkness.

CH**A**PTER 18

Fleeing like a fury down the storm-ravaged street, Chloë was observed by a rather startled Sergeant Williams. At first he thought the strange apparition must be one of the residents of the group home, terrified by the storm. On closer inspection he realized it was Chloë White, dressed only in wellingtons and a nightie. His initial amusement gave way to alarm when he stopped her to ask what had happened. Immediately he ushered her into this car and drove back up the street to the Manor. As he did so, he used his mobile to alert Beth that an ambulance might be needed. It was fortunate that Chloë was unable to hear Beth's reply: no ambulance could get to them in less than four hours. The storm was worsening and the roads not already flooded were littered with fallen power lines and trees.

But ten minutes later, Chloë was cheered by James's swift return to consciousness. By the time they got him to the safety and warmth of the church, he was blinking furiously, slurring his words – but very much alive. 'Thief,' he said, in answer to Beth's question. 'Went after him, didn't I?'

Kneeling by his side and now wrapped in a blanket, Chloë gripped his hand. 'Someone attacked him, Beth. The front door was opened from inside. Some money's missing. They must have stayed behind in the dark after we closed.'

Her words had James blinking again. 'Where's the money?'

'Don't worry about the money, darling.'

'If I catch the bugger—'

Jack, standing beside Beth, interrupted. 'Do you know who it was, James?'

'Course I do.' But James was looking vacantly at Jack, as if trying to work out who he was.

'Who was it, then?'

'The thief. He bloody hit me.'

At that, Jack and Beth exchanged worried glances. Chloë, noticing, was about to say something when James, puzzled by his surroundings, asked her what the hell he was doing in church in the middle of the night. Chloë couldn't think of a reply. James's injuries aside, they were in an almost amusing situation, huddled like refugees and sharing hallowed ground with most of Cardale's pensioners, an increasingly testy Mr Kelly – and Alice's hens. Instead, Chloë turned to Jack and Beth. 'How long will he have to stay here?'

'Until the ambulance arrives.'

Chloë looked suspiciously at Jack. 'And how long will that be?'

'A few hours yet.'

'Is there anything you're not telling me?'

'No.'

'You're worried, aren't you? I can tell that you and Beth are worried.'

Jack put a gentle hand on Chloë's shoulder and ushered her to one side. 'Chloë, it's just that anyone who's been unconscious, for however short a time, should be hospitalized and X-rayed as a matter of course. It's going to take a while to get him to hospital, that's all. He'll be fine. He has, after all, got a skull like a rock.'

But Jack's attempt at humour did nothing to diminish Chloë's anxiety. She looked at her husband and frowned. Something was wrong: she knew it and they knew it. There was something they weren't telling her.

Her thoughts, however, were interrupted by the voice of Mr Kelly. 'Er, Beth?'

The little group round James turned in unison to see the churchman leading a distraught woman towards them. Only Chloë recognized her. 'Marion!'

'Oh, Mrs White.' Marion seemed equally surprised to see Chloë.

'This,' said Mr Kelly to Beth, 'is Marion Daley. She's worried about her son.'

'Oh.' Then Beth smiled in recognition. 'Of course, you were helping out at the Manor tonight. Er . . . your son?' she prompted.

'Yes. Sean. He's always had asthma, but never like this. He can't breathe. I think . . . I think he's going to die.'

Beth wasted no time in ushering Marion out to her car. 'I drive, you direct,' she said succinctly.

Ten minutes later they reached Marion's house. Uninspiring was a polite way of describing it: most people in Cardale referred to the entire terrace of dilapidated council houses as 'an eyesore'. It wasn't that they had anything against council houses, just that they had a lot against a council which had the nerve to house people in such rundown accommodation. If Marion's son has asthma, thought Beth as she followed the woman inside, his environment certainly isn't going to help his health.

Sean, upstairs in his room, looked ghastly. Whiter than the sheets on his bed, he lay there, eyes wide in panic, fighting for every breath. Beth rushed straight over to him, lifted him into a sitting position and rested his hands on his knees. Then, listening to his chest, she asked him where his inhaler was.

'I must've lost it,' he gasped.

'Have you got any spares?'

Silently, Sean shook his head.

'I looked,' said his mother. 'All his spares are empty.'

Without further ado, Beth extracted her peak-flow meter from her bag. 'Sean, I want you to blow into this.' Handing him the tube, which registered his lung capacity, she watched as he inserted it into his mouth. It was difficult for Sean to summon any breath at all. Eventually he managed one wheeze: the arrow on the dial clicked round to measure less than 300 – substantially below average. Beth, worried, returned to her bag and selected a syringe. 'I'll give you a steroid injection to reduce the inflammation, and then we'll get you on the nebulizer which should—' She stopped, suddenly realizing that they would need electricity for the nebulizer. 'Damn, no power. Never mind, Sean, we can get you a good dose of salbutamol another way . . .'

As she prepared the syringe, Beth chatted to Marion in an attempt to ease the tension in the room. It was an exercise that worked for Marion – but not for Sean. As Beth prattled on about the Manor, Sean became even more agitated. 'Easy, Sean, easy.' Beth was trying to fit the mouthpiece of the volumatic spacer over his mouth. If he could breathe from that, it would be the equivalent of twenty-five puffs from his inhaler. 'You can help yourself best by staying calm.' Then she turned back to Marion. 'Can you do me a favour? Press star, one and send. Doctor Kerruish should answer. Tell him I need the battery device for the nebulizer here. Pronto.'

Marion, alarmed, did as she was told. She didn't like the look of Sean. She had never seen him as bad as this. After calling Jack, she tried desperately to think of something to take her mind off it all: there was only one thing she could think of. 'Would you like a cup of tea?' she asked Beth.

Beth turned round and nodded. The last thing she wanted was tea – but she did want a word alone with

Marion. 'Sure. That would be great. I'll come down in a minute.'

'Sean seems terribly wound up,' she said when they were alone in the kitchen, patiently waiting for the pan of water to boil on the gas ring. 'Has anything happened to upset him recently?'

Marion shrugged. 'Not that I know of. He's . . . well, he's had a bit of a tough time recently. Moving here, and then his father getting banged up.'

'Oh? Why?' The question was out before she realized how rude it was.

Marion turned round and smiled without humour. 'He robbed people. He was a thief and a prat – I'm well shot of him. So's Sean, if only he knew it.'

Beth was surprised at Marion's sharpness. 'Well, it must be hard for Sean.'

'It was hard for the people who got robbed as well.'

Beth tried to steer the conversation away from Sean. 'Poor old James and Chloë White have had a bit of trouble at the Manor tonight,' she began. Again, too late, she saw the tactlessness of her remark: with a thief for a husband, the last thing Marion needed was a conversation about burglars.

'Oh? What sort of trouble?'

Well, I'm in it now, thought Beth. 'Someone broke into the pub and stole the takings. Banged James on the head as well. He's conscious but we'll be happier when we get him into hospital.'

Marion's back was towards Beth as she spoke. It was just as well: Beth's words planted a horrible, gnawing suspicion in her mind and her expression was grim.

Marion's fears were confirmed when they went back upstairs. Seeing that Sean was almost blue with cold, Beth decided he would be better off in his bed rather than on top of it.

'No!' Suddenly Sean became animated – and even more

agitated. Beth took no notice. Lifting his legs, she pulled back the covers. As she did so, she heard the jingle of coins. Then, laughing, she held up a bundle of coins wrapped in a tea-towel. 'What's this? Your life savings?' What a peculiar place to keep your money, she thought. Or was it? The lingering smell of stale beer emanating from the towel rang a warning note in her head. Sean was looking terrified. 'Where'd you get this?'

But before he could reply, his mother advanced upon them and snatched the towel from Beth. Eyes blazing with fury, she glared at her son. 'You little sod! Where'd you get this? Tell me where you got it.'

Sean, petrified and again breathing with difficulty, started to shake.

'It was the pub, wasn't it? You attacked that poor man. What did you do, hide in the dark, then jump him? Did you? Did you?' With each question, her voice rose until it became a furious, impassioned scream. Then, losing control, she tried to hit her son.

'OK, Marion! Leave him. *Leave him!*' Although equally furious, Beth tried to drag Marion away. He was, after all, her patient.

'You'll end up like your sodding father – and it'll be good riddance!' With that, Marion threw the money on the floor and stormed out of the room. Sean, gasping, fell back against the pillow. Beth looked dispassionately at his terrified, white face. 'James White,' she said quietly, 'is one of my oldest friends. Let's hope you haven't hurt him badly. Now we'll try a bit more salbutamol. I know it's hard, but you're going to have to stay very calm.

But Sean didn't remain calm for very long: the arrival of Sergeant Williams saw to that. Feeling unable to leave James, Jack had passed the request for the nebulizer on to the policeman who duly drove off to Marion's. 'I brought this,' he said as she answered the door, 'for Doctor Glover.' Odd, he thought, the woman looks terrified.

Marion *was* terrified – at the sight of the policeman, not the nebulizer.

'She said,' Eddie Williams continued, 'that it was urgent.'

'Oh. Yes. Sorry, you'd better come upstairs.'

As soon as Sean saw the policeman he leaped out of bed and tried to make a run for the door. Williams, although taken by surprise, had him back on the bed in a flash. Then, chest heaving and eyes wild with fright, Sean had another, even more severe, asthma attack.

'Christ, he's a wild one,' panted Williams. 'What's wrong with him?'

The policeman wasn't the only one interested in Beth's answer. She saw Marion's frightened face, Sean's terrified one – and Williams's interest. 'Asthma attack,' she said, after a slight hesitation. 'It's a severe asthma attack, Eddie. I've *got* to have an ambulance.'

'I need you to stay strong, Chloë. James needs you to stay strong.'

'Don't give me that doctor bullshit, Jack. What's wrong with him? I don't know what's happening to him.' Chloë, near to tears, looked down at her husband. Five minutes previously, at two in the morning, he had suddenly lost consciousness. 'Jack? Please . . .'

Jack took Chloë and led her away from Alice North and Mr Kelly, James's self-appointed 'nurses'. 'I'm not sure, Chloë.'

'Then tell me what you think!'

'Right. What I think is that there's some bleeding under the skull. Maybe even a blood clot. It's putting pressure on the brain, made him lose consciousness.'

'What can you do about it?'

Jack hated feeling so helpless – especially when two of his greatest friends were involved. 'Nothing here. He needs to be operated on to relieve the pressure on the brain. It's simple enough – if he's in hospital.'

'Then we *have* to get him to hospital, don't we?'

Jack didn't answer. He knew that as well as she did. The only question was, how? Trevor, long since roused from an amorous evening with Leanda, had just told him that the ambulance had had to turn back five miles away as the road was under two feet of water. The only other way to get out of Cardale and to the hospital was over the hills, across farm tracks, and for that they needed a four-wheel drive. Jack looked at Chloë's desperate face. A four-wheel drive. Suddenly it came to him. They knew someone who had a four-wheel drive . . .

Will's evening at home had been a disaster. Not that Julian hadn't enjoyed his family birthday party: it had been a jolly affair, made better by the lights going out and the subsequent, inevitable game of hide-and-seek. The problem, for Will, was his relationship with Sarah. His forced intimacy with her since Tony's accident had, he only realized this evening, been more of a trial than a temptation. However determined they both were to present a façade of togetherness, they were – and probably always had been – too far apart.

Sarah, however, appeared to think differently. After the boys had gone to bed, she had changed into a sheer, Leanda-type nightie and had done her best to seduce her husband. Will had nearly succumbed. But, at the last minute, the voice of reason told him that they were treading on dangerous ground, ground they had been covering, unsuccessfully, for years. Yet this time, he listened when the voice told him that it would never, ever work.

Sarah was spared his rejection by the opportune call from Jack. Would he, asked his colleague, take his car and meet him at the church? Will, relieved, said he would. Sarah was livid. Yet as Will left the house she looked at the bedside clock and asked herself if she really wanted to go back to a life where moments of passion were constantly ruined by urgent call-outs at two o' clock in the morning. She debated the question for a long, long time.

Will didn't have time to debate anything. The minute he arrived at the church, Jack informed him of what had happened to James – and of the urgency of getting him to hospital. 'The only way,' he said, 'is over the hills. All the roads to Derby are blocked and the ambulances can't get through. The only road open – and even that's not certain – is the farm track past Braignton, so . . .'

'Christ!' Will had had no idea things were so bad. 'That's tricky at the best of times.'

'I know. That's why we need your Range Rover. It's our only chance.'

Will tried a smile and looked over to James's bed. 'Well, we'd better get him on board, then. At least the start of the Braignton track is only round the corner.'

'Ah. Well, I'm afraid we'll have to make a detour . . . We've got another patient to pick up.'

'Oh? Who?'

Jack sighed. 'The chap who attacked him.'

'We're going to get you to hospital, Sean,' said Beth as soon as she came off the phone to Jack. She couldn't help herself from adding, 'The man you hit, by the way, has collapsed again. He's in a coma.'

Sean was terrified: his breathing, yet again, was becoming jagged. 'I didn't mean to hurt him.'

'Didn't mean to?' Again Beth couldn't help herself. 'You nearly cracked his skull!' Seeing she was contributing to his panic, she took a deep breath. 'Whatever you meant, you have hurt him. Why, Sean?'

'I had to have the money.'

'Why?'

Sean couldn't meet Beth's eye. 'Kelly. My girlfriend.'

'What about her?' Again, Beth was sharper than she meant to be.

Instead of replying, Sean extracted a crumpled letter from his breast pocket. He handed it to her. 'Just read.'

Beth read. The letter was short and to the point. With a weary sigh, she handed it back to him. 'How old is she?'

'Sixteen.'

'You're definitely the father?'

'Yes.'

'So what were you going to do?' Beth looked at the money scattered all over the floor. 'Post the money to her? Just leave her to get rid of the baby?'

But Beth had done him an injustice. Fighting for every word, he looked up in anguish and shouted, 'No! No! I was going to go and get her – make her come away with me. Live with me.' He looked at Beth through dark, troubled eyes. 'Have the baby. Her and me.'

Beth didn't know what to say. Foolish, misguided, reckless – Sean was all of those things. But he was also, in his way, caring. 'The car will be here soon,' she said at length. 'It's a four-wheel drive. It'll get you over the hills.' She didn't tell him that it also contained James. While part of her felt that Sean deserved every punishment going, the other part – the doctor in her – knew that he had to remain as calm as possible. Informing him that he was going to share an ambulance with the man he had nearly killed was a sure way to push him over the edge. Anyway, he would find out when they got him into the car.

Ten minutes later Sean took one look at the back of the Range Rover and let out a piercing scream. Will and Jack, carrying him, had all their work cut out to restrain him from breaking free, and neither knew the source of his terror.

'Steady on!' Will couldn't understand the boy's panic.

'No! No!'

'Sean, we've got to get you to hospital.' Jack, who reckoned that Sean was alarmed by the prospect of travelling in a Range Rover instead of an ambulance, gestured towards the car. 'This is the only way. You've got to stay calm.'

Sean nodded dumbly. His initial reaction on seeing James lying like a corpse in the back of the vehicle had exhausted him. After a feeble attempt at carrying on the struggle, he gave up and allowed Will to lift him into a sitting position and to place the nebulizer beside him. His mother, standing beside Beth, looked on in disbelief: the sight of James had alarmed her almost as much as it had her son.

Chloë, bending over her husband, looked up and smiled.

'Marion . . .'

But Marion immediately backed off in guilty alarm. Hurt and puzzled, Chloë turned to look at Sean, and at the horrified expression on his face as he watched James. What on earth, she wondered, was going on here?

Will and Jack, joining Beth, were wondering the same thing.

'What the hell,' asked Jack, 'was all that about?'

'Guess.'

'Well,,he seemed petrified at the sight of James . . . Oh . . . no. Surely you don't mean . . .'

Beth nodded. 'We found the money on him.'

For a moment Jack was speechless, struck dumb by the awfulness of the situation. Then, as Beth had while waiting for them to arrive, he thought of the medical implications. 'Christ . . . but he's in a real state already. Maybe this isn't a good idea.'

'Is there another way?'

Both men looked at Beth. Her question didn't need an

answer. 'I'll have to go with him,' she continued. 'But one of us should stay here.'

There was a brief, awkward pause as Jack looked at Will. 'I hope you don't mind, but I think it's better if I go.'

Will looked piqued at this implied slight to his driving ability. 'I do mind, actually. It's my car.'

'I know, I know. But it's just that I've driven in worse conditions in Africa. And James is my patient.'

Will nodded. Now was not the time to quibble over details. 'Sure.' He handed Jack the keys. 'Just don't get it dirty, OK?'

Even Chloë, worried sick about her husband, managed a grin when she overheard that one.

The conditions inside the makeshift ambulance were less than ideal, but those outside were infinitely worse. As the Range Rover climbed steadily, the wind seemed to increase and, even though the wipers were on full, they could hardly cope with the rain lashing against the windscreen. Jack didn't say a word as he negotiated the steep slopes of the dales; the vehicle lurched from side to side as he tried to avoid the potholes and ridges of the windswept hill road. His knuckles, white with tension as he fought to control the steering wheel, spoke for him.

Beth and Chloë were also largely silent. Chloë seemed lost in a world of her own as she looked at James, warmly wrapped in blankets but still silent and inert. There was nothing she could do; she could neither help him nor communicate with him. And while he looked as if he were enjoying a happy, contented sleep, he could, for all she knew, be gradually drifting towards death.

Sean, on the other hand, was getting visibly worse by the minute. Sweating profusely, he was also alarmingly pale and his breathing was heavy, laboured and wheezy.

Desperately worried now, Beth wiped his brow with a cloth and silently willed Jack to go faster.

Half an hour into the journey, and when they were at the top of the ridge, the weather began to improve. Only Jack noticed that the rain had dwindled to a drizzle and that the wind had lessened. Sending up a silent prayer of thanks, he began the dangerous, muddy descent to the point where the ambulance would meet them.

There was no way he could have known about the tree. Rounding a bend past a high, rocky outcrop, he was suddenly forced to jam on the brakes at the sight of a fallen tree trunk that completely blocked the track. He yelled for the others to hold tight – to no avail. In the space of seconds which seemed, to him, to pass in slow motion, the vehicle went into a skid and, with a sickening thud, smacked into the tree. The silence that followed was brief and profound. Then Jack turned and, to his horror, saw that Sean had rolled off his makeshift stretcher and was lying face to face with James. His eyes were wide with fear and his mouth was opening and closing as if he were trying to summon words. Yet Beth, desperately trying to haul him off James, knew that he was fighting for breath.

'Is James OK?'

'Yes!' Beth and Cloë answered simultaneously. James hadn't moved. 'Get round here, Jack,' continued Beth. 'We've got to get the nebulizer! Oh, my God!'

'What?' Jack, out of the vehicle in a flash, was hauling open the rear door.

Beth looked at him in panic. 'Nebulizer's bust! Got to get him out, lay him flat!'

Outside in the darkness, in the air that was now clear and fresh – and abundant – Sean had to fight for breath. As Beth scrambled to her knees beside him, his chest heaved, his mouth opened and closed once more – and then he was silent.

'Shit! Shit!' Beth leaned over him, pinched his nose and

put her mouth over his. She yelled at him as she came up for air. 'Sean . . . Sean!'

Jack tried to take over. 'Let me have a—'

'No!' In a frenzy, Beth put her hands on his chest and began to pump with all her might. 'No! Don't! Don't die on me, you little bastard! Don't!' Going back to his mouth, she tried to breathe life into him, to breathe for him. She went from heart to mouth and from mouth to heart as Chloë and Jack watched in grim, desperate silence. And long before she stopped battling they both knew that Sean had breathed his last, and that his over-laboured heart had given up the struggle.

A minute later they heard the siren of the ambulance cutting through the eerie silence of the night. The noise seemed particularly high-pitched, yet at first it failed to register with one of the little group on the desolate hillside. Only when it became louder and clearer did the blank expression leave James's face. And as his eyelids flickered and opened, it was replaced by a smile.

CH**A**PTER 19

While the storm had lasted less then twelve hours, its aftermath endured for months. Its legacy of fallen trees, flooded farmland and broken windows stayed with the people of Cardale far longer than the memory of the dark, desolate night itself. Yet for some, that memory endured.

The night of the storm stayed with Marion Daley for the rest of her life. Although she left Cardale shortly after her son's death, she never forgot the village, the place to which she had moved with such hopes for her and Sean's future. With all those hopes dashed on that fateful night, she couldn't bear to stay. Nor could she bear to live in the same place as James and Chloë: every time she saw them, she was reminded of Sean and of what he had done. After she left, no one in Cardale heard from her again.

James made a full and rapid recovery – although his memory, he claimed, was not what it used to be. Chloë said that was complete rubbish. 'He's always been a dozy sod,' she said to Beth one day. 'Now he thinks he's got an excuse for it. But,' she added darkly, 'he'd better think again . . .'

For Will, the night of the storm marked the final demise of his marriage. It had ended, as it had previously endured, rather strangely. When he had finally returned home, it had been with the resolution to 'have it out' with Sarah and ask her to leave. She, however, had taken the wind out of his sails. 'I've been thinking,' she had said as soon as he walked in the door, 'about us – about our marriage. I know you want me to stay for the sake of the kids but . . . well, I'm sorry. The answer's no.'

Will had been too flabbergasted to reply.

'We'd have a few good days,' continued Sarah with an apologetic shrug, 'but then we'd just be at each other's throats again, wouldn't we?'

Will managed a smile. 'Yes. You're absolutely right.'

'Good. No hard feelings, then?'

'No. No hard feelings.'

In the following weeks they proceeded, amicably, with their divorce. Their last exchange before Sarah finally moved out had served to convince Will that they were doing the right thing. Had they ever, he wondered, really understood each other? How on earth had Sarah managed to gauge his feelings so badly?

Jack and Beth had a fight the night after the storm. While they were both exhausted and upset, Beth in particular was affected by Sean's death. Initially, she blamed herself for wanting him dead after what he'd done to James. 'I was with him for five or six hours,' she wailed, 'and yet he *died*! It's my fault: I didn't try hard enough. He wasn't really bad . . . He was trying to help his girlfriend.' In tears, she went on to tell Jack about the letter Sean had shown her. Jack had been sympathetic, but adamant that she had done nothing wrong. 'We could all have been killed up there. That tree could have come down a few minutes later. Luck, Beth. We try as hard as we can and sometimes we do make a difference. That's all we can do.' His words, however, gave him an idea that, when he articulated it, led to their argument.

'You know,' he said later, 'I've been thinking. Perhaps we should take on a trainee doctor.'

'Why? We're not a training practice.'

'Yes, but look what happened during the storm. We're overstretched, Beth. And if we have a baby . . . Well, have you thought about who would cover for you?'

'Oh, I see.' Beth's voice was heavy with sarcasm. 'You're assuming that I'll be the one stuck at home, feeding, nursing, changing however many babies we're lucky enough to have, while you run around free as a bird.'

'No!' Jack held up his hands in an attempt to stem her brittle words. 'For goodness sake, Beth, but do just think about it. I, for obvious reasons, can't actually give birth, so you'll *have* to be off for a while. And what if you decide to take longer than you planned. It does happen . . .'

Beth had to concede that indeed it did. She had lost track of the number of expectant mothers who had sworn blind they'd only take a few weeks off – and who had never worked again. She couldn't imagine never working again – but Jack did have a point.

At the next practice meeting, Jack raised the question of The Beeches becoming a training practice. He was careful not to mention anything about their hopes of Beth becoming pregnant: that would make the whole issue look like self-interest. Will, initially, was unenthusiastic. He cited the extra insurance cover they would need and the amount of time they would all have to spend bringing a new doctor up to speed. Furthermore, he was reluctant to employ a trainee none of them knew anything about. 'Is it a good idea,' he asked, 'to stake the good name of the practice on any old Tom, Dick or Harry?' The others had to concede that his objection was valid. The issue was temporarily shelved.

A few weeks later, Beth raised the subject again. She began by tackling Trevor on his own. Always keen to discuss possibilities of more contracts, more money and greater expansion, he agreed to talk to Will again. Perhaps, he suggested, they should ask the vocational training service to get them someone local, or at least someone with a background and interests sympathetic to the Cardale environment. 'Damage limitation,' he said importantly. 'If we narrow the parameters, we're less likely to end up with a Tom, Dick or a Harry.'

Will came round in the end – and a month after that they were contacted by the training service: Trevor's exercise in damage limitation meant that they were going to end up with an Andrew.

'Andrew Attwood,' said Will as he looked at the letter. 'What do you know about him?'

'Nothing.' Jack shrugged. 'All I've got is his name and his CV. It was all a bit last-minute.'

'Oh, well, let's hope we don't scare him off.' Will picked up his pint and drained it. 'One for the road?'

Jack looked at his watch. He seemed to recall telling Beth something about 'a quick drink': he and Will had been in the Manor for nearly two hours. Then he looked up and grinned. 'Sure, why not?'

Half an hour later, feeling extremely guilty, he ran most of the way home. Beth was waiting for him in the kitchen. He looked at her and at the elaborate meal she had prepared – and felt even worse.

But Beth seemed unperturbed. 'That was a *very* quick drink,' she said, with a twinkle in her eye.

'I didn't realize you were going to all this trouble. If only you'd said I – I would have got away earlier.' He hung his head. 'I'm sorry.'

Beth giggled. 'Never mind. Why don't we just sit down and eat. Drink?' she added, waving a bottle of wine.

Nodding, Jack went to fetch the glasses.

'Er . . . no, not for me,' said Beth, as he poured.

'Oh?' Concerned, Jack looked up at her. Beth *always* had a glass of wine with dinner: he could remember how pleased she had been when it had become 'official' that a couple of glasses of red wine a day were good for you. 'You all right, love?'

'I think so.'

Jack frowned. Something wasn't right here. Then he

noticed her slow smile – and suddenly he clicked. 'You're pregnant, aren't you?'

Beth threw back her head and laughed. 'Yes. I am.'

Jack, gawping at her, remained rooted to the spot. 'You are! You're sure? You're absolutely sure?'

'Yes, I'm sure. I did a home test last week – but I rang through and got confirmation this morning.'

Jack was ecstatic. He leaped towards her and swept her into his arms. Hugging her and laughing with delight, he found it difficult to summon any words. 'Beth!' he said at length. 'That's just wonderful. That's bloody wonderful! That's *better* than wonderful.'

Beth prised herself out of his increasingly bearlike hug and looked him in the eye. 'It is, isn't it?'

Jack's eyes were as moist as her own. He was still, however, almost inarticulate with joy. 'I'm so happy. We'll be so happy . . . we are so . . . I can't . . .' Then he fell quiet and looked at her with the beginnings of a frown. She was laughing at him.

'Who would ever have thought it?' She giggled. 'Jack Kerruish – speechless.'

Jack couldn't think of a reply.

Tom McGregor
Peak Practice   £3.99

Dr Jack Kerruish has been part of the Cardale community for a year now – but has he really been accepted? His senior partner at The Beeches surgery, Beth Glover, would like to think so – not least because she and Jack have fallen in love . . . But fellow partner Will Preston, as aloof as Kerruish is approachable, still has his doubts. Just as he has his doubts about the cause of the latest crisis in his famously rocky marriage . . . However, elsewhere in Cardale the villagers are preoccupied with their own troubles. Until rumours start to spread of an impending wedding . . .

Adapted from the second television series, here is the story of the characters and the casualties, the domestic dramas and the medical minefields of ITV's hugely popular *Peak Practice*.

Peak Practice is a Central Films production for Central Independent Television. Series devised by Lucy Gannon.

Tom McGregor
Kavanagh Q.C.   £4.99

To accompany the new ITV drama series starring John Thaw

James Kavanagh's profession is Justice. As a Queen's Counsel he is
one of the most able barristers of his generation, an astute criminal
lawyer who can master the most varied and challenging of briefs . . . A
vigilante accused of attempted murder; a Cambridge undergraduate
suspected of rape; a successful businessman desperate to regain
custody of his abused son; a prostitute accused of killing a tycoon . . .

From Manchester Crown Court to the awesome grandeur of The Old
Bailey, Kavanagh's only concern is to see that justice is done. But with
his personal life in crisis it is not always easy to keep on top of the
dramas taking place in the courtroom . . .

Kavanagh QC is a Central Films production for Central Independent
Television plc. Series created by Ted Childs and Susan Rogers.

Jill Arlon
Circles of Deceit   £4.99

A Major New Television Series starring Dennis Waterman

John Neil is a haunted man. His wife and child have been murdered
by a terrorist bomb and he has nothing left to lose. Now his SAS
training can be used by British Intelligence to deadly effect.

Going undercover to infiltrate the IRA in Belfast . . . Shadowing a
rogue ex-KGB agent in Paris . . . Investigating the mysterious murder
of a Military Intelligence specialist . . . Neil sees each mission as a
personal vendetta. And the more dangerous the better. For putting his
life on the line is the only way that John Neil can forget . . .

Circles of Deceit is a major new drama series from Yorkshire
Television produced by Yorkshire Television in association with
Waterman & Arlon Films.

Lynda La Plante
Award winning creator of *Prime Suspect* and
Widows
She's Out   £4.99

FROM TELEVISION'S MOST SUCCESSFUL WRITER . . .

. . . THE PHENOMENAL SEQUEL TO *WIDOWS!*

Dolly Rawlins is out. The unforgettable heroine of the most popular
and exciting TV drama of the 1980s is free after serving a nine year
sentence for the murder of her husband.

Waiting for Dolly are a group of women who all served time with her.
They know she has stashed millions of pounds worth of diamonds
from a raid and they want a cut. Also waiting is a Detective Sergeant
in the Metropolitan Police. He holds her personally responsible for the
death of his sister in the diamond raid ten years earlier. And now he
wants her back inside for that robbery.

Dolly Rawlins has other plans: to realise the dream that kept her going
for years in prison. But against such determined opposition, the
fantasy soon turns into a very different, tragic and violent reality . . .

Read LYNDA LA PLANTE's blockbusting bestsellers *The Legacy*, *The
Talisman*, *Prime Suspect*, *Entwined*, *Seekers*
Only in Pan Books

Lynda La Plante
The Governor   £4.99

Scarcely a day passes without an incident at one of Britain's most notorious top security prisons. But what happens when the tension boils over and there's a woman in charge?

Helen Hewitt is the boss. The first woman Governor of a top security men's prison – home to some of the country's hardest criminals. And case-hardened male officers who'll pounce at the first sign of weakness.

Helen Hewitt is tough. She has to survive. But she is also a woman. She can play the hard games too. But sometimes with a different set of rules . . .

The Governor. The exclusive novelisation of the hit TV series from Lynda La Plante. Hard-hitting, exciting, true-to-life drama from the phenomenally successful author of *Prime Suspect* and *Widows*.

All Pan books are available at your local bookshop or newsagent, or can be ordered direct from the publisher. Indicate the number of copies required and fill in the form below.

Send to: Pan C. S. Dept
             Macmillan Distribution Ltd
             Houndmills Basingstoke RG21 2XS
or phone: 0256 29242, quoting title, author and Credit Card number.

Please enclose a remittance* to the value of the cover price plus: £1.00 for the first book plus 50p per copy for each additional book ordered.

*Payment may be made in sterling by UK personal cheque, postal order, sterling draft or international money order, made payable to Pan Books Ltd.

Alternatively by Barclaycard/Access/Amex/Diners

Card No.   ☐☐☐☐☐☐☐☐☐☐☐☐☐☐☐☐☐☐☐

Expiry Date   ☐☐☐☐☐☐

———————————————————————————————
                    Signature:

Applicable only in the UK and BFPO addresses

While every effort is made to keep prices low, it is sometimes necessary to increase prices at short notice. Pan Books reserve the right to show on covers and charge new retail prices which may differ from those advertised in the text or elsewhere.

NAME AND ADDRESS IN BLOCK LETTERS PLEASE:

....

Name_____

Address_____

_____

_____

_____

6/92